MOUNTAIN MEN TRAIL BUILDERS

PEYTON LAWSON

Edited by Veronica Jauregui

Cover by Peyton Lawson

BEACHES AND TRAILS
PUBLISHING

FORBIDDEN MOUNTAIN MAN

A ONE-BED, FLIRT-TO-LOVERS ROMANCE
WITH A CURVY HEROINE

1

TROUBLE IN BOOTS

TALIA

Talia Fisher had spent her entire life following rules. Graduated top of her class. Finished her MBA by twenty-three. Said please, thank you, and excuse me in the right order. Never drank before twenty-one. Never slept around. Never risked anything worth losing.

But standing in the clearing with damp soil beneath her hiking boots and her internship paperwork clutched to her chest, she wondered if maybe—just this once—she should have broken that perfect streak.

She hadn't come here to fall in love. She'd come to prove something.

To herself. To her father. Maybe to the part of her that still equated perfection with worth.

But rules never held up well against wild places.

Because no one mentioned Sawyer Hall.

No one warned her that the Summit Trail Crew's resident chainsaw expert had eyes that could cut through you faster than his blade through pine. Or that his grin hit like lightning—bright, sudden, and promising inevitable destruction.

"You're Talia, right?" he asked, hooking his thumbs through his belt loops like he owned the mountain and everything on it. "Nash said they were sending another intern."

She swallowed. Nodded. Stuck her hand out like her father had taught her—firm grip, confident eye contact, never let them see you sweat.

"Yes. Environmental resources intern. Conservation focus." She cleared her throat. "Nice to meet you."

His eyes flicked to her outstretched hand, then back to her face. His mouth quirked.

He didn't take it.

Instead, he lifted his own—greased with chainsaw oil, dirt crusted under his nails—and wiggled his fingers.

"Wouldn't want to mess up those clean hands, princess." He heard the words land sharp, sharper than he'd meant. Damn it. Why did he always default to being a dick when he felt off-balance?

Her cheeks burned.

She kept her hand extended. Refused to break eye contact. Refused to back down.

After a beat too long, he chuckled. Wiped his palm on the thigh of his worn work pants. Took her hand.

His grip was solid. Warm. A little too tight and a little too long.

"I'm Sawyer. I'll be your team lead for the North Ridge restoration project."

"The what?" She frowned. "I was assigned to mapping at the south junction."

He shrugged, released her hand. "Plans changed an hour ago. Flash flood warning came through on the emergency radio. Half the south trail's already under. Nash reassigned you to my crew."

The dismay must have shown on her face because his grin widened—wolfish, knowing, dangerous.

"Sorry, princess. Looks like you're stuck with me."

She straightened her spine. Set her jaw. "I'm not a princess."

"Sure thing, Your Highness."

The title bit into her, not because it was inaccurate, but because it was the one her father had used too often—smiling with pride in public, scolding with disappointment in private. "Senator's daughter," he always said, like a brand. Not a person.

Before she could respond, he turned and strode toward the gathering of crew members by the edge of the trail. His shoulders were broad beneath his faded henley, the fabric stretched taut across muscle built from years of labor.

Talia exhaled slowly through her nose.

Eight weeks. It was just eight weeks.

She could survive anything for eight weeks.

Even Sawyer Hall.

SAWYER

Nash had warned him. Nash had been crew boss for six years, ever since the accident that took his partner and left him with scars he hid under long sleeves. The man who'd carved Laura's name into that cabin wall with shaking hands wasn't the type to give relationship advice. But he'd looked at Sawyer with something like understanding when he'd said, 'Some women change the game, Hall. Make sure you know what you're playing for.

"She's not one of your usual conquests, Hall. She's high-value. Daughter of a state senator. Harvard grad. Don't fuck this up."

Sawyer had snorted. "What, you think I can't keep it in my pants for two months?"

Nash had given him that flat stare—the one that made rookie crew members piss themselves.

"I think you don't know how to operate unless you're flirting or fighting. And neither one's going to work with her. She's here to work, to learn, to get credit. That's it."

"Message received, boss," he'd drawled. "I'll be a perfect gentleman."

And he'd meant it. Mostly.

But that was before he'd seen her.

Before he'd watched her climb out of that ridiculously pristine Subaru with her even more pristine hiking boots, survey the muddy clearing, and square her shoulders like she was marching into battle instead of a summer internship.

Sawyer had always had a weakness for women who looked like they were trying too hard to prove something. They were usually the most fun to unravel. Maybe because he'd once been one himself. Scrapping for attention, respect, and a reason to stay rooted. But roots were tricky things on mountains. They didn't always hold.

He slung his pack over his shoulder and headed to the trail entrance where his crew was assembling. Most were already listening to Micah's safety rundown—harness checks, emergency protocols, the usual bullshit.

Talia arrived at the edge of the group, looking like she was trying to blend in and failing spectacularly. Her gear was too new. Her stance too rigid. Her eyes too eager to take everything in.

Micah nodded at her. "You need the safety briefing, Fisher?"

"I've read the manual," she replied. "Three times."

Of course she had.

Sawyer stepped in. "Manual's nice, but it doesn't tell you what to do when a bear thinks your lunch box is more appealing than pine nuts."

Her eyes widened.

"I'm joking," he said. "The bears here prefer backpacks. More nutritional value."

A flicker of annoyance crossed her face. "I'm familiar with wildlife safety protocols, thank you."

"Protocols." He repeated the word, testing it on his tongue like it tasted funny. "Well, that'll be real comforting when you're halfway up a ridge with no cell service."

She didn't bite. Just adjusted the straps of her pack, and the movement pulled her shirt taut across curves that had no business being on a mountain trail. Sawyer forced his eyes back to the ridge, jaw tight. She tugged her ponytail tighter and looked at him expectantly.

Eight weeks of this torture.

"Are we hiking out today, or are you just going to stand there trying to unnerve me?"

Something hot sparked in his chest—and lower. He'd expected her to blush, stammer, maybe cry. Not fire back with that steady gaze and a voice that held steel wrapped in honey. The kind of voice that made him wonder what she'd sound like saying his name in the dark.

"Wouldn't dream of unnerving you, princess," he said, shouldering past her to lead the group. "But just so you know, where we're going? Your protocols won't mean shit."

He didn't have to look back to know she was glaring holes into his spine.

Eight weeks.

This might be more fun than he thought.

TALIA

The North Ridge trail was beautiful and brutal.

Switchbacks cut through dense forest, climbing steeper with every turn. The path grew narrower, rockier, and the air thinner. Her lungs burned. Thighs screamed. But she kept pace, refusing to be the one to ask for a break.

Sawyer led from the front, moving with the easy confidence of a man who knew every root and rock on the mountain. He barely seemed to sweat despite the summer heat. It was infuriating.

"Keep up, princess!" he called back, not bothering to mask the amusement in his voice.

She gritted her teeth and pushed harder.

By the time they reached the first survey point, her shirt was plastered to her back and she'd emptied half her water bottle. The three other crew members—Dani, Liam, and Evan—looked winded but not destroyed. They'd clearly done this before.

Nash's voice crackled over the radio to Sawyer—something about winter assignments and a crew member named Micah taking solo rotations. Talia caught fragments: *'reliability issues'* and *'family problems.'* She filed it away. Eight weeks on this mountain meant she'd learn everyone's story eventually.

Sawyer planted an orange marker flag, then turned to address the group. His eyes landed on her, lingering just a beat too long on the flush in her cheeks, the dampness of her shirt.

"We're marking damaged sections from the spring thaw. Flag anything that needs structural reinforcement. Log any wildlife interaction. Stay within sight line."

He pointed at a mossy patch of ground. "Fisher, you take point on this section. Document any endangered plant species you find. That's why you're here, right? Plants and shit?"

"Ecological conservation," she corrected.

"Right. Plants and shit."

She bit the inside of her cheek, holding back a retort. He was baiting her. She wouldn't give him the satisfaction.

The group dispersed. Talia pulled out her field journal and started documenting the undergrowth along the trail edge.

Kneeling in the moss, Talia inhaled the cool air, sharp with crushed fern and loamy soil. Her fingers brushed over slick leaves, damp with dew, and the chirp of a bird overhead echoed like a reminder—life here was quieter, but never still.

The work was calming. Familiar. The kind of methodical observation she excelled at.

She was so focused she didn't notice Sawyer approaching until his shadow fell across her notebook.

"Find anything worth saving, princess?"

She didn't look up. "Several species, actually. Including a rare variety of—"

"I'm gonna stop you," he interrupted, crouching beside her. "Because I don't actually care about moss."

She finally met his eyes. "Then why ask?"

"Just checking if you're still breathing. You look like you're about to pass out."

"I'm fine."

"You're red as hell and you haven't touched your water in twenty minutes."

She blinked. He'd been watching.

"Hydration is important, Fisher." He held out his own bottle. "Drink."

"I have water."

"Yours is almost gone, and we're not heading back for hours."

She hesitated.

"Jesus, I don't have cooties." He shook the bottle. "Just take it."

She accepted the bottle reluctantly. Took a sip. It was shockingly cold, like he'd filled it from a mountain spring right before offering.

It wasn't just the water. It was that he'd noticed. Her father noticed her only when she failed—when she didn't live up to the plan he'd laid out like a campaign strategy. But Sawyer noticed when she hadn't had enough to drink. That made it worse, somehow.

"Thank you," she said, because her mother had raised her with manners.

He stared at her a moment longer than necessary, something unreadable flickering in his eyes.

"Don't mention it." He stood. "And Fisher? Take a break when you need one. Mountains don't reward heroes. They bury them."

With that, he walked away, leaving her unsettled and annoyed —both at his presumption and the fact that he was right. She had been pushing too hard.

She took another sip of his water.

She wouldn't make that mistake again.

2

STRANDED

S AWYER
Of all the shit luck.

Sawyer stared at the muddy torrent where the lower trail had been just hours ago. The radio in his hand crackled with Nash's voice—static-laced and pissed.

"You need to get to the north shelter. Now. Storm intensifying. Flash flood advisory upgraded to warning."

"Copy that," Sawyer replied, scanning the darkening sky. "ETA thirty minutes."

"Make it twenty. Over."

He clipped the radio back to his belt and turned to the crew.

"Change of plans," he said. "Emergency shelter. Fisher, you're with me."

No one argued. They'd all seen the water level rising, heard the distant rumble of thunder that meant this wasn't just passing rain.

They moved fast, single file. Sawyer kept watch on the group, counting heads as they navigated each precarious turn. Four. All accounted for. All moving steady.

Until the ground shifted.

It happened fast—a section of trail crumbling beneath Liam's right foot. He stumbled, caught himself, but the edge gave way, creating a small landslide that took out the next ten feet of path.

"Shit!" Sawyer lunged, grabbing Liam by the back of his pack and yanking him to safety. "Everyone back!"

They scrambled away from the crumbling edge. A three-foot gap separated them from the continuation of the trail. They didn't have the right equipment to cross it, and the rain was turning everything slippery and treacherous.

"Can we jump it?" Evan asked, eyeing the gap.

"Not worth the risk," Sawyer replied. "One slip, and you're gone."

He unclipped the radio, called in their situation. Nash's reply was immediate and unhelpful.

"Get to the shelter. There's another route, an old hunting trail. Half mile north of your position."

Sawyer swore under his breath. The "old hunting trail" was barely a game path, and in this weather, it would be a mudslide.

"Copy that," he replied anyway.

He turned to find Talia watching him, her face pale but calm. Her rain jacket was zipped to her chin, hood pulled up, but water still dripped down her cheeks. Her eyes were clear, focused.

He watched her scan the crumbling trail edge, mentally calculating angles and stability points like she'd done this before. Most people would be freaking out. Talia Fisher pulled a small notebook from her jacket pocket and started sketching the landslide pattern. For her fucking environmental report. In a goddamn emergency.

That shouldn't have been sexy.

It was.

Something inside him shifted, just a fraction.

"Alright," he said, addressing the group. "We're taking the north route. It's rough, but it'll get us to the shelter. Stay close, watch your footing, and for fuck's sake, don't try to be heroes."

They moved out, picking their way through dense brush, climbing over fallen logs that were quickly becoming slick with rain.

Evan's radio crackled to life.

"Sawyer, do you copy?" Nash's voice, urgent now.

Evan handed the radio over. "I copy," Sawyer replied.

"River's crested. North route's compromised. How close are you to the upper shelter?"

Sawyer did a quick mental calculation. "Twenty minutes, maybe more in this shit."

A pause. Static. Then: "Make it happen. We're pulling everyone off the mountain. Rescue crews won't be able to reach you until morning at the earliest."

Great. Fucking great.

"Copy that," he said. "We'll check in when we're secure."

He clipped the radio back to his belt and turned to the group. "Change of plans. Dani, I need you, Liam, and Evan to take the high route. It's navigable, but barely. Get to the upper shelter and radio in."

"What about you?" Dani asked, eyes darting between him and Talia.

"I'll take Fisher to the small shelter by the old logging site. It's closer, and the terrain's more stable."

He saw the doubt. But no one argued. They knew better.

"It's the safest play," he added firmly. "You three know the high route. She doesn't."

As the group split, Sawyer caught Talia's eye. "You good with this, Fisher?"

She nodded once, tight and determined.

"Good. Stay close. And fair warning—where we're going isn't exactly the Four Seasons."

"I think I can manage one night without room service," she replied dryly.

He almost smiled.

TALIA

The "shelter" was a glorified shack.

The air inside was thick with the scent of old wood, damp earth, and the lingering smoke of long-forgotten campfires. It smelled like stories waiting to be told—and maybe a bit like wet socks.

A single room, maybe twelve by fourteen feet. Four walls, a roof, a tiny woodstove that looked like it predated electricity. One narrow cot pushed against the far wall. A shelf with emergency supplies. A basin for water collection.

And absolutely nowhere to hide.

Talia stood in the doorway, dripping onto the rough wooden floor, trying not to look as desperate as she felt. Her clothes were soaked through, her hair plastered to her scalp, and her fingers had gone numb about twenty minutes ago.

Sawyer moved past her with practiced efficiency, dropping his pack by the stove and immediately setting to work. His wet shirt clung to every muscle, outlining the kind of strength that came from years of hard labor.

'You planning to stand there all night?' he asked without looking up. 'Because watching you drip is distracting as hell.'

She stepped inside, closing the door against the howling wind.

Water pooled at her feet. The space felt smaller now, intimate in a way that had nothing to do with square footage.

"You planning to stand there all night?" he asked without looking up.

She stepped inside, closing the door against the howling wind. Water pooled at her feet.

"Is there a...bathroom?" she asked, knowing the answer before the words left her mouth.

He looked up then, amusement dancing in his eyes. "There's a bucket with a lid behind that screen, princess. And if you need to do more than that, there's a lovely rainstorm waiting outside."

She turned away, heart hammering louder than the rain. Not from fear. From him

Her face burned. "Right."

Sawyer turned his attention back to the stove, coaxing a small flame to life from kindling he'd apparently been carrying in a waterproof pouch in his pack. The man came prepared, she'd give him that.

"'Strip, Fisher."

Her eyes snapped up. He didn't flinch. Didn't soften. Just held her gaze with an intensity that made her stomach flip.

"You're soaked," he said. Voice lower now, rougher.

"Hypothermia's a bitch. And I'm not watching."

His eyes dropped to her mouth, then back up.

"Unless you want me to."

He didn't look at her, just continued feeding the growing fire.

"There are emergency blankets in the supply bin. They're not comfortable, but they're dry."

She hesitated, glancing around the tiny space. There was nowhere to change privately.

Sawyer sighed, as if reading her mind. "I'll turn my back. Scout's honor."

"Were you even a Boy Scout?"

"Hell no. Had better things to do than sell popcorn and learn knots." He paused. "Though the knots came in handy later."

The implication wasn't lost on her. Heat crawled up her neck, and it had nothing to do with the stove.

"Turn around," she said, more sharply than intended.

He raised his hands in mock surrender, then made a show of facing the wall.

Talia peeled off the jacket, then the shirt beneath. The tank clung to her, damp and thin. She didn't look at him. Didn't want to know if he was watching. Her hiking pants came next, peeled down with difficulty over goosebump-covered skin.

The emergency blanket crinkled loudly as she wrapped it around her waist like a makeshift skirt. It was silver, reflective, and about as dignified as a baked potato.

"Done," she announced.

He turned. Stared. Didn't blink.

That silver foil clung to her hips like sin dressed up as safety. Her shoulders were bare. Her lips parted.

His breath caught—and this time, he didn't bother to hide it.

"Hang those by the stove," he instructed, nodding at her wet clothes. "They won't dry completely overnight, but it's better than nothing."

She did as instructed, trying to maintain some semblance of dignity while arranging her pants and jacket over the edge of a rickety chair.

When she turned back, Sawyer had stripped off his own outer layers. His henley clung to his torso, outlining muscles that hadn't been as obvious under his rain gear. Water dripped from his hair onto his shoulders, trailing down his neck.

He caught her staring and raised an eyebrow.

"See something you like, princess?"

She forced her eyes away. "Just wondering if you're planning to change, too. Since, as you pointed out, hypothermia is a bitch."

His mouth quirked. "Didn't know you could swear."

"I'm full of surprises."

"Clearly." He pulled his shirt over his head in one fluid motion, revealing a torso that belonged on the cover of a calendar. The kind firefighters posed for.

Heat flooded her face. She turned away quickly, pretending to adjust her blanket.

"Modest, too," he commented, and she could hear the smirk in his voice. "Don't worry, Fisher. I'm not going to ravish you. Nash would have my balls."

"I wasn't worried," she said stiffly.

"No?"

"No." She forced herself to look at him. "I'm perfectly capable of saying no if the situation calls for it."

Something in his expression shifted. His eyes darkened, a challenge sparking."And what about saying yes? You capable of that, too?"

The question hit like a spark. Not loud, but hot—too hot.

Talia didn't flinch. Didn't step back.

"Try me," she said.

Sawyer's jaw ticked. He took one step closer—just one. But the air changed. The wind rattled the shelter, and her pulse thrummed louder than the storm.

"Careful, Fisher," he said, voice low, voice *rough*. "You tempt a man too long, eventually he stops asking."

She swallowed hard.

He didn't touch her. Didn't have to. That stare alone dragged heat to her cheeks, then lower.

She glanced down, saw his knuckles tighten at his sides. Controlled. Coiled. *And waiting.*

Her throat worked around the words that didn't come. So she turned, wrapped the emergency blanket tighter around her waist, and moved toward the corner to set up her makeshift bed— anywhere but the cot.

"Guess we'll never know," she said over her shoulder. But her voice wobbled. Just a little.

Behind her, Sawyer's low, dangerous laugh sent a shiver down her spine that had nothing to do with the cold.

3

BOUNDARY LINES

SAWYER
Sawyer had expected tears. Complaints. Maybe a
meltdown about the cot.

Instead, Talia Fisher sat cross-legged on the floor, wrapped in that ridiculous silver blanket, calmly reviewing her field notes by the light of the emergency lantern.

Like they weren't stranded in a 12x12 box in the middle of a raging storm.

Like she wasn't half-naked under that crinkly excuse for covering.

Like he wasn't watching her from the shadows, tracking the movement of her pen across paper, the way she tucked stray strands of damp hair behind her ear, the soft curve of her neck as she bent over her work.

"You always study during natural disasters?" he asked, breaking the silence.

She didn't look up. "This is hardly a disaster."

"Tell that to the trail that just washed away."

"Mmm." She made another note, then finally glanced up. "I like to be prepared. Even if that means working through... unexpected situations."

"Is that what I am? An unexpected situation?"

The corner of her mouth twitched. Almost a smile. "You're certainly something."

He leaned back against the wall, stretching his legs out in front of him. He'd changed into his spare pants, but his chest remained bare. The fire had warmed the small space enough that it wasn't uncomfortable but not so much that he'd sacrifice the way her eyes occasionally darted to his torso when she thought he wasn't looking.

"Something you want to keep your distance from? Or something you want to crawl closer to when the lights go out?"

She set her notebook aside. "Something complicated."

"I'm actually pretty simple."

"I doubt that."

He studied her face in the flickering light. Her cheeks were flushed, but her eyes were clear, direct. No bullshit. It was refreshing and unsettling all at once.

"You hungry?" he asked, changing topics.

"Starving," she admitted. "But I'm guessing you're not hiding a personal chef in the closet."

He laughed, genuinely surprised. "The princess has a sense of humor. Who knew?"

"Stop calling me that."

"Why? It fits."

"It doesn't." Her voice hardened slightly. "You don't know anything about me."

"You're a senator's daughter. Harvard. Probably never slept without Wi-Fi."

Her eyes narrowed. "You did a background check on me?"

"Nash did. I just listened while he read it."

"Invasion of privacy much?"

"That's rich, coming from the daughter of a man who votes on surveillance policies."

A flash of something—hurt, maybe, or resignation—crossed her face before she masked it.

"My father's politics aren't mine," she said quietly.

He hadn't expected that. Had assumed she was a carbon copy of her old man—conservative, reserved, boring as hell.

"No?" he challenged.

"No." She met his gaze steadily. "I'm here because I believe in conservation work. Not because it looks good on a resume or makes a nice press release."

He studied her for a long moment, then nodded once. "Fair enough."

He reached into his pack and pulled out two protein bars, tossing one to her. "It's not filet mignon, but it'll keep you from passing out."

She caught it with surprising dexterity. "Thanks."

They ate in silence, the storm providing background noise that filled the space between them. Rain drummed on the roof, occasional thunder punctuating the steady rhythm.

"You should take the cot," he said finally.

She glanced at the narrow bed, then back at him. "Where will you sleep?"

"Floor's fine. I've slept on worse."

"That doesn't seem fair."

He raised an eyebrow. "You offering to share, princess?"

She flushed. "No. I'm offering to take the floor."

"Not happening."

"Why not? Because I'm a woman? Or because I'm a 'princess'?" She made air quotes around the word.

"Because Nash would kill me if I let the senator's daughter sleep on a dirty floor when there's a perfectly good cot."

"I'm not made of glass."

"Never said you were."

"Then stop treating me like I am." Her voice rose slightly, a hint of real frustration breaking through her composed exterior.

Sawyer leaned forward, closing some of the distance between them.

"You want me to treat you like everyone else? Fine. Everyone else on my crew earns their place. They don't get special treatment because of who their daddy is or what school they went to."

Her eyes flashed. "I have never once asked for special treatment."

"You haven't had to. The world bends over backwards for girls like you without you having to say a word."

She stood abruptly, blanket clutched around her. "You know nothing about my life or what I've had to earn. Nothing."

He rose too, towering over her, close enough to see the angry flush spreading across her cheeks, the slight tremor in her hands.

"Then enlighten me, princess." His tone was sharp, harsher than he meant. He heard it echo and hated the way her face went still. That wasn't what he wanted. But he didn't know how to pull it back, so he pushed harder—like always.

For a moment, he thought she might slap him. Her free hand clenched at her side, knuckles white.

But she didn't. Instead, she took a deliberate step back.

"I don't owe you my life story," she said, voice low and controlled. "I don't owe you anything except professional courtesy and competent work. Both of which I'm providing, despite your best efforts to antagonize me."

The controlled fury in her voice hit harder than if she'd

shouted. Sawyer felt something shift in his chest—respect, maybe. Or regret at pushing too far.

"You're right," he said finally. "You don't owe me shit."

Her eyes widened slightly, clearly not expecting him to concede.

He stepped back, creating more space between them. "Take the cot, Fisher. Not because you're special. Because it's the right thing to do."

She hesitated, then nodded once. "Thank you."

He turned away, arranging his pack as a makeshift pillow against the wall. "Don't thank me yet. That thing probably has fleas."

He heard her laugh—soft, barely there—and something in his chest loosened.

"Goodnight, Sawyer."

"Night, princess."

This time, she didn't correct him.

And that scared her more than the storm.

TALIA

Talia didn't sleep.

She lay stiff on the cot, foil blanket crinkling with every breath. Behind her, Sawyer hadn't moved—but she could feel him. A presence. A furnace. A dare.

"You're cold," he said, voice low.

"You're observant."

"I'm also warm. Don't flatter yourself—it's basic thermo-dynamics."

She didn't answer.

"Slide over, Fisher. I'll keep to my side. Unless you ask nice."

She hesitated but shifted toward the wall. The cot dipped under his weight, her body rolling back into his. Not fully—just enough to feel it.

Heat poured off him like a fire stoked too high.

"This is wildly inappropriate," she murmured.

He didn't respond. Just threw his blanket over both of them.

They didn't touch. Not quite. But his leg brushed hers. His arm grazed her shoulder. Her breath caught.

If she turned her head, their mouths would be inches apart.

She didn't.

But she wanted to.

"If you say a word about this—"

"Relax," he murmured. "Your virtue's safe. For now."

"We're not kissing."

"Yet."

Her thighs clenched, slow and instinctive.

"Go to sleep," she snapped.

"Don't tell me what to do."

He laughed, low and wrecked and all heat. It vibrated through the cot. Through her.

An arm slid under her head. She didn't fight it. His chest pressed to her back, just enough to be known.

"Night, Fisher," he said.

It didn't sound like a goodbye.

And that scared her more than the storm.

4

FAULT LINES

TALIA

Warmth.

That was Talia's first conscious thought.

Not the clammy sort that came from too many blankets, but real warmth—radiating through her bones, curled around her like safety.

Her second thought?

Her pillow was breathing.

Her eyes snapped open.

Sawyer.

He was beneath her, one arm wrapped around her waist, her leg thrown over his. His bare chest rose steady under her cheek, and for a second, she just... froze. Sunlight filtered through the shelter's window, streaking golden across his skin, the dust motes and petrichor catching in her throat like a spell.

She moved to slip away.

His arm tightened.

"Five more minutes," he mumbled.

"Let me go."

His grip eased immediately. She rolled back, dragging the crinkling foil blanket with her, cheeks burning, trying to forget how her thigh had settled over his. Or how natural it had felt.

"Sleep well?" he asked, voice still rough with sleep.

"Fine." She cleared her throat. "Thanks for the body heat."

"Anytime, Fisher."

He stood and stretched, unapologetically shirtless. Her eyes darted up, then quickly away. His back was all long lines and hard labor. She hated how badly she wanted to trace the scar running over one shoulder.

What the hell was wrong with her?

She mumbled something about needing to pee and bolted, dragging on damp pants and boots before slipping outside.

The storm had passed. The world gleamed. Sunlight glinted off every leaf, water pooled in tree hollows, and the air smelled like earth and freedom.

But her chest felt tight.

She wasn't supposed to feel anything about Sawyer Hall. Not warmth. Not attraction. Not the echo of his breath against her neck or the way he said her name last night like it meant something.

This was fieldwork. Resume-building. Eight weeks of hard data, good impressions, and no distractions.

And yet...

She stepped back inside, trying to push every stupid thought out of her head.

Sawyer had the stove going. A metal pot steamed beside him. He held up two battered packets.

"Coffee?"

Her resolve cracked. "God, yes."

He handed her a tin mug. Their fingers brushed. Hers tingled.

"You're full of surprises," he said.

She took a cautious sip. Bitter. Burnt. Perfect. "And you're full of yourself."

He clutched his chest in mock pain. "Fisher has claws."

"I'm just not a fan of condescension with my caffeine."

"Noted." He sipped, then nodded toward the window. "Radio said we're grounded till noon. Trails are still sloppy."

She sighed. "Of course."

"You could be stuck with worse company," he added.

She didn't answer, just sipped again. The silence between them wasn't awkward. Just... full.

"About last night," he said eventually. "You held your own. Not bad for a princess."

"Still with that?"

"You're not denying it."

She rolled her eyes. "I went to Harvard, not Hogwarts. I don't turn into a pumpkin if I don't get turndown service."

Sawyer smirked. "That's a shame."

She arched a brow. "And what are you exactly?"

He stepped in a little closer. "Complicated."

She laughed once, quiet and sharp. "Is that what you call it?"

"You want the truth?"

"Sure."

"I push too hard. Say shit I shouldn't. And I've got a thing for women I shouldn't touch."

That last line lingered.

Talia froze. Then—without looking away—she asked, "Am I one of them?"

He didn't move. Just said, "You tell me."

Her breath caught, but she covered it with a sip of coffee. "I think you like the idea of chasing what you can't keep."

"And you don't?"

"I don't chase."

Sawyer's grin faded. Something darker settled in his eyes. "No. You don't."

They stood there too long. Close enough that she could see the faint stubble on his jaw, smell pine and fire smoke and something inherently male. Her heart pounded for all the wrong reasons.

She stepped back first. "We should check our gear."

"Running again?"

"Thinking ahead."

He let her move, but his eyes stayed on her.

She bent toward her pack, heart still thudding too fast. Her fingers curled around the wet strap of her field bag, grounding herself.

Sawyer moved behind her—not crowding, but not far.

"For what it's worth," he said softly, "I don't just chase things I can't have. I go after what I want."

She turned slowly. "And what is it you want?"

His voice dipped lower. "Right now? To kiss you. Badly."

The air went still.

Her lips parted—but no sound came.

Before either of them could move, the radio crackled. Nash's voice broke the spell, gruff and practical: "All trail crews report status."

Sawyer reached for the device but didn't look away from her.

"Hall here. Secure with Fisher. ETA base 1400 hours."

"Copy. Base out."

He clipped the radio back to his belt.

Silence.

Talia exhaled. "So that almost happened."

"Almost," he agreed. "But the day's not over."

She arched an eyebrow. "I thought we were keeping it professional."

"I haven't done a professional job of that since you stepped out of that SUV."

She turned away so he wouldn't see her smile.

Outside, the storm-washed forest shimmered like it knew something she didn't.

Maybe it did.

SAWYER

Talia Fisher was a goddamn problem.

Not because she complained. Not because she was delicate.

But because she wasn't.

She'd woken up tangled around him and hadn't screamed or shrieked—just pulled back, wrapped herself in foil, and squared her spine like nothing happened.

And that kiss they almost had? That wasn't nothing.

He couldn't stop thinking about how her voice had dropped.

How she hadn't said no.

And how close she'd been to saying yes.

Sawyer shouldered his pack before he did something stupid—like grab her and finish what they started.

They moved out just after noon, boots squelching through the soaked forest floor, the world glittering like it had been scrubbed clean. Storm runoff had carved new lines into the trail, branches scattered like matchsticks.

Sawyer didn't say much.

Didn't trust himself to.

Talia kept pace easily, breathing steady, eyes scanning the terrain like she'd done this before. He liked that. Liked that she didn't ask to rest. Liked that she didn't expect him to carry her pack.

They reached the ridge after half an hour. The damage was worse than expected—mud thick and unstable, one section completely collapsed.

Sawyer tested the edge with his boot. "Stay back."

"Problem?"

"Only if you like falling."

She didn't argue. He picked his way across the narrow ledge, boots sliding a little in the muck. He made it to the other side and turned.

"Okay. Your turn. Watch my steps exactly."

She nodded, crouched slightly, and moved with careful precision. But about halfway across, the ground betrayed her—just a small slide, but enough.

She gasped as her foot slipped, her balance gone.

Sawyer surged forward, heart slamming.

He caught her wrist just before she went over.

For a breathless second, she hung there—suspended between solid ground and a steep slope lined with rocks and regret.

He pulled.

Hard.

Her body crashed into his, momentum slamming her chest to his and knocking the wind from both of them. His arms closed around her instinctively, one hand pressing low on her back.

They didn't move.

Her breath was hot against his neck. Her hands gripped his shirt like she needed it more than balance.

"You okay?" he asked, voice lower than intended.

She nodded against his chest, but didn't step back.

Didn't want to.

And holy hell, neither did he.

Sawyer pulled his head back just far enough to look at her. Her eyes were wide, lips parted, cheeks flushed—but she wasn't scared.

She was staring at his mouth.

Dangerous.

He dipped his head—slow, measured, so she had time to stop him.

She didn't.

Their lips met in a collision of adrenaline and need. At first, it was a brush, tentative. Then deeper. Hotter. Her mouth opened under his. She made a soft sound—something between a sigh and a moan—and that undid him.

His hand slid to the back of her neck, thumb grazing her jaw as he kissed her like he'd earned it. Her fingers curled into his chest, pulled him closer, and that control he was so fucking proud of? Gone.

He wanted her.

Wanted her spread under him in back at the cabin. Wanted her out of those clothes. Wanted to know how many times he could make her say his name before it turned into something more than a warning.

The radio at his hip crackled.

He didn't stop.

Another burst of static. Then: "All trail crews, report status."

Reluctantly, he pulled back. Her breath was uneven. Her lips were pink and swollen. Her eyes... wrecked in the best possible way.

Sawyer unclipped the radio, trying to steady his voice. "Hall here. En route to base with Fisher. ETA ninety minutes."

"Copy. Base out."

He clipped it back. Silence swelled between them again—thick, complicated.

Talia cleared her throat. "That was—"

"Yeah."

They stared at each other.

Neither said, "That was a mistake."

Neither said, "Do it again."

But both of them felt the space where the kiss had lived—and what it could've turned into.

He took a step back.

She let him.

"We should move," he said, shifting his weight to hide the obvious. "Still a lot of trail to cover."

She nodded once, too quickly. "Right."

They started walking. Neither of them spoke. But every brush of her arm against his lit him up like a live wire.

Eight weeks, he told himself.

Just eight.

But he already knew that wasn't going to be long enough.

5

BREAKING POINT

TALIA

Five days since the kiss.

Five days of pretending she didn't feel the weight of Sawyer's gaze every time she passed. Of polite silence where there used to be sparks. Of lying awake in her bunk, replaying the exact tilt of his head when he leaned in—like he'd wanted her for years, not hours.

They hadn't talked about it.

Not once.

At camp, they worked clean. Efficient. No banter. No smirks. No mistakes.

But the air between them? Still heavy. Still humming.

Talia bent over her field journal, trying to focus on moss instead of the heat climbing up her neck.

"Earth to Fisher," Dani said.

Talia looked up, startled. "What?"

Dani gave her a smirk. "You've been staring at that sample like it holds the secrets of the universe. Or Sawyer's phone number."

"I'm thinking," she said, too sharp.

"Uh-huh. And he's not currently staring at you from the ridge line like a man contemplating sin."

Talia's head snapped up.

Sawyer stood above them, one hand braced against a tree, gaze locked on hers. When their eyes met, he didn't look away.

He never looked away.

Dani grinned. "So what happened in that shelter?"

"Nothing."

"Sure," she said. "And Nash isn't running a betting pool on when you two finally combust."

Talia nearly choked. "He what?"

"Well, Nash shut it down officially. But unofficially? Still going. Eighty bucks in the pot. I've got fifty on 'already happened.'"

Talia's face burned. "This is ridiculous."

"Maybe. But he's watching you like a man who's already tasted you and wants seconds."

"Stop."

Dani lifted her hands in surrender. "Hey, I'm just saying—you could do worse. Sawyer might be all flannel and sarcasm, but he's not a jerk. And you've been wound so tight since day one. Maybe you need someone who makes you forget the rules."

Before she could fire back, his voice cut through the trees.

"Fisher. With me. Ridge assessment."

Dani mouthed a dramatic "Oooh" as Talia gathered her gear, cheeks still flushed. "Coming," she called, immediately regretting the word.

She followed him up the incline, silence stretching long and thick.

When they stopped, he turned to face her. No smile. No smirk. Just heat.

"You're avoiding me."

"That's impossible. I'm working with you."

"You know what I mean."

Talia exhaled. "We kissed. It happened. But it shouldn't have."

"Why not?"

"Because it was adrenaline. Circumstance. A mistake."

That word cracked something between them.

"A mistake?" he echoed. "So I'm what? Fieldwork regret?"

She didn't answer.

"Look me in the eye and say it meant nothing."

Talia opened her mouth, but nothing came out.

He stepped closer.

"You're scared," he said.

"I'm not."

"You're terrified. Not of me—of what this means. Because you've spent your whole damn life playing by someone else's rules, and now there's this thing between us that doesn't fit your plan."

Her spine straightened. "You don't know anything about my plan."

"No, but I know chemistry. And I know what your face looked like after that kiss."

She backed up until her shoulders hit the trunk of a tree.

He didn't touch her. But he leaned in just enough to make her breath hitch.

"This is more than attraction, Fisher. You feel it. Same as me."

She wanted to deny it.

Couldn't.

"I don't know what this is," she said finally.

"It's messy. It's inconvenient. But it's real."

"And temporary."

His jaw ticked. "Maybe. But that doesn't make it worthless."

A silence pulsed between them, thick with want and wariness.

He reached up—slow, deliberate—and tucked a piece of hair behind her ear. His fingers lingered on her neck, warm and sure.

"Tell me you haven't thought about kissing me again."

She didn't move.

"I can't," she whispered.

That was all it took.

His hand slid to her jaw. Her breath caught.

And just when she thought he'd lean in, when her body braced for it.

The radio on his belt crackled.

"Hall, report. You at the ridge?"

Sawyer's eyes closed for half a second. A heartbeat of frustration.

"Copy," he said, stepping back.

"Base in thirty. Another front's moving in."

He clipped the radio silently, then looked at her—gaze steady, voice low.

"This isn't over."

And God help her, she didn't want it to be.

SAWYER

The second storm hit harder than the first.

Rain slammed the main cabin's roof like it held a grudge. Wind howled down the ridge. Lightning painted the valley in brief, electric snapshots. It was the kind of night you double-checked the gear and prayed the trees stayed upright.

Sawyer stood at the map table, arms crossed, pretending he was paying attention.

Nash pointed to high-risk sections with his Sharpie. "East trail's borderline. No crew out till morning. Hall, you're on night watch. Fisher's on supply detail with Dani. Everyone else, stay dry and stay put."

The crew scattered. Sawyer didn't move. Not because he had a job to finish, but because Talia had just walked in.

She didn't look at him. Not directly. Not anymore.

But he watched her tuck that same stubborn strand behind her ear. The one he'd touched on the ridge.

The one he wanted to touch again.

Nash's voice cut in. "You still here to brood, or are you planning to gear up?"

"I don't brood."

"Right. You just glare out windows like a guy in a breakup montage."

Sawyer didn't laugh. Didn't deny it either.

Nash sighed and stepped beside him. "You're off your game, Hall."

"I'm fine."

"You're not." He lowered his voice. "You're in line for crew lead next season. Keep this up, and that shot disappears."

The words hit. Crew lead wasn't just a promotion. It was the plan. The path out. The thing he'd been chasing since he quit trying to prove shit to his dad and started building something real.

"I'm not jeopardizing anything."

"You sure? Because you've been checking the door every five minutes like you're waiting for someone."

Sawyer didn't answer.

Nash didn't need him to.

"I don't care what's going on between you and Fisher—as long as it doesn't compromise the crew. Or her. She's got a future riding on this internship. Don't screw that up for her."

With that, Nash clapped him on the shoulder and walked off, boots thudding across the cabin floor.

Sawyer stayed by the window. Watched the rain streak down the glass and tried not to think about the way Talia's mouth had felt under his.

It didn't work.

He turned when he heard the door open—and there she was.

Rain slicker. Clipboard. No smile.

"Dani needs the supply logs. Nash said you had them."

He pointed to the drawer. "Bottom left."

She crossed the room, calm and collected. All professional polish. Except her hands shook a little when she pulled the folder.

"Forecast says the storm will pass by morning," she said, not looking at him.

He nodded. "You could stay in the cabin. Bunk here tonight."

She stiffened. "That wouldn't be appropriate."

Right. Of course not.

She turned to leave.

"Screw this," he said.

She froze. "What?"

"This. Pretending. Acting like I didn't kiss you five days ago. Acting like you didn't kiss me back."

She faced him slowly, eyes wary. "It doesn't matter."

"It matters to me."

"Why? So you can scratch the itch and move on?"

His jaw flexed. "You really think that's all this is?"

"I think I'm not built for temporary."

"Then don't make it temporary."

"I leave in a few weeks."

"I know."

"What happens when I go?"

"I don't know, Fisher," he said honestly. "But I know what's happening right now. And I know I don't want to keep pretending we're nothing."

She stared at him. Something in her face cracked—just a little.

"This is stupid," she whispered.

"Probably."

She set the folder on the table and stepped toward him. One step. Then another.

"If we do this," she said, voice low, "there are rules."

"Name them."

"No one knows. Not Nash, not Dani. No one."

He nodded. "Done."

"It ends when I leave. No drama. No guilt."

Another nod.

"If it interferes with my work, we stop."

"I won't get in your way."

She was standing in front of him now. Close enough to see the pulse in her throat. The way her breath hitched.

"One more thing," she added.

He tilted his head. "Yeah?"

"Don't make me ask twice."

Then she grabbed his shirt.

And he kissed her like he'd been waiting since the shelter. Like he was starving for it. Like he didn't care if the whole damn mountain came down around them.

6

THE FALL

TALIA

He didn't kiss her like he was trying to win.

He kissed her like he already had.

Talia had expected urgency. Swagger. The kind of pressure a man like Sawyer Hall might use to prove a point. But instead, his mouth had moved over hers like he was memorizing her. Like every pass of his lips, every flick of his tongue was a lesson in how to make her fall apart slowly.

And God, she was falling.

Hard.

His hands had stayed respectful—firm on her waist, steady against her back—but the way he touched her was anything but distant. He kissed like someone who didn't just want her body. He wanted the parts she didn't show anyone. The ones buried under layers of control and polish and performance.

When he finally pulled back, breath ragged, she wasn't sure she remembered what she'd been so determined to protect.

Then boots hit the porch.

Sawyer froze. She turned toward the sound just as the door swung open.

Dani.

Soaked through. Scowling. Eyes narrowed the second she stepped inside.

"There you are. I've been—" She stopped mid-sentence, gaze flicking between Talia and Sawyer, zeroing in on the blush in Talia's cheeks and the tilt of her lips. "Am I interrupting something?"

Talia coughed. "No. We were just... going over trail erosion notes."

"Uh-huh." Dani crossed her arms. "And that involved smudging your lipstick how?"

Talia's hand flew to her mouth.

Sawyer didn't even try to hide the smirk.

"The papers are there," he said casually, nodding to the counter. "Fisher was just leaving."

"Was I?" she shot back before she could stop herself.

"Unless you've got more... ground shifts you want to analyze."

His tone was innocent. His eyes were anything but.

Dani made a sound that could only be described as a gleeful snort. "Don't mind me. I'll just grab these and let you two get back to your... sediment evaluation."

"Ecology," Talia corrected weakly.

"Sure. Whatever you're calling it now."

The door shut behind her, and the air thickened all over again.

Talia groaned and dropped her face into her hands. "So much for subtle."

Sawyer's laugh was warm and wicked. "You're adorable when you panic."

"This isn't funny. She's going to tell everyone."

"She won't need to. They've already figured it out."

Talia lifted her head and glared at him. "You're enjoying this."

"Absolutely." He stepped close again, eyes dropping to her lips. "You kiss like a woman who hasn't let herself want something in a long time."

"That's none of your business."

"It is now."

He brushed his thumb over her cheek, and damn it, she leaned in.

Just a fraction.

But it was enough.

Talia backed up fast, putting a table between them. "We're not doing this here. Not with half the camp wandering around."

He didn't argue. Just waited.

She crossed her arms. "After your shift. Late."

He arched a brow. "You're inviting me somewhere?"

She hesitated, then gave him the name. "Storage shed. Behind the gear cache."

A slow smile spread across his face. Not cocky—just pleased. Like she'd given him something he wasn't sure he'd get.

"I'll be there."

"Don't be obvious."

"I'm not the one leaving with smudged lipstick."

"Shut up."

He winked. "See you tonight, princess."

Then he was gone, leaving her heart racing and her stomach in knots.

She didn't return to the bunkhouse right away. Couldn't. Instead, she paced the narrow trail between the cabin and the equipment cache, the hem of her hoodie twisted in her fists.

What the hell was she doing?

This was reckless. Stupid. She was here for her future. A prestigious internship. A chance to prove herself in a field still dominated by men with head starts and family money.

She was not here to sneak into storage sheds for secret make-out sessions with the crew lead's favorite hothead.

And yet...

Her lips still tingled. Her thighs still clenched every time she replayed the sound Sawyer made when she'd pulled him close.

She wanted him.

Not as a rebellion. Not for a story.

Because he saw her.

Because when she wasn't fighting him, she felt like someone she didn't hate.

At 11:45, she changed into dry clothes—soft cotton, no lace, practical as hell—and pulled her hair into a loose braid. No makeup. No pretense.

She slipped out the back of the bunkhouse with her jacket slung over one shoulder and a flashlight tucked in her hand.

Every step toward the shed felt like crossing a line.

And she didn't stop.

Because tonight wasn't about her five-year plan or her father's expectations. It wasn't about resume building or being the best girl in the room.

Tonight was about her.

She opened the door.

Saw him there—waiting, calm, prepared, eyes locked on her like she was the only damn thing that mattered.

And for once, she let herself believe it.

SAWYER

Sawyer waited in the storage shed, trying not to pace like a man about to lose his goddamn mind.

The tarp he'd laid out earlier didn't squeak this time. The old sleeping bags were tucked around the edges, softening the corners. A battery lantern flickered low in the corner, throwing gold shadows across the walls.

Outside, rain hissed on the metal roof.

Inside, his pulse thudded like footsteps.

He checked the time again. Midnight. Exactly.

He'd been early. Of course he had. The second she said, "after your shift," he'd been planning it like a goddamn mission op. Condoms? Check. Whiskey? Optional. Nerves? Way too real.

He hadn't done this in a long time—not like this. Not with someone who mattered.

And Talia Fisher? She mattered.

He'd kissed a lot of women. But none like her. None who kissed him back like she'd been holding her breath for five years and he was the first inhale.

Then the latch creaked.

She stepped in. Hood down. Hair damp. Cheeks pink. A breathless smile just barely hidden behind her usual steel.

"You came," he said.

"You doubted me?"

He shook his head. "No. But I thought maybe you'd come to your senses."

"Maybe I did." She stepped further inside, door clicking shut behind her. "And I came anyway."

Sawyer's jaw flexed.

God, she was dangerous.

"I set up a place to sit," he said. "Or lie down. Or talk. Or not."

She walked past him, brushing close. "You always this prepared?"

He grinned. "Only for emergencies."

"And is this an emergency?"

"Feels like one."

He reached for her slowly—giving her room to step back.

She didn't.

Their mouths met in the center of the shed, and this time, there was nothing tentative. Just heat. Her hands were in his hair. He gripped her waist. He spun them, backing her toward the makeshift bed, not breaking the kiss.

"Tell me to stop," he whispered against her mouth.

"No."

He leaned his forehead to hers, breath ragged. "You sure?"

"Yes."

One word. That's all it took.

She pulled her rain jacket off and he helped with the rest, peeling her down to a simple white tank and cotton underwear that made his hands shake more than any lace ever had.

He shed his shirt, felt her eyes drag over his chest, linger on the compass tattoo just above his heart.

"I always wondered where that pointed," she said.

He caught her hand. Placed it flat over the ink. "Right here."

Talia stared at him like she was trying to memorize the moment.

Then she whispered, "Take me apart."

He groaned—low and wrecked—and laid her back with more care than he'd ever given to anything off the trail.

Their clothes fell away like they were never needed. He kissed her slowly. Reverently. Traced her with his mouth, her stomach, her thighs, that perfect curve of her hip.

When she gasped and arched, he smiled against her skin. "That spot?"

"That spot."

He stayed there. Until her hands clawed for his shoulders. Until her legs trembled and her voice broke open on his name.

He slid up her body, cupped her face. "Talia."

"Yes," she said.

Condom. Heat. Her.

When he pushed into her, her mouth fell open in a soundless cry. His name again—soft, broken, reverent.

"Okay?" he asked, holding still even as every muscle begged to move.

She nodded. Pulled him deeper.

They moved slow at first. Then harder. Then like they couldn't get close enough.

Every kiss, every thrust, every gasp was a confession.

And when she came again—tight, clenching, eyes locked to his —he followed her over, lost in her body and whatever the hell this was between them.

After, they stayed tangled in silence. His hand on her waist. Her breath steady against his neck.

She whispered, "That wasn't a one-time thing."

He kissed her hair. "No. It really wasn't."

TALIA

The next three weeks passed in a blur of work and stolen moments.

By day, they maintained their professional distance—Talia documenting ecological impacts, Sawyer leading trail restoration, their interactions formal and appropriate.

But nights—nights belonged to them alone.

The storage shed became their sanctuary. They met whenever they could, sometimes just for an hour, sometimes until dawn threatened to expose their secret. They talked more than she'd expected, about everything and nothing—childhood dreams, favorite books, the philosophical implications of conservation work.

And they touched. God, how they touched. Each encounter more intense than the last, as they learned each other's bodies with the same dedication they brought to their work.

No one knew. Or at least, no one said anything directly. Dani's knowing smirks, Nash's occasional pointed looks, the way conversations sometimes stopped when they entered a room together—all hints that their secret wasn't as well-kept as they pretended.

But Talia didn't care. Not anymore. She was living fully, perhaps for the first time in her life, and the approaching end of her internship felt increasingly like a looming shadow rather than a welcome conclusion.

Tonight, she reached the shed first, slipping inside while the rest of the camp focused on dinner preparations. She'd begged off with a headache, knowing Sawyer would join her as soon as he could escape unnoticed.

The space had evolved over the weeks—a proper mattress now instead of sleeping bags, pillows pilfered from the supply closet, and even a small battery-powered speaker that sometimes played soft music as they explored each other.

It felt almost like a home. Their home.

The thought should have terrified her.

She settled on the mattress, pulling her knees to her chest, and allowed herself to acknowledge what she'd been avoiding for days: she was falling for him. Hard. Beyond chemistry. Beyond the physical connection that still took her breath away.

She was falling for his laugh. His unexpected gentleness. The way he looked at her when he thought she couldn't see—like she was something precious and rare.

She was falling for Sawyer Hall, and in exactly seven days, she would leave him behind.

The door creaked open, and there he was—hair damp from a hasty shower, smile wide and unguarded in a way it only ever was when they were alone.

"Hey, princess." He closed the door, crossing to her in three long strides. "Missed you at dinner. Dani was asking questions."

"What did you tell her?"

"That you were making a long-distance call to catching up with some Harvard friends before the gala." He dropped beside her on the mattress, pulling her into his arms. "She didn't buy it for a second."

Talia sighed, settling against his chest. "Does it matter anymore? I'm leaving soon anyway."

She felt him tense slightly, his arms tightening around her. "Six days, fourteen hours. Not that I'm counting."

"You're counting?"

He kissed the top of her head. "Hard not to."

The admission knocked something loose in her chest—a dam breaking, feelings flooding through.

"This wasn't supposed to happen," she whispered.

"What wasn't?"

"This. Us. I wasn't supposed to..." She trailed off, afraid to name the thing growing between them.

Sawyer shifted, turning her to face him. "Wasn't supposed to what, Talia?"

Her given name on his lips—rare and deliberate—made her heart stutter.

"Care," she admitted finally. "I wasn't supposed to care. This was supposed to be temporary. Simple. A summer fling to remember when I'm back in my real life."

"And now?"

"Now I don't know what this is. Or how to let it go."

His expression softened, thumb brushing across her cheek. "Who says you have to?"

"We did. Remember? Rule number two: clean break when I leave."

"Rules can change."

Hope fluttered in her chest, dangerous and tempting. "What are you saying?"

"I'm saying..." He hesitated, uncharacteristically cautious. "I'm saying maybe this doesn't have to end. Maybe there's a way to make it work."

"How? I'll be in Cambridge. You'll be here. That's over 3,000 miles."

"I hear they have these newfangled things called airplanes now. And phones. Even video calls."

She didn't smile. "Long distance is a slow death. I've seen it happen."

"It doesn't have to be." He took her hands in his. "I'm not asking for promises," he said, then hesitated. "I just... I don't want to screw this up. But I don't know what I'm doing here, Talia. Not with you. Not when it actually matters."

"Where could it go, Sawyer? Really? You belong on this mountain, with your crew, doing what you love. And I—"

"Belong with your color-coded planner and your five-year

goals and your prestigious future?" There was no mockery in his tone, just a simple acknowledgment of who she was.

"Yes," she said, but the word lacked conviction.

He studied her face, seeing too much, as he always did. "You know what I think? I think you're scared. Not of distance, but of disruption. Of something that doesn't fit neatly into your plan."

"That's not—"

"It is." He squeezed her hands gently. "And it's okay. Plans are comfortable. Safe. But sometimes the best things happen when we let them go."

The truth of his words resonated through her, painful in its accuracy.

"I don't know how to do that," she confessed. "I've spent my whole life following a path, being what everyone expected. Responsible, focused, and disciplined. This—us—doesn't fit anywhere in that picture."

"So draw a new picture." He cupped her face, eyes intense. "Life isn't a straight line, princess. It's messy and complicated and full of detours that end up being the best parts."

Tears pricked at her eyes. "When did you get so philosophical?"

His smile was soft, a little sad. "When I realized I was falling in love with a woman who thinks she has to choose between happiness and success."

The words hit her like a physical blow. Love. He'd said love.

"Sawyer, I—"

"Don't," he interrupted gently. "Don't say anything right now. Just... think about it. About us. About what you really want, not what fits into the plan."

He kissed her then, slow and deep and full of everything they hadn't said. And Talia kissed him back, pouring her confusion and hope and, yes, love into the connection.

Later, as they lay tangled together, sweat cooling on their skin, she traced the compass tattoo on his chest and wondered if maybe, just maybe, he could be her true north—the fixed point around which a new plan could form.

But as sleep claimed her, doubt crept in. Because wanting wasn't the same as having. And some distances couldn't be bridged, no matter how much love tried to span them.

7

AFTER THE FALL

SAWYER

Sawyer had said the words.

Not "I love you," not directly. But close enough. Close enough that Talia had heard the truth behind them, had seen it in his eyes, had felt it in the way he'd held her afterward like she might disappear if he let go.

Three days had passed since that night. Three days of Talia retreating into herself, focused on completing her work, on documenting everything, on preparing for her departure.

Three days of her slipping away, even as she still came to him each night, her body speaking what her words could not.

He hadn't pushed. Hadn't asked for an answer. Had given her the space to process what he'd said, what it meant, what came next.

But time was running out. In four days, she'd be gone.

And he was terrified that the silence between them meant she'd already made her choice.

They were working side by side today, the first time in weeks. A new section of trail needed ecological assessment before construction could begin, and Nash had assigned them to work together.

Coincidence? Unlikely. Nash saw too much, knew too much, though he never said it directly.

Talia knelt a few feet away, carefully measuring soil composition, making notes in her field journal with that precise handwriting that was so quintessentially her. The summer sun had darkened her skin, lightened her hair, and burned away the last traces of the hesitant intern who'd arrived two months ago.

She was beautiful. Confident. Completely in her element.

And completely avoiding his gaze.

"Finding anything interesting?" he asked, breaking the silence that had stretched between them for over an hour.

She glanced up briefly. "Some unusual erosion patterns. Might indicate underground water movement we didn't account for."

"Want me to take a look?"

"If you want."

He moved closer, crouching beside her, close enough to smell the faint vanilla scent that clung to her skin. Close enough to see the tension in her shoulders, the careful way she maintained distance between them despite their proximity.

"Talia."

She kept her eyes on her work. "Hmm?"

"Look at me. Please."

Reluctantly, she raised her head, meeting his gaze. There was something guarded in her eyes, something that hadn't been there before his ill-timed confession.

"We need to talk," he said quietly.

"We are talking."

"No, we're exchanging information about soil. That's not talking."

She sighed, setting down her tools. "What do you want me to say, Sawyer?"

"Anything. The truth. What you're thinking. What you're feeling." He lowered his voice, though there was no one around to hear. "What happens after you leave."

She looked away, focusing on the distant mountains. "I don't know."

"Don't know, or don't want to say?"

"Both." She met his eyes again. "I've been thinking about what you said. About us. About... possibilities."

"And?"

"And I'm scared." The admission came out soft, vulnerable. "Scared that if I try to hold onto this, to you, I'll end up losing both my focus and what we have now."

His heart twisted. "Or maybe you gain something better than what either of us planned."

"Maybe." She didn't sound convinced. "But maybe we're just caught up in this place, this situation. Maybe in the real world, outside this mountain, this doesn't work."

"There's only one way to find out."

She shook her head. "It's not that simple."

"It could be." He reached for her hand, relieved when she didn't pull away. "I'm not asking you to change your life. I'm not asking you to choose me over your career or your goals. I'm just asking for a chance to see if we can find a way."

"And if we can't?"

"Then at least we tried." He squeezed her hand gently. "Isn't that better than always wondering what if?"

She was quiet for a long moment, her expression thoughtful. Then she looked at him with those clear, direct eyes that had captivated him from the start.

"I care about you," she said finally. "More than I expected to. More than is probably wise."

Hope flickered in his chest. "I care about you too, princess. A lot."

"I know." A small smile curved her lips. "And that terrifies me."

"Why?"

"Because it's real." She took a deep breath. "And real means it can really hurt."

He wanted to promise he'd never hurt her. Wanted to swear that they'd figure it out, that distance wouldn't matter, that love would conquer all.

But he couldn't make those promises. Not honestly.

"I can't guarantee what happens next," he said instead. "But I can promise you this: what we have is worth fighting for. At least to me."

She looked down at their joined hands, then back up at him. "I need time. To think. To figure out what I want."

It wasn't the answer he'd hoped for. But it wasn't a rejection either.

"How much time?"

"Until I leave." She squeezed his hand. "Can you give me that?"

Four days. Four days to wait, to hope, to prepare himself for either possibility.

"I can do that," he said, though it cost him to say it. "But Talia?"

"Yes?"

"Whatever you decide, these weeks with you... they've changed me. And I wouldn't take them back for anything."

Her eyes softened, filling with something that looked danger- ously like the love he felt but wouldn't name again until she was ready to hear it.

"Neither would I," she whispered.

It wasn't a promise. It wasn't a commitment.

But for now, it was enough.

TALIA

Her last night on the mountain.

Talia stood in the darkness outside the storage shed, heart hammering against her ribs, decision heavy in her chest.

She'd spent four days thinking, weighing, and analyzing. Four days of working alongside Sawyer during daylight hours and losing herself in him each night. Four days of watching how he moved through the world—confident, competent, and kind in ways most people missed.

Four days of imagining her life without him, and finding the picture hollow.

She'd made her choice. Now she just had to find the courage to voice it.

Taking a deep breath, she pushed open the door.

Sawyer was already there, sitting on the edge of the mattress, hands clasped between his knees. He looked up when she entered, his expression a mixture of hope and resignation.

"I wasn't sure you'd come," he said.

"It's our last night. Of course I came."

She closed the door behind her, leaning against it, suddenly unsure how to begin.

"So," he said, after the silence had stretched too long. "Did you decide?"

Direct. Straightforward. No games. It was one of the things she loved about him.

Loved.

The word echoed in her mind, no longer frightening but right. Fitting. True.

"I did," she said, moving toward him slowly. "I've been thinking about what you said. About plans and detours and... possibilities."

He nodded, watching her approach but not reaching for her. Giving her space to say what she needed to say.

"I've spent my whole life on a path," she continued. "The right schools, the right internships, the right connections. Always knowing exactly where I was going and how to get there."

"And now?"

"Now I'm standing at a fork in that path." She stopped in front of him, close enough to touch but not touching. "And for the first time, I don't know which way to go."

"You don't have to choose, Talia." His voice was gentle. "That's what I've been trying to tell you. You can have your career, your goals, your future—and still see where this goes."

"Can I? Really?" She sat beside him, turning to face him. "Because I've never been good at dividing my focus. I put every-thing into whatever I'm pursuing."

"I know." He smiled slightly. "It's part of what makes you so damn incredible."

"But it's also what makes this so hard." She took a deep breath. "I go back to Cambridge tomorrow. Classes start in three weeks. My thesis proposal is due by mid-term. I'll be working sixty-hour weeks minimum."

His expression fell, though he tried to hide it. "I understand."

"No, you don't." She reached for his hand, threading her fingers through his. "Because I'm not saying no. I'm saying it's going to be hard. Really hard. And I need to know that when I'm stressed and busy and can't call for three days straight, you'll still be there."

His eyes widened as her meaning became clear. "You want to try?"

"I want more than that," she said, confidence growing with each word. "I want to come back for Thanksgiving. I want you to visit during winter break. I want to figure out how to fit you into my plan because I've realized my plan isn't worth much if it doesn't include people I care about."

The smile that broke across his face was like a sunrise—warm and bright and full of promise.

"Say that again," he said.

"Which part?"

"The part where you want me in your life. In your future."

She laughed, a sound of surprise and joy and release. "I want you, Sawyer Hall. In my life. In my future. In whatever ways we can manage across 3,000 miles until we figure out something better."

He pulled her to him then, kissing her with a tenderness that made her heartache.

"I love you," he said against her lips, no hesitation this time. "I love you, Talia Fisher, plans and all."

She'd thought the words would scare her. Would send her running in the opposite direction.

Instead, they felt like coming home.

"I love you too," she whispered. "God help me, but I do."

They sealed the confession with another kiss, deeper now, filled with promise and potential and the sweet ache of time running short.

Later, much later, as they lay tangled together in the aftermath of love made more intense by the knowledge of impending separation, Talia traced the compass on his chest and smiled.

"You know," she said. "Your compass is pointing north."

"So?"

"Cambridge is east."

He laughed, the sound rumbling through his chest beneath her ear. "Good thing I've got a great sense of direction."

"And frequent flyer miles?"

"Those too." He kissed the top of her head. "Tomorrow's going to suck."

"Yeah." She couldn't deny it. "But the day after tomorrow, and all the days after that? Those could be pretty amazing."

"Could be?"

"Will be," she corrected, certainty filling her voice. "I'm very thorough in my research, you know. And all evidence suggests that what we have is worth the work."

"Look at you," he murmured. "Using science to justify breaking your own rules."

"Not breaking them," she said. "Rewriting them. With a co-author."

His arms tightened around her. "I like the sound of that."

Outside, the mountain stood as a silent witness to their promises. The same mountain that had brought them together, forced them to see each other clearly, taught them both that some rules were meant to be broken.

And as Talia drifted toward sleep in the arms of her unlikely love, she realized that sometimes, the most beautiful views came from the paths you never planned to take.

EPILOGUE

Three months later, Talia stood in the arrivals terminal at Boston Logan, shifting her weight nervously from foot to foot.

The flight from Portland had landed twenty minutes ago. Any second now, he would walk through those doors.

Her phone buzzed with a text.

> Just grabbed my bag. Almost there. I love you.

She smiled, typing back quickly.

> Love you more. Hurry up before I cause a scene.

The doors slid open, and there he was—scruffier than she remembered, shoulders broader, eyes locked on her like she was the only thing in the damn terminal.

Time seemed to stop as recognition hit, her breath catching.

Then she was running, launching herself into his arms without a second thought.

He caught her mid-sprint, lifting her off her feet, face buried in her neck like she was already home.

"You're here," she whispered, pulling back just enough to see his face. "You're really here."

"Told you I would be." He set her down gently, keeping her close. "Nice welcome, by the way. Very dignified."

She laughed, the sound filling all the empty spaces the past three months had carved inside him.

"Dignity is overrated," she said, rising on tiptoes to kiss him properly. "I missed you."

"Missed you more."

"Not possible."

His phone buzzed again, interrupting the moment. He ignored it, but it buzzed three more times in quick succession.

"Someone really wants to reach you," Talia said.

Sawyer sighed, pulling out his phone. "It's Nash. Hang on."

He scrolled through the messages, his expression shifting from annoyance to concern.

"Everything okay?" she asked.

"Not sure. "Micah's gone off-grid. Last three check-ins? Silence. Not even weather pings."

Talia frowned. "No way. That's not like him."

"Exactly," Sawyer muttered. "He doesn't flinch at storms, doesn't ghost during winter isolation. If Micah's quiet—it's either bad luck or something worse."

"Micah? The quiet one who always carried that book of poetry?"

Sawyer nodded, still reading. "Yeah. He took a winter assignment at the north cabin. Solo rotation, just basic maintenance and storm monitoring. But he missed his last three check-ins."

"That doesn't sound like him."

"It's not." Sawyer typed a quick reply, then looked at Talia. "Nash is sending a crew up to check on him next week."

"Is he worried?"

"Nash doesn't worry. He prepares." Sawyer pocketed his phone. "But yeah, something's not right. Micah's the most reliable guy on the crew. He doesn't just disappear."

"Maybe he just needs space. After what happened with his brother last spring..."

Sawyer's jaw tightened. "Maybe. But that mountain's unforgiving in winter. And Micah's been carrying too much weight for too long."

Talia touched his arm, drawing his attention back to her. "Hey. There's nothing you can do from here."

"I know." He pulled her close again, pushing the worry aside. "And I've got better things to focus on for the next five days."

She smiled, though concern still lingered in her eyes. "Like what?"

"Like showing the Harvard princess how the other half survives," he teased, slinging his bag over his shoulder.

As they walked toward the exit, Talia leaned into him. "Your crew will find him. They'll make sure he's okay."

"Yeah," Sawyer said, but there was doubt in his voice. "Unless he doesn't want to be found."

His phone buzzed once more. Another message from Nash:

Road to north cabin washed out. Single mother and kid stranded nearby. Sheriff's office requesting assist. Keep your phone on. Might need your expertise if this goes sideways.

Sawyer stared at the message, a chill that had nothing to do with Boston's November air settling in his chest.

"Sawyer?" Talia's voice pulled him back. "What is it?"

He forced a smile, tucking the phone away. "Nothing important. Just crew stuff."

But as they stepped into the cold afternoon, a low thrum of unease settled in his gut.

Something was shifting on that mountain, and it wouldn't be kind. It would change more lives than just Micah's.

Because the mountain had its own way of bringing people together. Of forcing them to face what they'd been running from.

He should know. It had done the same for him.

"Lead the way, princess," he said, forcing the grin. "I'm all yours."

For five days.

After that, the mountain might be calling him back—

and this time, it wasn't just the weather he'd be walking into.

THE END

DEVOTED MOUNTAIN MAN

A SINGLE MOM, SILENT PROTECTOR, CURVY GIRL MOUNTAIN MAN ROMANCE

1

BREAKDOWN

G RACE
The car died with a shudder that sounded like surrender.

Grace pressed her forehead to the steering wheel, watching steam rise from under the hood. Twenty-six hours since leaving Portland. Six since the last gas station. And now this—stranded on a mountain road that looked like it led to absolutely nowhere.

In the backseat, Lily stirred, dark curls plastered to her flushed cheek. Five years old and already carrying more loss than most adults. The divorce papers were still warm in Grace's purse, Jon's signature barely dry. *Irreconcilable differences,* the lawyer had said. What he meant was that *your husband found someone younger and less broken.*

"Mommy?" Lily's voice was small, confused. "Are we there yet?"

"Not yet, baby." Grace forced her voice steady. "The car needs a little break."

She stepped into the mountain air that bit through her jacket.

No cell signal. No houses. Just trees that stretched up like cathedral walls and a silence so complete it made her ears ring.

Then she saw it—a flicker of light through the trees. Golden. Steady.

Fire.

Grace grabbed their emergency bag and gently shook Lily awake. "Come on, sweetheart. We're going to take a little walk."

When they started on the narrow path, it started raining. Lily stumbled twice before Grace picked her up, carrying her daughter's sleepy weight as she followed the light through trees that seemed to close behind them.

The cabin appeared like something from a fairy tale. Log walls. Stone chimney. Warm light spilling from windows that looked hand-cut. And on the porch—

A man.

Grace's breath caught.

He was *massive.* Broad shoulders that filled the doorframe. Arms that looked like they could split wood all day and still have energy to spare. Dark hair that needed cutting. A beard that couldn't quite hide the sharp line of his jaw.

And eyes. Jesus, those eyes. Gray like winter sky, watching her with an intensity that made her stomach flip.

"Help," she called out, hating how her voice cracked. "Our car broke down."

He didn't move. Just stared at her like she was something he'd been expecting. Something he'd been waiting for.

"Please," she added, shifting Lily's weight. "My daughter—"

"Inside." His voice was gravel and whiskey. "Now."

Not a question. A command that made something deep in her belly clench with want instead of fear.

What the hell is wrong with me?

He stepped aside, creating space in the doorway. As Grace passed him, she caught his scent—pine, woodsmoke, and something darker. Something that made her want to lean closer instead of away.

The cabin was warm. Clean. Sparse in a way that spoke of a man who didn't need much but took care of what he had.

"Sit," he said, nodding toward a chair by the fire.

Grace set Lily down, watching as her daughter immediately gravitated toward the warmth. The man—she didn't even know his name—moved to the kitchen with economic precision. Poured water into a kettle. Set it on a woodstove that looked older than she was.

"I'm Grace," she said, because someone had to break the silence. "This is Lily."

He turned, gray eyes locking onto hers. "Micah."

One word. But the way he said it—like he was giving her something precious—made her skin prickle with awareness.

"Thank you for—"

"Storm's coming." He cut her off, moving to the window. "Road'll wash out. You're staying."

Staying. Not *you can stay* or *you should stay.*

You're staying.

Like it was already decided. Like she belonged here.

"I couldn't impose—"

"Not imposing." His eyes found hers again, and the heat in them made her forget what she was protesting. "You're here. That's enough."

MICAH

She was perfect.

That was Micah's first thought as she stood in his doorway—soaked, desperate, holding a child like a shield against the world. Dark hair escaping from a messy ponytail. Eyes the color of whiskey in firelight. Curves that her wet clothes clung to like they had every right.

His second thought was more dangerous: *Mine.*

Which was insane. He didn't know her name. Didn't know why she was running—and she was definitely running. Women with children didn't end up on his mountain by accident.

But something in his chest had cracked the moment he saw her. Something that had been locked down tight for three years, ever since he'd decided that wanting led to losing and losing led to the kind of pain that could kill a man.

"I'm Grace," she said, and even her name sounded right in his space. "This is Lily."

The little girl was already asleep again, curled in his chair like she'd been born to it. Dark curls long lashes, and the kind of trust that only came from being loved completely.

"Micah," he said, giving her his name because she'd earned it just by existing.

Grace's eyes widened slightly, like she hadn't expected him to answer. Like men had been letting her down for a while now.

The thought made something violent stir in his chest.

"Thank you for—" she started.

"Storm's coming. Road'll wash out. You're staying."

The words came out harder than he'd intended. Not a request. A decree.

But Grace didn't flinch. Instead, something flashed in her eyes —surprise, maybe. Or recognition. Like she was seeing him for the first time.

"I couldn't impose—"

"Not imposing." He stepped closer, watching her pulse jump at her throat. "You're here. That's enough."

And it was. She was enough. More than enough.

She was everything he hadn't known he'd been waiting for.

The kettle whistled, breaking the moment. Micah forced himself to turn away, to focus on making tea instead of the way Grace's breath had quickened when he moved closer.

But he could feel her watching him. Could feel the weight of her gaze as he moved around his kitchen, and it took every ounce of control he had not to turn around and show her exactly what she was doing to him.

Three years of solitude, he reminded himself. *Three years of carefully controlled isolation.*

All shattered by a woman with whiskey eyes and a broken-down car.

He poured hot water over the tea bags, added honey because she looked like she needed sweetness. When he turned back, she was still watching him, and the hunger in her eyes nearly undid him.

"You live here alone," she said. Not a question.

"Yeah."

"Why?"

The directness of it caught him off guard. Most people danced around his isolation, treated it like a character quirk instead of a deliberate choice. The same way his supervisor had accepted his "personal leave" request without prying— temporary break, they thought. Time off to get his head straight.

"Safer that way."

Her head tilted, studying him. "Safer for who?"

For everyone. For the people who might depend on him. For the women who might trust him to keep them safe and whole.

But he didn't say that. Instead, he handed her the mug, careful not to let their fingers touch because he wasn't sure he could handle that much contact without breaking.

"Drink," he said. "Get warm."

She wrapped both hands around the mug, and he watched her shoulders relax for the first time since she'd appeared at his door.

"How far to town?" she asked.

"Twenty miles."

Her face fell. "Shit. Sorry," she added quickly, glancing at her sleeping daughter. "I didn't mean—"

"She's fine. And you're not walking twenty miles in a storm."

"I have to. I can't just—" She stopped, something vulnerable flickering across her features. "We can't stay here. You don't know us."

I know enough. He knew she was running from something. Knew she was protecting her daughter. Knew she hadn't been held properly by anyone else in a long time, if the way she flinched from his proximity was any indication.

And he knew that letting her leave would be the biggest mistake of his life.

"You're staying," he said again, softer this time. "Both of you. Until the storm passes."

Grace stared at him for a long moment, and he could see her weighing her options. Could see the exact moment she realized she didn't have any.

"Okay," she whispered. "Thank you."

The gratitude in her voice made something twist in his chest. Made him want to promise her things he had no right to promise.

Made him want to be the kind of man who could keep her safe.

Dangerous thinking. But as he watched her sip her tea, watched the tension slowly leave her body, Micah found he didn't care.

For the first time in three years, he wanted something more than solitude.

He wanted *her.*

Outside, the rainstorm was raging. Soon it would be a deluge, washing out roads and cutting off escape routes.

Trapping them together.

Micah should have felt confined. Instead, he felt like something had finally clicked into place.

Like he'd been waiting his whole life for Grace to break down on his mountain.

Like everything that came before had just been preparation for this moment.

For *her*.

2

ONE BED

GRACE

The storm hit like a living thing.

Grace jolted awake to the sound of wind screaming through the trees, rain hammering the roof in sheets. She'd been dozing in the chair by the fire, Lily curled in her lap, when the temperature dropped and the world outside turned violent.

"Jesus," she breathed.

"Language, Mommy," Lily mumbled against her shoulder, not quite awake.

Across the room, Micah stood at the window, silhouetted against flashes of lightning. He'd changed his clothes—flannel that stretched across his shoulders, jeans that hung low on his hips. Every line of him screamed danger and safety in equal measure.

"How long will it last?" Grace asked.

"Hours. Maybe through tomorrow." He turned, gray eyes finding hers in the firelight. "Road's already gone. Creek's rising."

The finality in his voice made her stomach clench. Not fear—something else. Something that felt suspiciously like relief.

You're trapped, her rational mind whispered. *With a stranger who looks at you like he wants to devour you.*

Good, replied a voice she didn't recognize. A voice that had been silent since her marriage started falling apart. *Let him try.*

"Lily needs sleep," she said, because focusing on her daughter was safer than thinking about the way Micah's eyes darkened when he looked at her.

"Bed's through there." He nodded toward a doorway she hadn't noticed. "Only one, but it's big enough."

Grace's mouth went dry. "Where will you sleep?"

"Floor's fine."

"Absolutely not." The words came out sharper than she intended. "You're already giving us shelter. I won't take your bed too."

Something shifted in his expression. "You think I can't handle discomfort?"

"I think you've done enough." She stood, settling Lily more securely in her arms. "We'll take the couch."

"No." One word, but it hit like a command. "Kid needs proper rest. So do you."

"Micah—"

"Grace." The way he said her name—low, rough, like he was tasting it—made her breath catch. "Take the bed."

She should argue. Should insist on the couch, maintain some distance between them. But Lily was a warm weight in her arms, and exhaustion was pulling at her like gravity.

And maybe—God help her—maybe she wanted to see what would happen if she pushed back.

"Fine," she said. "But you're not sleeping on the floor. The bed's big enough for three."

The words hung between them like a challenge. Micah's jaw tightened, and she saw something flicker in his eyes—want, sharp and sudden, before he locked it down.

"That's not—"

"What? Appropriate?" Grace lifted her chin. "We're adults, Micah. And you said it yourself—it's a big bed."

What are you doing? Her rational mind screamed. *This is insane.*

But her body was already moving toward the bedroom, carrying Lily with her, not giving him time to argue.

The bedroom was small, simple. A bed that dominated the space, a handmade quilt pulled tight over crisp white sheets. Everything was neat and ordered, like the man who slept here.

Grace laid Lily down gently, tugging off her shoes and pulling the quilt up to her chin. Her daughter barely stirred, exhaustion keeping her deep under.

When Grace turned around, Micah filled the doorway.

"She's beautiful," he said quietly, eyes on Lily's sleeping form.

"She looks like her father." The words slipped out before Grace could stop them, and she saw Micah's expression shutter.

"Where is he?"

"Denver. With his secretary." Grace kept her voice level, matter-of-fact. "Apparently, I wasn't enough anymore."

Micah stepped into the room, and the space suddenly felt smaller. Intimate. Charged with electricity that had nothing to do with the storm outside.

"His loss," he said simply.

Two words. But the way he said them—like he meant them, like he could see what her ex-husband had thrown away—made something crack open in her chest.

"You don't know me," she whispered.

"I know enough." He moved closer, and she could smell that scent again—pine and smoke and something darker. Something that made her want to press closer instead of backing away. "I know you're stronger than you think. Braver than you believe."

"How could you possibly—"

"Because you're here." His voice dropped, rough with something that sounded like hunger. "Standing in my bedroom. Not running."

The air between them crackled. Grace's heart hammered against her ribs as Micah took another step forward, close enough now that she could see the flecks of silver in his gray eyes.

"I should run," she breathed.

"But you won't."

It wasn't a question. It was a certainty that made her core clench with want.

"No," she admitted. "I won't."

MICAH

She was going to kill him.

Standing there in his bedroom, lips parted, eyes wide with something that looked like hunger—Grace was going to be the death of him.

Three years of celibacy. Three years of telling himself he didn't need this, didn't want the complications that came with caring about someone.

All shattered by a woman who looked at him like she wanted to be devoured.

"You should get some sleep," he said, his voice rougher than he intended.

"Should I?" She tilted her head, studying him with those whiskey eyes. "Or should I ask why you're looking at me like that?"

"Like what?"

"Like you want to eat me alive."

The directness of it hit him like a physical blow. His hands clenched into fists at his sides, fighting the urge to reach for her, to show her exactly how accurate her assessment was.

"Grace—"

"I'm not fragile, Micah." She stepped closer, and he caught a hint of her scent—something sweet and warm that made his mouth water. "I'm not going to break if you touch me."

Touch her. Christ, he wanted to do more than touch her. He wanted to pin her against the wall and map every inch of her skin with his tongue. Wanted to make her scream his name until she forgot every other man who'd ever disappointed her.

"You don't know what you're asking for," he said through gritted teeth.

"Don't I?" Another step. Now she was close enough that he could feel the heat radiating from her skin. "I'm asking for you to stop treating me like I'm made of glass. I'm asking you to look at me like a woman instead of a charity case."

"You think I see you as charity?"

She shrugged, but he caught the vulnerability that flashed across her features. "Don't you? Poor abandoned woman with a kid, grateful for your help—"

He moved before he could stop himself, backing her against the wall beside the bed. His hands braced on either side of her head, caging her in, close enough that her breath ghosted across his lips.

"You want to know how I see you?" His voice came out as a growl. "I see a woman who's strong enough to walk away from a man who didn't deserve her. Who's brave enough to start over with nothing but her daughter and a broken-down car."

Grace's eyes widened, but she didn't try to escape. If anything, she pressed closer, her body a line of heat against his.

"I see a woman who makes me want things I swore I'd never want again," he continued, his voice dropping to barely above a whisper. "Who makes me forget every reason I have for staying alone."

"Micah—"

"You want to know what I want to do to you?" He leaned down, his mouth a breath away from her ear. "I want to strip you naked and worship every inch of your body. Want to make you come so hard you forget your own name. Want to fuck you until you're mine."

She gasped, her hands fisting in his flannel. "Then why don't you?"

The question hung between them, heavy with promise and danger. Micah pulled back to look at her, searching her face for any sign of doubt, any hint that this was just adrenaline talking.

He found nothing but want. Pure, honest hunger that matched his own.

"Because once I start," he said quietly, "I won't stop. Once I have you, I won't let you go."

Something flashed in her eyes—not fear, but recognition. Like she understood exactly what he was offering. What he was threatening.

"Promise?" she whispered.

The single word shattered his control.

He kissed her hard, desperate, three years of loneliness and want pouring into the contact. Grace melted against him, her mouth opening under his, hands pulling him closer like she couldn't get enough.

She tasted like honey and sin, like everything he'd been denying himself. He backed her harder against the wall, his hands sliding down to grip her hips, grinding against her until she moaned into his mouth.

"Micah," she gasped against his lips. "Please—"

A soft sound from the bed made them both freeze.

Lily, shifting in her sleep, one small hand reaching out across the quilt.

Reality crashed back like cold water. Micah stepped back, his chest heaving, hands shaking with the effort it took not to reach for Grace again.

"Fuck," he breathed.

"It's okay," Grace whispered, but her voice was unsteady, her lips swollen from his kiss. "She's still asleep."

"It's not okay." He dragged a hand through his hair, trying to get his breathing under control. "I'm sorry. I shouldn't have—"

"Don't." Her voice was sharp enough to cut. "Don't you dare apologize for that."

He stared at her, taking in the flush on her cheeks, the way her chest rose and fell with rapid breaths. She looked thoroughly kissed and absolutely beautiful.

And she was looking at him like she wanted him to finish what he'd started.

"Grace—"

"I know we can't. Not with Lily here." She pushed off from the wall, smoothing down her clothes with hands that trembled slightly. "But don't apologize."

The storm outside had intensified, wind howling through the trees, rain lashing against the windows. But the real storm was in this room, crackling between them like live electricity.

"I'll take the couch," Micah said, his voice rough.

"No." Grace moved to the far side of the bed, putting distance between them. "The bed's big enough. And Lily will sleep better with both of us here."

Both of us. Like they were already a unit. Already something more than strangers thrown together by circumstance.

"I don't think that's wise."

"Probably not." She pulled back the quilt, slipping under the covers next to her daughter. "But wisdom is overrated."

Micah stared at her for a long moment, this woman who'd walked into his life six hours ago and turned everything upside down. This woman who kissed like fire and looked at him like she could see straight through to his soul.

This woman who was going to destroy him completely.

"Get in the bed, Micah," she said softly. "I promise I'll keep my hands to myself."

I won't, he thought. *I can't promise the same.*

But he was already moving, already pulling off his flannel and settling on the far edge of the mattress. The bed was big, but not big enough to escape the heat radiating from Grace's body. Not big enough to ignore the soft sound of her breathing in the dark.

"Good night," she whispered.

"Good night."

But sleep was the last thing on his mind. All he could think about was the taste of her mouth, the sound she'd made when he'd pressed against her. The way she'd looked at him like he was something worth wanting.

Outside, the storm raged on. Inside, Micah lay in the dark and tried not to think about the woman lying just inches away.

Tried not to think about how right it felt to have her in his bed.

How much he already dreaded the moment she would leave.

3

MORNING AFTER

GRACE
Grace woke to sunlight and the sound of an axe splitting wood.

For a moment, she lay still, disoriented. The bed was unfamiliar, the scent of pine and smoke surrounding her like an embrace. Then memory crashed back—the storm, the cabin, the kiss that had nearly set her on fire.

Micah.

She turned her head, expecting to see him beside her, but his side of the bed was empty. Cold. Like he'd been gone for hours.

Lily was still fast asleep, curls spread across the pillow, one small hand clutching the edge of the quilt. Safe. Protected. Exactly where she needed to be.

The sound of the axe continued outside—rhythmic, powerful, hypnotic.

Grace slipped from the bed, careful not to wake her daughter, and padded to the window. What she saw made her breath catch all over again.

Micah stood in the clearing behind the cabin, shirtless in the morning sun. His back was to her, muscles flexing with each swing of the axe, sweat gleaming on skin that looked carved from marble. Dark hair fell across his forehead as he worked, and when he paused to wipe his brow, she caught a glimpse of his profile—sharp jaw, focused expression, the kind of concentrated power that made her thighs clench.

Jesus.

She pressed closer to the glass, drinking in the sight of him. The way his shoulders bunched when he lifted the axe. The flex of his forearms as he brought them down. The devastating efficiency of every movement.

This was what she'd kissed last night. This beautiful, dangerous man who looked like he could take apart the world with his bare hands.

Her lips tingled with the memory—the desperate hunger in his mouth, the way he'd pressed her against the wall like he wanted to crawl inside her skin. The things he'd whispered in that rough voice that made her core ache even now.

I want to strip you naked and worship every inch of your body.

I want to fuck you until you're mine.

Grace's hand drifted to her throat, fingers tracing the spot where his mouth had been. She could still feel the ghost of his touch, still taste him on her tongue. Still feel the hard length of him pressed against her belly, promising things that made her dizzy with want.

What had she awakened last night? What had that kiss unleashed in both of them?

More importantly—what was she going to do about it?

Grace had been married for six years. Had thought she understood desire, passion, the pull between two people. But what she'd felt with Micah last night... that was something else entirely.

Something raw and primal that had nothing to do with love and everything to do with *need.*

The kind of need that could consume a person if they weren't careful.

The kind of need she'd forgotten she was capable of feeling.

Outside, Micah set down the axe and reached for his shirt, pulling it over his head with easy grace. Even fully clothed, he was devastating. All controlled power and quiet intensity.

He turned toward the cabin, and for a moment their eyes met through the glass. The impact hit her like a physical blow—heat, recognition, hunger that hadn't dimmed in the light of day.

If anything, it had grown stronger.

Grace stepped back from the window, her heart hammering. She needed coffee. Needed to get her head straight before she faced him. Before she did something completely insane like walking outside and finishing what they'd started last night.

But as she moved toward the kitchen, one thought echoed in her mind:

I'm in so much trouble.

MICAH

She'd been watching him.

Micah had felt her eyes like a physical touch, burning into his back as he worked. When he'd finally turned, the sight of her framed in his bedroom window had nearly brought him to his knees.

Sleep-mussed hair. Bare legs. His flannel shirt hanging loose on her frame—when had she put that on?—the soft fabric doing nothing to hide the curves underneath.

She'd looked like sin and salvation wrapped in morning light.

Now she was in his kitchen, making coffee with the easy confidence of a woman who belonged there. Her hair was pulled back in a messy knot, and she'd found pants somewhere, but she was still wearing his shirt. The sight of it—of *her* in his clothes—made something possessive and primal roar to life in his chest.

"Morning," he said, hanging his axe on its hook by the door.

"Morning." She didn't look at him, focused intently on the coffee pot. "Sleep well?"

No. He'd spent the night listening to her breathe, fighting the urge to roll over and bury his face in her neck. Fighting the urge to wake her with his mouth between her thighs.

"Fine," he lied. "You?"

"Like a rock." Now she did look at him, and the heat in her eyes made his blood surge south. "Lily's still out cold. I think yesterday exhausted her."

"Big day," he agreed, moving closer. Close enough to catch her scent—warm skin and something sweeter. Something that was just *Grace.*

"Speaking of yesterday..." She turned to face him fully, and he saw the moment her gaze dropped to his mouth. Saw the way her tongue darted out to wet her lips. "About what happened—"

"Regrets?" The word came out sharper than he'd intended.

"No." Her answer was immediate, certain. "Do you?"

"No." He stepped closer, close enough that he could see the rapid flutter of her pulse at her throat. "But we need to talk about it."

"Do we?" She tilted her head, studying him with those whiskey eyes. "Or do we need to decide what happens next?"

The directness of it caught him off guard. Most women would dance around this, make him guess what they wanted. But Grace met his gaze head-on, no games, no artifice.

"What do you want to happen next?" he asked.

She was quiet for a moment, the only sound the bubble of the coffee pot and the distant call of birds outside. When she spoke, her voice was steady, sure.

"I want you to kiss me again. But not with my daughter ten feet away." Her eyes darkened. "I want to see what you do when there's no one to stop you."

Heat slammed through him so hard he had to grip the counter to stay upright. "Grace—"

"I know it's crazy. I know we barely know each other." She stepped closer, and he could feel the warmth radiating from her skin. "But I also know I've never felt anything like what I felt last night. And I'm tired of being careful."

Tired of being careful. Christ, she was testing him."You don't know what you're asking for," he said, his voice rough with want.

"I'm asking you to want me back." Her hand came up to rest on his chest, right over his heart. "I'm asking for you to stop holding back."

The coffee pot started to boil over. Neither of them moved.

"I haven't stopped thinking about it," she continued, her voice dropping to barely above a whisper. "About your hands on me. Your mouth. The things you said."

Micah's control snapped. He backed her against the counter, his hands framing her face, thumbs stroking along her cheekbones.

"You want to know what I haven't stopped thinking about?" His voice was pure gravel. "The sound you made when I kissed you. The way you melted against me like you'd been waiting for it your whole life."

Her breath hitched. "Micah—"

"The way you looked at me when I told you I wanted to make you mine." He leaned down, his mouth a breath away from hers. "Like you wanted that too."

"I do," she whispered. "I want that too."

The admission hung between them, raw and honest and dangerous as hell.

"Mommy?"

They sprang apart like they'd been burned. Lily stood in the doorway, rubbing her eyes, dark curls sticking up at odd angles.

"Hey, baby." Grace's voice was steadier than it had any right to be. "Sleep good?"

"Uh-huh." Lily looked between them with the shrewd awareness of a five-year-old. "Are you making breakfast?"

"Coffee," Grace said. "But I could make eggs. If Micah has some."

"I do," he confirmed, moving to turn off the burner before the coffee destroyed itself completely. "There are chickens out back."

Lily perked up. "Real chickens? Can I see them?"

"After breakfast," Grace said quickly. "And after you brush your teeth."

As Lily wandered back toward the bedroom, grumbling about teeth brushing, Grace caught Micah's eye.

"Later," she said quietly. It was a promise and a threat wrapped in one word.

Micah nodded, not trusting his voice. But as he watched her move around his kitchen, making breakfast for her daughter like she belonged there, one thought echoed in his mind:

Later couldn't come fast enough.

And when it did, he wasn't going to hold back.

Not anymore.

4

BREAKING POINT

GRACE

The roof repair should have been simple.

Grace stood on the ladder, holding the shingles steady while Micah hammered them into place. What should have been a straightforward morning task had turned into exquisite torture—three hours of his hands brushing hers as he passed tools, his body radiating heat whenever he leaned close, the controlled power in every movement making her dizzy with want.

"Hand me that one," he said, nodding toward the bundle beside her.

Grace reached for it, her fingers grazing his as she passed it over. The contact sent electricity shooting up her arm, and from the way his jaw tightened, he felt it too.

"Thanks," he said, his voice rougher than it needed to be.

Below them, Lily played with a collection of pinecones, chattering to herself as she arranged them in elaborate patterns. Completely oblivious to the tension crackling overhead.

"How much more?" Grace asked, shifting her weight on the ladder.

"Almost done." Micah positioned the shingle, muscles flexing as he drove in the nails. "Few more pieces."

His shirt had ridden up as he worked, revealing a strip of tanned skin above his belt. Grace found herself staring at the flex of his lower back, remembering how those muscles had felt under her hands last night.

"Grace."

Her eyes snapped up to find him watching her, heat darkening his gray eyes.

"You're not paying attention," he said quietly.

"I'm paying attention to exactly what I want to pay attention to," she replied, not caring that it was basically an admission.

His hands stilled on the hammer. "Dangerous thinking."

"Is it?" She shifted closer on the ladder, close enough that her thigh brushed his. "Or is it honest thinking?"

The question hung between them, loaded with everything they weren't saying. Everything they were both trying not to do with a five-year-old twenty feet away.

"Mom!" Lily's voice cut through the tension. "Can we have lunch soon? I'm hungry!"

"In a minute, baby," Grace called back, not taking her eyes off Micah.

"Few more shingles," he said, but his voice had gone rough.

They worked in charged silence, every accidental touch sending sparks through Grace's system. When Micah leaned across her to reach the far corner, his chest pressed against her back, and she had to bite her lip to keep from making a sound.

"Sorry," he murmured, but he didn't move away immediately.

"No, you're not," she breathed.

His laugh was low, dangerous. "No. I'm not."

The admission sent heat spiraling through her core. This careful, controlled man was coming undone, and she was the cause.

Finally, blessedly, the last shingle was in place. Micah climbed down first, then held the ladder steady as Grace descended. When she reached the bottom, his hands found her waist, steadying her.

But he didn't let go.

"Grace," he said, and her name sounded like a prayer on his lips.

"I know." She looked up at him, seeing her own hunger reflected in his eyes. "I feel it too."

MICAH

She was going to break him.

Standing there in his arms, looking up at him like she wanted to be devoured, Grace was systematically destroying every wall he'd built around his heart.

"Lunch," he said, forcing himself to step back. "Should make lunch."

"Right. Lunch." But she didn't move either, just stood there staring at him like she was memorizing his face.

"Mommy, I'm starving!" Lily's voice carried across the clearing.

"Coming!" Grace called, finally breaking eye contact. But as she turned toward her daughter, her hand brushed his, fingers lingering just long enough to send fire through his veins.

They made sandwiches in careful silence, working around each other in his small kitchen. Every time Grace reached for something, every time she passed behind him, the air crackled with electricity.

Lily chattered through lunch, telling them elaborate stories about her pinecone families and the adventures they were having. Micah enjoyed her creativity, her boundless imagination. He could barely focus on anything except the way Grace's lips closed around her water glass, the soft sound she made when she laughed at her daughter's stories.

"Can we explore after lunch?" Lily asked. "I want to see everything!"

"That depends," Grace said, glancing at Micah. "How much of 'everything' is safe for a five-year-old?"

"Trail to the creek's easy," he said. "Good for beginners."

"Can we, Mom? Please?"

Grace smiled at her daughter's enthusiasm. "Alright. But you stay close and listen to Micah, okay?"

The hike was meant to be a distraction. A way to burn off some of the tension that had been building all day. Instead, it became another form of torture. Even the muddy trail couldn't keep his focus.

Grace walked ahead of him on the narrow trail, her hips swaying with each step. When she paused to point out a bird to Lily, bending slightly to get down to her daughter's level, Micah had to stop and grip a tree trunk to keep from reaching for her.

At the creek, Lily immediately became fascinated with the smooth stones, collecting them in careful piles while Grace and Micah sat on a fallen log nearby.

"She's amazing," he said, watching Lily's intense concentration as she arranged her treasures.

"She is." Grace's voice was soft, full of love. "She's been my anchor through everything. The divorce, the move... I don't know what I would have done without her."

Something in her tone made him look closer. "It was bad. The divorce."

It wasn't a question, but Grace nodded anyway.

"He didn't just leave," she said quietly. "He made sure I knew exactly why. How I'd failed him. How I wasn't enough anymore."

She picked up a pebble, turning it over in her hands. "Said I'd let myself go after Lily was born. That I was boring. Predictable."

Rage, white-hot and consuming, flooded Micah's system. "He's an idiot."

Grace's laugh was hollow. "Is he? I mean, look at me. Single mom with stretch marks and trust issues. Not exactly a prize."

"Stop." The word came out harsher than he'd intended, making her flinch. "Don't talk about yourself like that."

"It's just the truth—"

"Bullshit." He turned to face her fully, taking the pebble from her hands and tossing it aside. "You want to know what I see when I look at you?"

She shook her head, but he continued anyway.

"I see a woman who's strong enough to rebuild her life from nothing. Who loves her daughter more than her own comfort. Who kisses like fire and looks at me like I'm worth something." His voice dropped. "You're not boring, Grace. You're fucking magnificent."

Her breath caught, eyes wide with something that looked like shock.

"You don't mean that," she whispered.

"I never say things I don't mean." He reached out, touching her cheek with gentle fingers. "He was threatened by you. By your strength. So he tried to tear you down."

A tear slipped down her cheek, and he caught it with his thumb.

"I haven't felt beautiful in so long," she admitted.

"Then he was blind." Micah's voice was fierce with conviction. "And stupid. And he lost the best thing that ever happened to him."

Grace stared at him for a long moment, something shifting in her expression. Something that looked like hope.

"Micah," she started, but Lily chose that moment to splash into the creek, sending water flying.

"Mom! Look! There's fish!"

The moment shattered, but something had changed between them. Something deeper than lust, more dangerous than desire.

On the walk back, Lily ran ahead, full of energy and creek water. Grace fell into step beside Micah, her shoulder occasionally brushing his arm.

"Thank you," she said quietly. "For what you said back there."

"Just the truth."

"Maybe. But it's been a long time since someone saw me that way." She looked up at him, and the vulnerability in her eyes made his chest tight. "You make me feel like myself again. Like the woman I was before everything fell apart."

"You never stopped being her," he said. "You just forgot for a while."

They walked in comfortable silence, but the air between them hummed with possibility. With promises unspoken but understood.

That night, after Lily was asleep, they would stop fighting this thing between them.

Tonight, he was going to make Grace his.

And from the way she kept looking at him—like she was counting down the minutes until her daughter's bedtime—she was thinking the exact same thing.

5

CLAIMED

GRACE

The waiting was killing her.

Grace stood at the kitchen sink, washing the same plate for the third time, hyperaware of Micah moving through the cabin behind her. He was banking the fire, checking the windows, doing all the small rituals of settling in for the night.

But every movement felt charged. Every sound amplified.

Lily had been asleep for an hour, exhausted from their day at the creek. An hour of stolen glances and careful distance, of pretending they weren't both counting down the minutes until they could stop pretending.

"She's out," Micah said quietly, emerging from the bedroom. "Deep sleep."

Grace set down the plate with hands that weren't quite steady. "Good. She needs it."

Silence stretched between them, thick with everything they'd been holding back. Grace turned slowly, leaning against the counter, and found Micah watching her with an intensity that made her breath catch.

"We're really going to do this," she said. Not a question.

"Are we?" His voice was rough, careful. Still giving her a choice. Still letting her be the one to cross the line.

Instead of answering with words, Grace reached for the hem of his flannel shirt—the one she'd been wearing all day—and pulled it over her head.

She heard his sharp intake of breath as the fabric hit the floor. Felt the weight of his gaze as it traveled over her bare skin, taking in the simple black bra, the soft curve of her waist, the way her nipples peaked under his scrutiny.

"Grace." Her name was a growl, a warning, a plea.

"Don't you dare stop this time," she whispered, moving toward him. "Don't you dare pull away."

He met her halfway, his hands finding her waist, pulling her against him with bruising force. This kiss was nothing like the one from last night—no hesitation, no holding back. Just pure hunger, months of want compressed into the meeting of mouths and tongues.

Grace moaned into his mouth, her hands fisting in his shirt, pulling him closer. She could feel the hard length of him pressing against her belly, could taste the desperation on his lips that matched her own.

"Sofa," she gasped against his mouth.

"No." His hands dropped to her ass, lifting her onto the counter. "Here. Now."

The cold surface against her bare back made her arch, and Micah took advantage, his mouth trailing down her throat to the valley between her breasts.

"You're so fucking beautiful," he murmured against her skin, hands working the clasp of her bra. "So perfect."

The fabric fell away, and then his mouth was on her, hot and demanding, tongue circling one nipple before drawing it between his teeth. Grace's head fell back, a soft cry escaping before she could stop it.

"Shh," he breathed, moving to her other breast. "Quiet, baby. Don't want to wake her."

The endearment sent heat spiraling through her core. *Baby.* Like she belonged to him already.

MICAH

She tasted like honey and sin.

Micah worked his way down her body, mapping every inch with his mouth, committing the soft sounds she made to memory. When he reached the waistband of her jeans, he looked up to find her watching him, eyes dark with want.

"Please," she whispered.

He made quick work of the denim, pulling it down along with the scrap of lace beneath. Grace was bare before him now, beautiful and flushed and completely his.

"Spread your legs," he commanded softly.

She obeyed without hesitation, and the trust in that simple action nearly undid him. He kissed the inside of her thigh, tasting salt and sweet skin, feeling her tremble under his touch.

When his mouth found her center, Grace's back arched off the counter, one hand flying to cover her mouth to muffle her cry. She was already wet, already ready for him, and the knowledge that he'd done this to her—that she wanted him this much—made him dizzy with possession.

He worked her with tongue and lips, learning what made her gasp, what made her thighs clench around his head. When he found the spot that made her entire body shake, he focused there, relentlessly, until she was writhing against his mouth.

"Micah," she breathed, hand tangling in his hair. "I'm going to—"

"Come for me," he growled against her. "Let me taste it."

She shattered with a silent scream, her body convulsing as waves of pleasure crashed over her. Micah stayed with her through it, gentling his touch as she came down, pressing soft kisses to her inner thighs.

When she finally opened her eyes, they were glazed with satisfaction and renewed hunger.

"Your turn," she said, pushing him back.

But before she could reach for his belt, he was lifting her off the counter. Instead of the couch, he lowered them both to the thick rug in front of the fireplace, the flames casting dancing shadows across their skin.

Grace's back met the soft wool, Micah's body covering hers, solid and warm and perfect. He stripped off his clothes with precise movements, the firelight playing across the planes of his chest, the corded muscle of his arms.

Grace's eyes went wide as he revealed himself completely—all hard muscle and controlled power, his cock thick and ready for her.

"Come here," she whispered, reaching for him.

He settled over her, bracing his weight on his forearms, the head of his cock nudging against her entrance. The fire crackled beside them, bathing them in golden light as they stared at each other, both understanding that this would change everything.

"You sure?" he asked, even though stopping might kill him.

"I've never been more sure of anything in my life," she replied.

He pushed into her slowly, watching her face as her body adjusted to accommodate him. She was tight, perfect, hot as silk around him. When he was fully seated, they both went still, overwhelmed by the sensation of being completely connected.

"You feel incredible," he breathed against her ear.

Grace wrapped her legs around his waist, pulling him deeper. "Move," she whispered. "Please, Micah. I need you to move."

He began to thrust, slow and deep, building a rhythm that made her breath hitch with every stroke. This wasn't just sex—it was claiming, marking, the complete surrender of two people who'd been alone too long.

"Harder," Grace gasped, nails digging into his shoulders.

Micah obliged, driving into her with increasing force, the firelight dancing across their sweat-slicked skin. Grace bit her lip to keep from crying out, her body rising to meet every thrust.

"You're mine," he growled, the words torn from somewhere deep in his chest. "Say it."

"Yours," she breathed. "I'm yours."

The admission pushed him over the edge. His rhythm faltered as his release built, and Grace sensed it, her hand sliding between their bodies to touch herself.

They came together, muffling their cries against each other's necks, bodies shaking with the force of their mutual climax.

Afterward, they lay tangled together on the soft rug, breathing hard, skin slick with sweat. Micah pulled the throw blanket over them, not ready to break the connection, not ready to let her go.

"That was..." Grace started, then trailed off.

"Yeah," he agreed, understanding perfectly.

She turned in his arms to face him, something vulnerable in her expression. "What happens now?"

The question hung between them, loaded with implications. Micah smoothed a strand of hair from her face, his touch gentle despite the possessiveness still thrumming through his veins.

"Now you stay," he said simply. "Both of you. For as long as you want."

"And if I want forever?"

The hope in her voice made his chest tight. "Then forever it is."

Grace's smile was radiant, transformative. She kissed him softly, a promise sealed with lips and breath.

Outside, the wind had picked up again, but inside the cabin, wrapped in each other's arms, they were safe from any storm.

They had found their shelter in each other.

And neither of them intended to let it go.

6

MORNING RECKONING

GRACE

Grace woke to the sound of Lily's voice and the absence of Micah's warmth.

"Mommy, why are you sleeping on the floor?"

Grace's eyes snapped open to find her daughter standing over her, head tilted with five-year-old curiosity. The throw blanket was pulled up to her chin, but underneath, she was naked, and the memory of last night hit her like a freight train.

Micah's hands. His mouth. The way he'd claimed her on this very rug.

"I... the couch was too small," she managed, sitting up carefully, clutching the blanket. "Where's Micah?"

"Outside chopping wood. He made me cereal." Lily plopped down beside her, apparently unconcerned by her mother's floor-sleeping habits. "He said not to wake you. Said you needed rest."

Heat flooded Grace's cheeks. Had he told Lily that? And more importantly—what exactly had her daughter seen or heard last night?

"Did you sleep okay, baby?"

"Uh-huh. I dreamed about the fish in the creek." Lily studied her with those sharp eyes that missed nothing. "You look different, Mommy."

"I need coffee," Grace said, which was true but barely scratched the surface of what she needed. "And a shower. Can you play quietly for a few minutes?"

Lily nodded and wandered back to her cereal, leaving Grace alone with her racing thoughts and the lingering scent of woodsmoke and sex.

She gathered her scattered clothes quickly, heat blooming in her core as she remembered how they'd been removed. How Micah had touched her, tasted her, made her come apart in his hands.

How she'd begged for it.

What have I done?

But as she pulled on her clothes, Grace caught sight of herself in the small mirror by the door. Her lips were swollen, her neck marked with faint bruises from Micah's mouth. She looked thoroughly debauched.

She looked *alive.*

MICAH

He'd been up since dawn, splitting wood with more force than necessary.

Not because he regretted last night—Christ, no. Every moment was burned into his memory like a brand. The taste of her. The sounds she'd made. The way she'd looked at him afterward, like he'd given her something precious.

No, he was chopping wood because he needed to do something with his hands before Grace woke up and he did something stupid like pin her against the nearest wall and fuck her again.

Which he wanted to do. Desperately.

But they needed to talk first. About what this meant. About what happened next. About the very real complications of a woman with a child wanting to stay in his carefully ordered life.

The cabin door opened, and Grace emerged, hair damp from a shower, wearing fresh clothes. She looked beautiful and uncertain, and Micah had to grip the axe handle to keep from reaching for her.

"Morning," she said, not quite meeting his eyes.

"Morning." He set down the axe, wiping his hands on his jeans. "Sleep well?"

A flush crept up her neck. "Eventually."

They stared at each other across the clearing, the memory of last night hanging between them like live electricity. Micah wanted to cross the distance, wanted to kiss her until she stopped looking so worried.

But Lily's voice carried from inside the cabin, a reminder of all the reasons they needed to be careful.

"We should talk," Grace said quietly.

"Yeah. We should."

They walked to the edge of the clearing, close enough to keep an eye on the cabin but far enough for privacy. Grace wrapped her arms around herself, suddenly looking small and vulnerable.

"I don't usually—" she started, then stopped. "Last night was..."

"A mistake?" The words came out harsher than he'd intended.

"No." Her response was immediate, fierce. "Not a mistake. But maybe... reckless."

Micah studied her face, seeing the war between what she wanted and what she thought she should want.

"Regrets?" he asked, echoing their conversation from yesterday.

"About what we did? No." She looked up at him, vulnerability shining in her eyes. "But Lily and I are living out of suitcases. I don't even have a job. And last night I let a man I've known for two days fuck me senseless while my daughter slept twenty feet away." Her voice cracked. "What kind of mother does that make me?"

The self-recrimination in her voice made something violent stir in his chest. "The kind who's human. Who has needs."

"But what if I'm wrong about this? About you?" She stepped closer, her hand finding his chest. "When you touch me, I forget everything that went wrong before. I feel safe in a way I haven't since I was a kid. Like I could fall asleep in your arms and nothing bad would ever happen again." Her voice dropped to a whisper. "And that terrifies me."

The admission cracked something open in his chest. He covered her hand with his, holding it against his heartbeat.

"Then why are you fighting it?"

"Because I have to think about Lily. About what's best for her." Grace's voice was stronger now, more certain. "She's already lost so much. Her father, her home, her entire life as she knew it. I can't let her get attached to someone who might not stick around."

Micah was quiet for a moment, absorbing her words. Understanding, for the first time, the weight of what she was offering him.

Not just herself. But her daughter. Her entire future.

"You think I won't stick around," he said finally.

"I think you've been alone for a long time. And I think the reality of instant family might be different than the fantasy."

She wasn't wrong. Three days ago, the thought of sharing his space with anyone—let alone a woman and her child—would have sent him running for the hills.

But that was before Grace. Before Lily's endless questions and infectious laughter. Before he'd tasted forever on a stranger's lips and realized he'd been starving for it.

"What if it's not?" he asked.

Grace blinked. "What?"

"What if the reality is better than the fantasy?" He stepped closer, his free hand cupping her face. "What if I want this? All of it. You, Lily, the chaos and noise, and the mess that comes with a family."

"Micah—"

"I haven't felt alive in three years, Grace. Not until you showed up at my door." His thumb stroked along her cheekbone. "You think I'm going to let that go without a fight?"

Tears gathered in her eyes. "It's crazy. We barely know each other."

"So we'll learn. We have time."

"Do we?" She pulled back slightly, fear creeping into her voice. "What happens when the road clears? When we have to make real decisions about real life?"

Before Micah could answer, the sound of an engine cut through the morning air. They both turned to see a pickup truck navigating the washed-out sections of the road, coming steadily toward the cabin.

"Expecting someone?" Grace asked, tension creeping into her voice.

Micah's jaw tightened. "No."

The truck pulled into the clearing, and Micah recognized the driver immediately. Jake Reeves, his closest neighbor, probably coming to check on him after the storm.

Which meant their private bubble was about to burst.

The truck door slammed, and Jake emerged with a knowing grin already plastered across his weathered face. He took in the scene—Micah standing close to a beautiful woman, both of them looking like they'd been caught doing something interesting—and his smile widened.

"Well, I'll be damned. Storm knocked out half the county, but you look like you weathered it just fine, Micah." His eyes shifted to

Grace, taking inventory with the practiced ease of a man who lived for gossip. "And who might this lovely lady be? Don't think I've seen you around these parts before."

Grace straightened, squaring her shoulders like she was preparing for battle. Micah felt a surge of pride at her courage, even as he dreaded the conversation to come.

"Grace," he said quietly, catching her hand. "Whatever happens next, whatever anyone says—last night wasn't a mistake. And neither is this."

She squeezed his fingers, some of the fear leaving her eyes. "Promise me something."

"Anything."

"Promise me you'll tell me if you change your mind. If this gets too real, too complicated. Promise me you won't just disappear."

The request hit him like a gut punch, revealing just how deeply her ex-husband's abandonment had cut.

"I promise," he said, meaning it with every fiber of his being. "I'm not going anywhere, Grace. You're stuck with me."

Jake cleared his throat loudly, clearly enjoying the show. "Hope I'm not interrupting anything important here."

Because Jake wasn't just a neighbor. He was a gossip, a busy-body, and the unofficial town crier for everything that happened in a fifty-mile radius.

Which meant by evening, half the county would know that the hermit of Pine Ridge had taken in a woman and her child.

And by tomorrow, everyone would be speculating about whether she was just a temporary visitor—or something more permanent.

The morning of reckoning had officially begun.

7

CARVED IN STONE

G RACE
Jake Reeves had the biggest mouth in three counties.

Grace learned this within five minutes of meeting him, as he peppered her with questions disguised as friendly small talk while his eyes catalogued every detail—her rumpled clothes, Micah's protective stance, the way they kept gravitating toward each other like magnets.

"So you're just passing through?" Jake asked, accepting the coffee Micah had grudgingly offered. "Hell of a storm to get caught in."

"Car broke down," Grace said simply, not elaborating.

"Lucky Micah was here to help." Jake's grin was pure mischief. "Man's handy with all sorts of repairs, aren't you, Micah?"

Micah's jaw tightened. "Jake."

"What? Just making conversation." Jake turned back to Grace, clearly fishing. "You got people expecting you somewhere? Husband probably worried sick."

"No husband," Grace said, lifting her chin. Let him chew on that.

Jake's eyebrows shot up. "Well, now. That's interesting."

"Jake." Micah's voice carried a warning that made the older man chuckle.

"Alright, alright. I can take a hint." Jake drained his coffee and stood. "Just wanted to check you made it through the storm okay. Road should be passable by this afternoon, if you're planning to head out."

The statement hung in the air like a challenge. Grace felt Micah's eyes on her, waiting for her answer. Waiting to see if she'd run.

"Actually," she said, her voice steady, "I'm thinking of sticking around for a while. If there's work to be found."

Jake's grin widened. "Work, huh? What kind of work?"

"I'm a nurse. Emergency medicine."

"Well, shit—sorry, ma'am—but Doc Henderson's been looking for help at the clinic for months. Can't keep staff this far out. You interested in small-town medicine?"

Grace's heart leaped. A job. An actual reason to stay that had nothing to do with the man standing beside her.

"Very interested," she said.

"I'd head down there today if I were you. Folks in town love good news." Jake's knowing wink made it clear he'd be spreading his own version of good news before his truck even reached the main road.

After Jake left, his truck disappearing down the mountain road with suspicious speed, Grace and Micah stood in the clearing, the weight of her decision settling between them.

Grace squeezed his fingers. "What do you think Jake will tell people?"

"Everything." Micah's mouth quirked. "By tonight, half the county will know I'm off the market. Including my crew."

"Your crew?"

"Trail builders. Good men, mostly. Though Reese might have his hands full soon—heard there's a Forest Service assessor coming to evaluate the north ridge damage. Government type with a clipboard."

Grace grinned. "That could be interesting."

"Could be a war zone," Micah corrected. "Reese doesn't play nice with authority."

"You meant it," Micah said, bringing them back to the moment. "About staying."

"If there's work. If I can make it work for Lily." She looked up at him. "If you want us to."

His answer was to back her against the nearest tree and kiss her breathless, his hands fisting in her hair, his body pressing her into the rough bark.

"Is that answer enough?" he growled against her mouth.

"Getting there," she gasped, but she was smiling.

MICAH

The clinic job was hers by noon.

Doc Henderson took one look at Grace's credentials and hired her on the spot, relief evident in his weathered face. The pay wasn't much, but it came with housing—a small apartment above the clinic that would work perfectly for her and Lily.

Which should have been good news.

Instead, Micah felt something cold settle in his chest as Grace explained the details over lunch.

"It's perfect," she was saying, cutting Lily's sandwich into triangles. "Walking distance to the school, stable income, our own place..."

"Sounds ideal," he said, his voice carefully neutral.

Grace looked up, catching something in his tone. "What's wrong?"

"Nothing's wrong."

"Micah." She reached across the table, her fingers finding his. "Talk to me."

He was quiet for a moment, trying to articulate the fear clawing at his chest. The apartment was in town. Twenty miles from his cabin. Twenty miles from him.

"You'll be in town," he said finally.

"So?"

"So I'm not."

Understanding dawned in her eyes. "You think I'm leaving you."

"Aren't you?"

Grace was quiet for a moment, studying his face. Then she turned to Lily, who was absorbed in arranging her sandwich pieces by size.

"Lily, baby, why don't you go check on the chickens? Make sure they have enough water."

Lily perked up. "Can I collect eggs too?"

"Of course. Take the basket."

Once Lily was gone, Grace turned back to him, her expression serious.

"I took the job because I need to be able to support myself," she said. "Because I need to know I can take care of Lily on my own. Not because I'm planning to run."

"But you'll live in town."

"For now." She leaned forward, her eyes holding his. "Until we figure out what this is. What we want it to be."

"I know what I want it to be."

"So do I." Her voice dropped. "But I also know that moving in with a man I've known for three days, no matter how incredible he is, isn't something I can explain to my daughter. Or to myself."

Micah nodded, understanding her reasoning even as his chest tightened with the thought of her leaving.

"How long?" he asked.

"I don't know. A few weeks? A month? However long it takes for us to be sure." She squeezed his hand. "I'm not running, Micah. I'm being careful. There's a difference."

Before he could respond, Lily's voice carried from the chicken coop.

"Micah! Come quick! Ghost laid a really big egg!"

He looked at Grace, seeing his own reluctance to break the moment reflected in her eyes.

"Go," she said softly. "She's excited to show you."

As he walked toward the coop, Micah felt something shift in his chest. Grace was right to be careful. Right to want stability before making promises. But that didn't make the thought of her leaving any easier.

He found Lily holding an enormous egg, her face glowing with pride.

"Look how big it is!" she exclaimed. "It's the biggest one yet!"

"That's a good one," he agreed, admiring her find. "Ghost's been busy."

"Will you miss me when we move to town?" Lily asked, the question coming out of nowhere with the brutal honesty of childhood.

Micah crouched down to her level, meeting her eyes. "Yeah, kiddo. I'll miss you a lot."

"Will you visit us?"

"If your mom says it's okay."

Lily nodded solemnly. "I'll ask her. But I think she'll say yes. She likes you."

"I like her too."

"And you like me?"

"Very much."

Lily grinned, apparently satisfied with this arrangement. "Good. Then everything will be fine."

If only it were that simple.

8

COMING HOME

GRACE

They left after dinner. Micah had fixed her car—a clogged fuel filter—with practiced ease before she even knew what was wrong with it. Now, it was loaded with her few possessions and a basket of eggs from Micah's chickens. Grace had expected the goodbye to be awkward, emotional. Instead, it felt strangely like a see-you-later.

Maybe because Micah had pressed something into her hand as they walked to the car. A small wooden figure, carved with the same careful precision as everything he made.

A mountain. Simple, elegant, unmistakably his work.

"So you don't forget where you belong," he'd said quietly.

Now, as she tucked Lily into the narrow bed in their new apartment, Grace turned the carving over in her hands, feeling the smooth wood warm under her fingers.

"I like our new place," Lily said sleepily. "But I miss Micah's cabin already."

"Me too, baby."

"When can we see him again?"

"Soon," Grace promised, though she wasn't sure what soon meant. A few days? A week? However long it took for her to feel steady on her own feet again.

She kissed Lily's forehead and moved to the window, looking out at the small town settling into the evening. Somewhere in the distance, beyond the trees and hills, Micah was banking his fire, checking his windows, settling into his solitary routine.

But now that routine had a hole in it shaped like her and Lily.

The thought should have made her feel guilty. Instead, it made her feel powerful.

She had marked him as thoroughly as he had marked her.

Her phone buzzed. A text from an unknown number.

> Sleep well. Both of you.

Grace smiled, recognizing Micah's style. She typed back quickly.

> You too. Thank you for everything.

His response came immediately.

> Not everything. Not yet.

Heat flooded her cheeks at the promise in those words. He wasn't done with her. This wasn't an ending—it was an intermission.

A pause between the first act and whatever came next.

Grace set the phone aside and moved to unpack their things, but her hands kept returning to the wooden mountain, to the solid weight of it in her palm.

So you don't forget where you belong.

She wouldn't forget. Couldn't.

Because for the first time in her life, she had found a place—a person—worth fighting for.

Worth staying for.

Worth building a future around.

The mountain wasn't just carved wood. It was a promise. A claim. A reminder that some things, once found, were too precious to let go.

Tomorrow she would start her new job, begin building a life in this small town. But tonight, she held Micah's promise in her hands and knew, with absolute certainty, that this was just the beginning.

MICAH

Three weeks later, Micah stood on his porch, watching a familiar car navigate the winding road to his cabin.

They came every weekend now. Grace and Lily, loaded with groceries and stories from town, filling his space with laughter and chaos and everything he'd been missing.

But today felt different. Grace moved with purpose as she climbed out of the car, her eyes holding something he couldn't quite read.

"Hey," she said, approaching the porch steps.

"Hey yourself." He studied her face, noting the flush in her cheeks, the way she bit her lower lip when she was nervous. "Everything okay?"

"More than okay." She reached into her purse, pulling out an envelope. "I got something in the mail today."

Micah took the envelope, recognizing the return address immediately. Divorce decree. Final and official.

"It's done," Grace said quietly. "Completely, legally done."

He looked up to find her watching him, something vulnerable and hopeful shining in her eyes.

"Grace—"

"I know what I want, Micah." She stepped closer, her hands finding his chest. "I want you. This. Us. Not someday, not eventually. Now."

"You sure?"

"I've never been more sure of anything in my life." She smiled, the expression radiant with certainty. "I love you. Lily loves you. And I'm tired of pretending that living twenty miles away changes any of that."

Before he could respond, Lily came barreling around the side of the cabin, arms full of pinecones.

"Micah! I found the biggest pine cone ever! And Mom said we could stay for dinner and maybe—" She stopped, taking in their proximity, the intensity of their locked gazes. "Are you guys going to kiss now?"

Grace laughed, the sound bright and free. "Maybe."

"Good," Lily declared. "You're both much nicer when you kiss."

And so Micah kissed her, there on his porch, with her daughter cheering and the mountain stretching out around them like a blessing.

When they finally broke apart, Grace rested her forehead against his.

"Take us home," she whispered.

"You already are," he replied.

And they were.

THE END

UNTAMED MOUNTAIN MAN

AN ENEMIES-TO-LOVERS CABIN ROMANCE WITH A GRUMPY BUILDER AND A CURVY RULEBREAKER

1

TERRITORY LINES

DANI

The GPS had been off for the last ten miles.

Danielle Vargas stood at the edge of what used to be a trail, staring at a landscape that looked like Mother Nature had gone wild with a sledgehammer.. Washouts carved fresh scars down the mountainside. Trees lay scattered like discarded toothpicks. And somewhere in this mess, she was supposed to assess environmental impact for the Forest Service.

"Perfect," she muttered, shouldering her pack. "Just fucking perfect."

The storm damage was worse than the satellite images had shown. Which meant more paperwork, more site visits, and more time dealing with mountain men who thought permits were polite suggestions rather than federal law.

She'd already had three confrontations this week with locals who'd taken "emergency trail maintenance" into their own hands. Apparently, waiting for official clearance was for people who didn't have chainsaws and opinions about government efficiency.

Dani picked her way through the debris field, boots slipping on loose gravel. The air smelled like pine sap and recent rain, crisp enough to clear her head after six hours in a rental car that reeked of cherry air freshener and disappointment.

She found a decent clearing about fifty yards off what used to be the main trail. Level ground, decent drainage, far enough from any obvious wildlife corridors. Perfect for a base camp while she surveyed the area.

Her hammock went up between two sturdy pines, rain fly stretched tight above it. Solar charger clipped to a branch where it could catch morning sun. Portable weather station assembled and calibrated.

Efficient. Professional. Exactly what she'd been hired to do.

The fact that she was technically camping without a permit on federal land? Well, sometimes you had to bend rules to enforce bigger ones.

Dani stripped off her hiking shirt, grateful for the mountain air on her overheated skin. The tank top underneath was soaked with sweat, clinging to her curves in ways that would've made her self-conscious back in the city. Out here, with nothing but trees and wildlife for an audience, she didn't give a damn.

She grabbed her field notebook and spread the survey map across a flat boulder, weighing down the corners with rocks. According to her research, the worst damage was concentrated in a three-mile radius from here. Slope failures, erosion channels, and—according to one particularly irate phone call from her supervisor—"unauthorized trail reconstruction by persons unknown."

Which meant someone was out here playing Johnny Apple-seed with heavy machinery, and she got to track them down and explain why federal land came with federal rules.

"Persons unknown, my ass," she said, making notes in the

margin. In her experience, "persons unknown" were usually local contractors with too much equipment and not enough patience for bureaucracy.

A branch cracked somewhere behind her.

Dani looked up from her map, scanning the tree line. Nothing moved except a squirrel chattering indignantly from a nearby pine.

Probably just wildlife. Maybe a deer picking through the storm debris.

She went back to her notes, marking potential survey points on the map. The squirrel's chittering grew louder, more agitated.

"What's your problem?" she asked it.

The squirrel responded by launching itself from the tree directly at her head.

"Jesus Christ!" Dani ducked, grabbing the first thing her hand found—a rock the size of a baseball—and hurled it at the furry little terrorist.

The rock sailed wide, missed the squirrel entirely, and connected with a sickening *thunk* against something metallic in the trees.

The squirrel fled. The chittering stopped.

And from the direction of the thunk came a sound that made her blood run cold:

A man clearing his throat. Slow. Deliberate. Pissed.

"Well," said a voice like gravel and whiskey. "That's gonna leave a mark."

REESE

Reese Carter had been having a decent morning until he found a government trespasser stringing camping gear between his trees.

He'd been checking the new drainage channels behind his cabin when he'd spotted the flash of orange nylon through the pines. A rental car with government plates parked at the trail access. Expensive gear scattered around a campsite that was definitely on the wrong side of his property line.

And now, apparently, the trespasser was hurling rocks at his truck.

Reese stepped out from behind the pine where he'd been watching, surveying the damage to his driver's side door. Fresh dent. Right through the paint job he'd touched up last month.

"Nice arm," he said.

The woman spun around, and Reese's annoyance shifted into something more complicated.

She was beautiful in a way that had nothing to do with makeup or careful styling. Dark hair pulled back in a messy ponytail. Olive skin flushed from exertion. Brown eyes that flashed with temper and intelligence in equal measure.

And curves. Christ, the curves. Her tank top clung to every line of her body—full breasts, narrow waist, hips that would fit perfectly in his hands.

She was also holding a clipboard and glaring at him like he was the one who didn't belong here.

"You always sneak up on people like that?" she asked, not backing down an inch.

"You always camp on private property without permission?"

Her eyebrows shot up. "Private property? This is federal land."

"Up to the tree line, yeah. You're twenty feet past it." Reese crossed his arms, enjoying the way her gaze dropped to his chest before snapping back up. "That hammock's hanging on my trees."

She looked at the hammock, then at the trees, then back at him with an expression that could've melted steel.

"Bullshit."

"Survey stakes are right over there if you want to check." He nodded toward the barely visible markers. "Been here since '98."

The woman—government contractor, judging by her gear—grabbed her map and stalked over to the stakes. Reese watched her move, taking in the efficient stride, the way she crouched to examine the markers, the curve of her ass in those hiking pants.

When she straightened, her jaw was tight with irritation.

"Fine. I'm twenty feet over your line." She turned to face him, hands on her hips. "You want me to move my camp?"

"I want you to tell me why you're here."

"Environmental impact assessment. Post-storm damage evaluation." She lifted her chin. "And you are?"

"The guy whose truck you just dented."

"That was an accident."

"Was it?"

Her mouth curved in what might've been a smile if it hadn't been so sharp. "Depends. You the type who thinks accidents happen to people who deserve them?"

Reese found himself fighting a grin. Most people apologized when they damaged his property. This one looked like she might throw another rock if he gave her reason.

"Depends," he said. "You the type who throws rocks when she's caught trespassing?"

"I was aiming for the squirrel."

"My truck's bigger than a squirrel."

"Your truck got in the way."

They stared at each other across the clearing, tension crackling between them like electricity before a storm. She was magnificent when she was pissed—eyes flashing, chest rising with quick breaths, every line of her body radiating controlled fury.

Reese had spent two years avoiding exactly this kind of complication. Smart, beautiful women with authority and attitude problems. Women who looked at him like they could see past the walls he'd built around himself.

Women who made him want things he'd sworn off.

"Environmental assessment," he repeated. "What kind of assessment?"

"The kind that determines whether recent trail work meets federal guidelines." Her smile turned predatory. "You wouldn't happen to know anything about unauthorized excavation in the area, would you?"

And there it was. The real reason she was here.

Someone had complained about his repair work. Probably Henderson, the weekend warrior who'd gotten his ATV stuck in one of Reese's drainage ditches last month. Or maybe the county, pissed that he'd diverted the washout before it took out the main access road.

Either way, this woman with the clipboard and the smart mouth was here to shut him down.

"Can't say I do," he said.

"Interesting." She made a note on her clipboard. "Because according to my information, someone's been doing extensive trail maintenance without proper permits. Someone who knows the area well enough to work at night and avoid the ranger patrols."

"Sounds like you've got a mystery on your hands."

"I love mysteries." Her gaze swept over him, taking inventory—his work clothes, the calluses on his hands, the mud on his boots that matched the mud around the fresh repair work. "Especially ones involving chainsaws and excavation equipment."

Reese kept his expression neutral. "You accusing me of something?"

"Should I be?"

The question hung between them, loaded with challenge and something else. Something that made his blood run hot and his hands itch to grab her.

"Move your camp," he said finally. "Or I'll call the ranger station and report you for illegal camping."

"Go ahead." She stepped closer, close enough that he could smell her shampoo over the pine and sweat. "I'll file a complaint about unauthorized trail work while you're at it."

"You do that."

"I will."

They were standing close enough to touch now, close enough for Reese to see the gold flecks in her brown eyes. Close enough to feel the heat radiating from her skin.

Close enough to do something supremely stupid.

Reese took a deliberate step back.

"Twenty-four hours," he said. "Then I want you gone."

"Or what?"

"Or we'll have problems."

Her laugh was sharp, dangerous. "Mountain man, we already have problems."

She turned away, dismissing him, and began packing her gear with efficient movements. Reese watched her stuff the map into a waterproof case, disassemble the weather station, and clip the solar charger to her pack.

Professional. Competent. Completely unintimidated by him.

Which should've been a relief.

Instead, it made him want to stay and watch her work. Made him want to see what other smart comments she'd make. Made him want to find out what she'd do if he grabbed that clipboard and used it for kindling.

"Hey," he called as she shouldered her pack.

She looked back, eyebrows raised.

"Name's Reese. Reese Carter. Since you'll probably need it for your report."

"Dani," she replied. "Danielle Vargas. And trust me, you'll be in my report."

"Looking forward to it, Danielle."

Her grin was pure trouble. "You shouldn't be."

She walked away without looking back, heading deeper into the forest with the confidence of someone who knew exactly where she was going.

Reese stood in the clearing, watching her disappear into the trees, and felt something twist in his chest. Something he'd been ignoring for two years.

Want. Pure, honest, dangerous want.

Which was exactly why he needed her gone.

Because Danielle Vargas with her clipboard and her smart mouth and her curves that could stop traffic?

She was going to be nothing but trouble.

And God help him, he was already looking forward to it.

DANI

Dani made it half a mile before she stopped to catch her breath and reassess her situation.

Situation one: She'd just dented a mountain man's truck and pitched camp on his property.

Situation two: Said mountain man was approximately six feet of solid muscle wrapped in flannel and a bad attitude.

Situation three: He was also, almost certainly, the "person unknown" who'd been rebuilding trails without permits.

Situation four: She'd threatened to report him, and he'd threatened to evict her, and neither of them had backed down.

Situation five: She was more turned on than she'd been in months.

"Professional," she muttered, dropping her pack beside a fallen log. "Stay professional."

But professional was hard to maintain when the subject of her investigation looked like he could bench press a tree and had eyes like winter sky. When he'd stepped back from her in the clearing, she'd caught the scent of pine sap and clean sweat, had seen the way his jaw tightened when she'd moved closer.

Had felt the electricity crackling between them like a live wire.

Dani pulled out her phone, hoping for a signal. Nothing. The nearest cell tower was probably twenty miles away, and the mountains made coverage spotty even on good days.

Which meant she was on her own until she hiked back to her car.

She opened her field notebook and started making notes:

Subject: Reese Carter Age: Early 30s Physical description: 6'2", brown hair, gray eyes, extensive manual labor conditioning Residence: Cabin, private property adjacent to federal land Attitude: Hostile, territorial, uncooperative Likelihood of unauthorized trail work: 95%

She paused, pen hovering over the page.

Additional notes: Significant sexual tension. Recommend requesting different assessor.

Dani scratched out the last line before the ink was dry.

She was here to do a job. Environmental assessment. File a report. Move on to the next assignment.

She was not here to fantasize about what Reese Carter looked like without that flannel shirt. Or wonder what his hands would feel like on her skin. Or imagine what it would be like to wipe that cocky expression off his face with her mouth.

Her phone buzzed. Text message from her supervisor.

Status report? Storm damage worse than expected?

Dani typed back quickly.

Initial survey complete. Some complications with local contractor. Will file full report by Friday.

Complications?

She stared at the screen, considering her options. She could report the unauthorized trail work now, get Reese shut down before he knew what hit him. Quick, clean, professional.

Or she could stick around, gather more evidence, and build a stronger case.

The fact that sticking around meant more time sparring with the most attractive man she'd met in years had nothing to do with her decision.

Nothing at all.

Minor permitting issues. Nothing I can't handle.

Copy that. Keep me posted.

Dani put the phone away and shouldered her pack. She had three days to complete her assessment. Three days to document the storm damage, evaluate the unauthorized repair work, and file a report that would either shut down Reese Carter's operation or give him the permits he should've applied for in the first place.

Three days to figure out why a man who clearly knew what he was doing had chosen to work outside the system.

And three days to ignore the fact that she'd rather strip him naked than write him up.

She started back toward the trail, already planning her next move. She'd set up a proper camp on federal land, well away from his property line. Document the trail work from a scientific perspective. Approach this like the professional she was.

But as she walked, Dani couldn't shake the memory of those gray eyes, the controlled tension in his voice when he'd said her name.

Danielle.

Like he was testing how it felt on his tongue.

Professional was going to be a lot harder than she'd thought.

Especially when the subject of her investigation looked at her like he wanted to devour her.

And especially when she was starting to think she might let him.

2

PRESSURE DROP

REESE

The storm hit at three in the morning with the fury of something personal.

Reese woke to the sound of wind screaming through the pines and rain hammering his tin roof like artillery fire. He pulled on jeans and boots, grabbed his flashlight, and stepped onto the porch to assess the damage.

The clearing behind his cabin had turned into a lake. Water poured down the mountainside in torrents, carving fresh channels through the soil he'd spent months stabilizing. His generator shed was already ankle-deep in runoff.

"Shit," he muttered, splashing toward the shed.

The generator sputtered and died just as he reached it. Emergency fuel pump, probably flooded. Which meant no power for the radio, no way to contact the outside world until the storm passed.

Lightning split the sky, illuminating the forest in stark black and white. In the distance, toward the federal land boundary, Reese caught a glimpse of orange fabric whipping in the wind.

The government assessor's camp.

He stood in the rain for a long moment, water streaming down his face, weighing his options. She'd pitched her tent in a drainage area that would be underwater within the hour. Her car was parked at the trail access, probably already cut off by the washout developing near the main road.

None of which was his problem.

Except the part where she'd drown if he left her out there.

"Fuck," he said, and started toward the tree line.

DANI

Dani's tent was disintegrating around her.

The rain fly had torn loose twenty minutes ago, and water was pouring through the mesh ceiling like a broken faucet. Her sleeping bag was soaked. Her gear was floating. And somewhere in the darkness outside, she could hear the creek rising, rushing toward her campsite with the sound of a freight train.

She stuffed her essentials into her waterproof pack—radio, first aid kit, emergency rations. The radio crackled with static when she tried to call for pickup, but no human voices came through the white noise.

A gust of wind caught her tent, lifting it off the ground with her still inside. Dani grabbed the door zipper and fought her way out into the storm.

The world outside was chaos. Rain fell in sheets so thick she could barely see her own hands. The creek had jumped its banks, rushing between the trees in a brown torrent that carried logs and debris like battering rams.

Her car was half a mile away, across ground that was rapidly becoming impassable.

Dani shouldered her pack and started moving, picking her

way through the storm debris by feel. Her boots slipped on wet rocks, and she went down hard, catching herself on her hands as cold water soaked through her jacket.

When she looked up, a figure emerged from the darkness like something out of a nightmare.

Reese Carter, water streaming from his hair, shirt plastered to his chest, moving toward her with the determined stride of a man who didn't let weather slow him down.

"You alive?" he shouted over the wind.

"Unfortunately!" she shouted back.

He reached her in three strides, grabbed her arm, and hauled her to her feet. His hands were warm even through her soaked jacket, strong enough to steady her when another gust of wind tried to knock her down.

"Your camp's gone!" he said. "Creek took it!"

Dani looked back toward where her tent had been. Nothing but rushing water and floating debris.

"My car—"

"Road's washed out! You're not driving anywhere!"

They stared at each other through the rain, the implications settling between them like a physical weight. She was stranded. Her extraction point was gone. And the only shelter for miles was the cabin belonging to the man she'd threatened to report.

"Come on!" Reese said, not waiting for her decision.

He turned and started back toward his property, not looking to see if she followed. But his pace was measured, careful, designed for someone struggling to keep up in the storm.

Dani followed.

REESE

His cabin felt too small the moment she stepped inside.

Reese had built the place for solitude, for the kind of space that didn't require sharing or compromise. One main room with a kitchen area, a door leading to a bedroom barely big enough for his bed, and a bathroom that counted as luxurious only because it had running water.

Now Danielle Vargas stood dripping in his doorway, hair plastered to her skull, clothes molded to every curve, and the walls seemed to contract around them both.

"Towels," he said, because staring at her was not an option. "And dry clothes."

He disappeared into the bedroom, grabbed an armload of flannel shirts and wool socks, tried not to think about her stripping out of those wet clothes in his living room.

When he returned, she was peeling off her jacket with careful movements, wincing as she lifted her arms.

"You hurt?"

"Just banged up." She gestured toward her pack. "I've got dry clothes in there. If you could just—"

"Bathroom's through there. Take what you need."

She nodded and disappeared with her pack, leaving Reese alone with the scent of rain and something else—something warm and female that had nothing to do with the storm.

He busied himself building up the fire, adding logs until the flames roared, throwing heat and light across the small room. Outside, the wind howled like something wounded, and debris crashed against the cabin walls with irregular thuds.

The bathroom door opened.

Reese didn't turn around. Couldn't. Because he'd heard the rustle of fabric, the soft sound of bare feet on wood floors, and his imagination was already running wild.

"Better," Dani said behind him.

He turned slowly.

She'd changed into dry hiking pants and a thermal shirt that hugged her curves like a second skin. Her hair was loose now, falling in damp waves around her shoulders. She'd removed her boots, and something about her bare feet in his space hit him like a physical blow.

Intimate. Domestic. Wrong in every way that mattered.

"Fire feels good," she said, moving toward the warmth.

Reese nodded, not trusting his voice. She stood close enough to the flames that the light played across her face, highlighting the sharp angle of her cheekbones, the soft curve of her mouth.

Close enough that he could see she wasn't wearing a bra under that thermal shirt.

"How long will the storm last?" she asked.

"Hours. Maybe through tomorrow." He forced himself to look away, focusing on the window where rain lashed against the glass. "Road will be impassable for days after it passes."

"Days?"

"Washouts take time to clear. Assuming the county gets out here before next week."

The silence stretched between them, loaded with implications. Days. In this cabin. Together.

"I'll sleep on the couch," Dani said finally.

"You'll take the bed."

"It's your cabin."

"It's my decision."

She turned to face him, eyebrows raised. "You always this charming with houseguests?"

"Don't usually have houseguests."

"I can see why."

Despite everything—the storm, the circumstances, the dangerous current running between them—Reese almost smiled.

"You always this grateful when someone saves your life?"

"You didn't save my life. You prevented mild hypothermia."

"Creek was rising fast. Another hour and you'd have been swimming."

"I'm a good swimmer."

"In flood conditions? With debris?"

Dani's jaw tightened. "I can take care of myself."

"Sure you can. That's why you were face-down in a puddle when I found you."

"That was a tactical fall."

"Tactical fall."

"I was assessing ground stability."

"With your face."

She glared at him, but there was something else in her expression now. Something that looked like reluctant amusement.

"You're an ass," she said.

"And you're trouble."

"Good thing we're stuck together, then."

The words hung in the air between them, heavy with unspoken possibilities. Reese felt something shift in his chest, some carefully maintained wall developing a crack.

Outside, thunder rolled across the mountains like cannon fire. Inside, the fire crackled and spat, casting dancing shadows across walls that suddenly felt like they were closing in.

Dani moved to the window, pressing her palm against the glass. The storm had intensified, wind bending the trees nearly horizontally, rain coming down in torrents that turned the world outside into an abstract painting of water and darkness.

"It's beautiful," she said quietly. "Terrifying, but beautiful."

Reese found himself standing behind her, close enough to feel the heat radiating from her skin. Close enough to catch her scent —clean rain and something warmer, something uniquely her.

"First time in a mountain storm?"

"First time trapped in one." She glanced back at him, and he saw something vulnerable in her expression. "With a stranger who may or may not be planning to murder me."

"If I was planning to murder you, I'd have left you in the creek."

"Comforting."

"I'm not much for comfort."

"No kidding."

They stood like that for a moment, her back almost touching his chest, both of them watching the storm rage outside. The air between them crackled with tension that had nothing to do with the weather.

Dani turned slowly, and suddenly they were face to face, close enough that he could see the water droplets still clinging to her eyelashes.

Close enough to do something they'd both regret.

Reese stepped back.

"You should get some sleep," he said, his voice rougher than intended. "Tomorrow's going to be a long day."

Dani nodded, but she didn't move away immediately. Just stood there looking at him like she was trying to solve a puzzle.

"Reese?" she said finally.

"Yeah?"

"Thank you. For coming to get me."

The simple gratitude in her voice hit him harder than her sarcasm had. Made something twist in his chest that he didn't want to examine too closely.

"Don't mention it."

She headed toward the bedroom, pausing in the doorway. "And Reese?"

"What?"

"Tomorrow we're going to talk about those trail modifications. The ones you didn't do."

With that, she disappeared into his bedroom, leaving him

alone with the storm and the scent of her shampoo lingering in the air.

Reese sank into his chair by the fire, listening to the soft sounds of her settling into his bed, and wondered what the hell he'd gotten himself into.

Because one thing was becoming clear: Danielle Vargas was going to be a lot more dangerous than any storm.

DANI

Dani lay in Reese Carter's bed, staring at the ceiling, hyper-aware of every sound from the next room.

The creak of floorboards as he moved around. The soft thud of logs being added to the fire. The scratch of a chair being dragged across wood floors.

His bed smelled like him—pine and clean laundry and something indefinably male that made her stomach clench with want.

Which was completely inappropriate under the circumstances.

She was stranded in his cabin. Dependent on his hospitality. Professionally obligated to investigate his activities.

Getting involved with him would be career suicide.

But as she listened to him settling onto what was probably an uncomfortable couch, Dani couldn't stop thinking about the moment by the window. The way he'd stood behind her, close enough to touch. The heat radiating from his body. The careful distance he'd maintained even as the air between them sparked with electricity.

He'd wanted to touch her. She was certain of it.

The question was: what was she going to do about it?

Outside, the storm raged on, trapping them together in a space too small for the tension building between them.

And in the morning, they'd have to face the reality of what came next.

Professional assessment. Official reports. The kind of bureaucratic dance that could end with him shut down and her transferred to a different assignment.

Unless she found another way.

Dani closed her eyes and tried to sleep, but her mind kept drifting to the man on the other side of the wall. The careful way he'd helped her out of the storm. The flash of humor beneath his gruff exterior. The controlled strength in his hands when he'd steadied her.

Tomorrow, she'd have to choose between doing her job and following the pull she felt toward him.

Tonight, she just had to survive being twenty feet away from the most intriguing man she'd met in years.

The storm outside seemed to echo the chaos in her chest—wild, uncontrolled, and gathering strength.

And Dani had the feeling that by the time it passed, nothing would be the same.

3

FLASH POINT

DANI

Morning came with the sound of a chainsaw and the smell of fresh coffee.

Dani woke in Reese's bed, tangled in sheets that carried his scent, and for a moment forgot where she was. Then reality crashed back—the storm, the rescue, the fact that she was stranded with the subject of her investigation.

The chainsaw revved outside, followed by the crash of falling timber.

She pulled on her boots and stepped into the main room, noting the precise way Reese had folded the blanket he'd used on the couch. Coffee waited in a thermal carafe, still hot. A plate of eggs and toast sat covered with a paper towel.

He'd fed her and disappeared without waking her up.

Thoughtful. Considerate. And completely infuriating.

Dani poured coffee and stepped onto the porch, following the sound of work. She found Reese fifty yards from the cabin, stripped to the waist, attacking a massive pine that had fallen across what looked like a drainage channel.

Sweet Jesus.

She'd known he was built—the flannel shirts didn't hide much
—but seeing him shirtless was a whole different level of torture.
Broad shoulders that tapered to a narrow waist. Arms that corded
with muscle as he worked. A chest covered with the kind of hair
that made her want to run her fingers through it.

And scars. Lots of them. Burn scars, by the look of them, scattered across his ribs and shoulder like a map of old pain.

Reese looked up, catching her staring. Water dripped from his
hair, and sweat gleamed on his skin despite the cool morning air.

"Sleep well?" he asked, not pausing in his work.

"Fine." Dani forced herself to focus on the fallen tree instead of
the way his muscles flexed. "Storm damage?"

"Some. This one was already diseased." He gestured toward the
trunk with his saw. "Would've come down eventually."

"But you decided to help it along."

"Decided to keep it from taking out my water line."

Dani stepped closer, examining the precision of his cuts. This
wasn't random tree removal—it was surgical. Strategic. The kind
of work that required years of experience and an intimate knowledge of forest management.

"You do this often? Emergency tree removal?"

"When necessary."

"Without permits?"

Reese straightened, wiping sweat from his forehead with the
back of his hand. "You conducting an interview, Inspector?"

"Just making conversation."

"Bullshit." He set down the chainsaw and faced her fully.
"You're building a case."

"I'm doing my job."

"Your job is environmental assessment. Not interrogating me
over morning coffee."

Heat flashed through her—part anger, part something else entirely. The way he said her title, like it was an insult. The casual dismissal in his voice.

"My job," she said, stepping closer, "is evaluating whether recent activity in this area meets federal guidelines. Activity like unauthorized trail reconstruction."

"Prove it."

"I will."

"Good luck with that."

They were standing close now, close enough that she could see the flecks of gold in his gray eyes. Close enough to feel the heat radiating from his bare chest.

"You think I won't find evidence?" she asked.

"I think you're fishing."

"I think you're hiding something."

"Everyone's hiding something, sweetheart."

The endearment hit like a slap. Patronizing. Dismissive. Designed to put her in her place.

"Don't," she said, voice sharp.

"Don't what?"

"Don't 'sweetheart' me like I'm some tourist who wandered off the trail."

Reese's eyes darkened. "Then don't act like one."

"Excuse me?"

"Standing there with your accusations, thinking you know everything about how this mountain works." He stepped closer, close enough that she had to tilt her head back to maintain eye contact. "You've been here two days. I've been here for three years."

"Long enough to think federal law doesn't apply to you?"

"Long enough to know the difference between law and bureaucracy."

"They're the same thing!"

"Are they?" His voice dropped, rough with something that made her pulse spike. "Then why did you camp on my land without a permit?"

The question hit like a physical blow. Because he was right. She'd bent the rules to get her job done, just like he had.

"That's different."

"How?"

"Because I'm not changing the landscape! I'm not cutting trees or diverting water or—"

"Or what? Fixing the damage before it gets worse?" Reese moved closer, backing her against the fallen tree trunk. "You want to see unauthorized work? I'll show you unauthorized work."

He grabbed her hand, his calloused fingers wrapping around her wrist, and pulled her toward the drainage channel he'd been clearing.

"See that?" He pointed to where water flowed in a controlled channel between carefully placed rocks. "Storm runoff. Without this channel, it would've carved a gully straight through the main trail. Made it impassable for months."

Dani stared at the precision of the work. The way each stone had been placed directed water flow without creating erosion downstream. It was engineering, not destruction.

"You did this overnight?"

"Took three nights. Had to work around the ranger patrols."

"Why didn't you just apply for permits?"

"Because permits take six months and three environmental assessments." His grip on her wrist tightened. "The mountain doesn't wait for bureaucracy."

She could feel his pulse against her palm, fast and hard. Could smell the scent of pine sap and clean sweat on his skin. They were standing close enough that his bare chest nearly brushed her shirt with each breath.

"So you just... took matters into your own hands."

"Someone had to."

"That's not how the system works."

"The system's broken."

"The system protects—"

"The system protects careers and budgets." His voice turned rough, dangerous. "I protect the mountain."

"You're not God, Reese."

"Never said I was." His free hand came up to brace against the tree trunk beside her head, caging her in. "But I know this land. Know what it needs."

"And what does it need?"

Their faces were inches apart now. She could see the silver threads in his gray eyes, could feel his breath against her lips when he spoke.

"Less talk," he said quietly. "More action."

The words hung between them, loaded with double meaning. Dani's heart hammered against her ribs as she stared up at him, caught between anger and attraction so sharp it made her dizzy.

"Is that a threat?" she whispered.

"It's a fact."

His thumb brushed across her pulse point, and she couldn't suppress the small sound that escaped her throat. Heat pooled low in her belly, need sparking along every nerve ending.

"Reese," she breathed.

"What?"

She didn't know. Didn't trust herself to speak. Because what she wanted to say—*touch me, kiss me, show me what you mean*— would be career suicide.

Professional suicide.

Personal disaster.

But God, she wanted it anyway.

REESE

She was killing him.

Standing there against the tree trunk, lips parted, pulse racing under his thumb—Dani was systematically destroying every wall he'd built around his self-control.

He could see the want in her eyes, dark and honest and dangerous as hell. Could feel the way her body responded to his proximity, the small tremor that ran through her when he'd touched her wrist.

She wanted him. And Christ, he wanted her back.

Wanted to pin her against that tree and kiss her until she forgot about permits and regulations and every reason they shouldn't be doing this. Wanted to taste the salt on her skin, feel her nails dig into his shoulders, hear his name on her lips when he made her come.

But she was government. Here to shut him down. And getting involved with her would be handing her the knife to gut him with.

Even if every instinct he had was screaming at him to close the distance between them.

"You should go," he said, his voice rough.

"Should I?"

"Before you find something you don't want to find."

"Like what?"

Like how much I want you. Like how hard it is not to touch you right now.

"Like evidence," he said instead.

Her laugh was shaky. "Too late for that."

"Dani—"

"I've already seen enough to write my report." She looked up at him, something vulnerable flickering in her expression. "The question is what I put in it."

The admission hung between them like a loaded gun. She was

giving him an out. A chance to play politics instead of facing consequences.

"What's that supposed to mean?"

"It means your work is good, Reese." Her voice dropped. "Really good. The kind of forest management they should be teaching in textbooks."

He didn't move, didn't breathe. "But?"

"But it's still unauthorized. Still outside the system."

"So you'll recommend shutting me down."

"I should." Her eyes searched his face. "Except shutting you down means this mountain loses the only person who actually gives a damn about it."

The honesty in her voice cracked something open in his chest. She saw what he was trying to do. Understood the choice he'd made between following rules and protecting something that mattered.

"So what happens now?" he asked.

"I don't know."

They stared at each other in the morning sunlight, the weight of unspoken possibilities pressing between them. Her hand was still trapped in his grip. His body was still caging hers against the tree.

One move. One kiss. One moment of giving in to what they both wanted.

And everything would change.

"Dani," he said quietly.

"Don't." Her voice was barely a whisper. "Don't say whatever you're about to say."

"Why not?"

"Because I'm already in trouble here." She looked up at him, eyes bright with something that might have been tears. "Because I want things I shouldn't want."

"Like what?"

"Like you."

The confession hit him like a physical blow. Raw. Honest. Dangerous as hell.

"Fuck," he breathed.

"Yeah."

His thumb found her pulse point again, stroking across the rapid flutter of her heartbeat. She gasped, eyes fluttering closed, and he felt his control slip another notch.

"This is insane," she whispered.

"Completely."

"I could lose my job."

"I could lose everything."

"Then why—"

"Because I haven't felt anything in two years." The words tore out of him, rough with honesty he hadn't meant to give. "Haven't wanted anything. Until you showed up with your clipboard and your smart mouth."

Her eyes opened, locked on his. "Reese—"

"Tell me to stop," he said quietly. "Tell me to walk away."

"I can't."

"Why not?"

"Because I want you too much."

He leaned down, his mouth a breath from hers, close enough to taste the coffee on her lips. Close enough to feel the small sound she made when his body pressed against hers.

Close enough to kiss her.

To cross the line they'd been dancing around since the moment they met.

His phone rang.

The sound cut through the moment like a blade, sharp and

insistent. Reese closed his eyes, cursing every piece of technology ever invented.

"Ignore it," Dani whispered.

"Can't." He stepped back, creating space between them that felt like a physical wound. "Satellite phone. Emergency only."

He pulled the phone from his pocket, noting the caller ID. Nash.

"Yeah?"

"Reese? Thank God. Been trying to reach you since the storm hit." Nash's voice was tight with concern. "You okay up there?"

"Fine. What's wrong?"

"County called. Said there's a government assessor missing in your area. Car found at the trail access, but no sign of her."

Reese looked at Dani, who was listening with obvious interest.

"She's here," he said. "Safe."

"Jesus. What's her condition?"

"Wet. Annoyed. Alive."

Nash's relief was audible. "Thank fuck. County's been scrambling search teams. I'll call it off."

"Good."

"Need extraction? Road's washed, but we could get a chopper in this afternoon."

Reese met Dani's eyes, seeing his own conflict reflected there. Extraction meant safety. Meant returning to their separate lives before they did something stupid.

It also meant losing whatever was building between them.

"Reese?" Nash prompted. "She needs a pickup?"

"Yeah," he said finally. "Send the chopper."

Because whatever was happening between him and Danielle Vargas, it was too dangerous to pursue.

Too dangerous for both of them.

Even if walking away from it felt like tearing out a piece of his chest.

DANI

The helicopter arrived at noon, cutting through the mountain air with military precision.

Dani stood beside Reese in the clearing behind his cabin, watching the aircraft settle onto the improvised landing zone he'd cleared with his chainsaw. Professional distance maintained. Careful space between their bodies.

Like they hadn't almost kissed two hours ago.

Like she couldn't still feel the heat of his skin, the weight of his body pressing her against that tree.

"Inspector Vargas?" The pilot jumped down, extending his hand. "Mike Torres, county search and rescue. You okay?"

"Fine." Dani shouldered her pack, avoiding Reese's gaze. "Ready to go."

"Good. Weather's turning again. I want to get you out before the next front hits."

She nodded, started toward the helicopter, then stopped. Turned back.

Reese stood where she'd left him, hands in his pockets, gray eyes unreadable. Like he was already forgetting she'd been here.

"Thank you," she said. "For everything."

"Don't mention it."

The dismissal in his voice stung more than it should have. Professional. Polite. Nothing like the man who'd pressed her against a tree and told her he wanted her.

"My report—"

"Do what you have to do."

Dani stared at him for a long moment, memorizing the sharp line of his jaw, the careful distance in his expression. Then she turned and walked toward the helicopter without looking back.

Because looking back would mean admitting that leaving felt like the biggest mistake of her life.

And she couldn't afford that kind of honesty.

Not when she had a job to do.

Even if that job might destroy the first man she'd wanted in years.

The helicopter lifted off, carrying her away from the mountain and the man who'd shown her what it felt like to want something more than professional success.

As the cabin disappeared below them, Dani pressed her hand to the window and tried not to think about what she was leaving behind.

Tried not to think about the report she'd have to write.

And tried not to think about the fact that she was already planning to come back.

Because some things were worth fighting for.

Even if the fight might cost her everything.

4

BREAKING POINT

REESE

Three days.

Reese had been alone on his mountain for three days, and the silence was driving him insane.

He'd thrown himself into work—clearing storm debris, reinforcing drainage channels, rebuilding sections of trail that had washed out completely. Physical labor that should have exhausted him enough to sleep without dreaming about dark eyes and smart mouths.

It wasn't working.

Every time he closed his eyes, he saw Dani pressed against that tree trunk, lips parted, pulse racing under his thumb. Heard her voice saying she wanted him. Felt the moment when everything between them had shifted from antagonism to something raw and honest and dangerous.

Now she was gone, probably writing the report that would shut him down permanently. And he was stuck on his mountain, replaying their almost-kiss like some lovesick teenager.

"Pathetic," he muttered, driving another stake into the trail barrier he was building.

The sound of an engine cut through his self-recrimination. Reese looked up to see a familiar pickup truck navigating the repaired section of road, moving too fast for the conditions.

Nash. Which meant news. Probably bad news, given the speed.

The truck pulled up beside the trail marker, and Nash climbed out with the careful movements of a man delivering unpleasant information.

"Afternoon," Nash said.

"Thought you were working the north section today."

"Was. Got a call." Nash leaned against his truck, studying Reese's face with uncomfortable intensity. "From the Forest Service."

Reese's blood went cold. "And?"

"Seems there's been a complaint filed. Unauthorized trail modification. Violation of federal land use regulations." Nash's voice was carefully neutral. "Know anything about that?"

"Might."

"Reese—"

"How bad?"

Nash sighed. "Bad. They're sending an enforcement team next week. Full investigation, cease and desist orders, possible criminal charges."

The words hit like physical blows. Criminal charges. Which meant fines he couldn't afford, legal battles that could drag on for years. Possibly jail time.

"Who filed the complaint?"

But he already knew. There was only one person who'd had access to enough evidence to build a case.

"Inspector Vargas," Nash confirmed. "Filed her report yesterday."

Something twisted in Reese's chest, sharp and bitter. She'd played him. Let him think she understood what he was trying to do, then stabbed him in the back the moment she got home.

"Fuck."

"Yeah." Nash straightened. "Look, I might be able to—"

The sound of another engine cut him off. A rental car this time, moving carefully up the mountain road. Reese recognized the vehicle immediately.

Dani.

She parked beside Nash's truck and climbed out, wearing the same hiking clothes she'd had on three days ago. Same clipboard. Same determined expression.

But something was different. Something in her posture, the set of her shoulders.

"Inspector," Nash said politely. "Thought you'd returned to Denver."

"I did." Dani's eyes found Reese's, held them. "I came back."

"To watch the arrest?" Reese asked, his voice rough with anger.

"To stop it."

The words hung in the mountain air like a challenge. Nash looked between them, clearly sensing undercurrents he didn't understand.

"I'll leave you two to talk," he said diplomatically. "Reese, call me later."

Nash climbed back into his truck and drove away, leaving them alone in the clearing. Dani stood beside her car, chin lifted, waiting for the explosion she had to know was coming.

"Stop it," Reese repeated. "How exactly do you plan to stop the investigation you started?"

"By filing an amended report."

"Bit late for that, don't you think?"

"Not if I have new evidence."

She reached into her car and pulled out a thick folder, official seals visible on the documents inside.

"What's that?"

"Emergency permits. Retroactive authorization for all trail work performed in the last six months." Her voice was steady, professional. "Filed under the Federal Emergency Management Act, subsection twelve."

Reese stared at her, not understanding. "That's impossible."

"Is it?" She moved closer, and he caught the scent of her shampoo, the same smell that had haunted his dreams for three days. "Turns out there's a provision for emergency trail maintenance when it prevents significant environmental damage."

"You can't just—"

"I can if I document a clear and present danger to the watershed." Her eyes sparked with something that might have been satisfaction. "Which I did. Extensively."

She opened the folder, showing him pages of technical documentation, photographs of his work, detailed analysis of erosion patterns and water flow.

"You spent three days writing this?"

"I spent three days fighting bureaucrats who think mountains wait for paperwork." Her voice turned sharp. "I called in every favor I had. Threatened to resign twice. Made enemies who will probably torpedo my career."

"Why?"

The simple question seemed to catch her off guard. She looked away, focusing on the papers in her hands.

"Because you were right," she said quietly. "The system is broken. And what you're doing here matters more than my career."

The honesty in her voice did something to his chest, cracked open the anger he'd been nursing for three days. But underneath the anger there was something else. Something that felt danger-ously like hope.

"So that's it? Case closed?"

"Case closed." She looked up at him. "You're in the clear."

"And you?"

"I've been reassigned. Different district, different projects."

"You're leaving."

"I have to."

They stared at each other across the small distance. She'd saved him. Sacrificed her career to protect his work. And now she was walking away.

"Dani—"

"Don't." Her voice was sharp enough to cut. "Don't say what-ever you're thinking."

"You don't know what I'm thinking."

"I know you're going to thank me. Maybe apologize for assuming the worst." Her laugh was hollow. "Then you're going to tell me it's better this way. That I should go back to my life and forget about whatever happened between us."

The accuracy of her words hit like a slap. Because that was exactly what he'd been about to say.

"Am I wrong?" she challenged.

Reese looked at her standing there in his clearing, chin lifted in defiance, eyes bright with hurt she was trying to hide. This woman who'd risked everything to save him. Who'd fought bureaucrats and regulations to give him what he needed.

Who'd come back when she could have stayed safely away?

"Yeah," he said roughly. "You're wrong."

"About what?"

"About all of it."

He crossed the distance between them in three strides, backing her against her rental car, hands braced on either side of her head.

"I wasn't going to thank you," he said. "I was going to ask why you came back."

"I told you—"

"Bullshit." His voice dropped, rough with three days of wanting. "You could have filed those permits from Denver. Could have called with the news."

Her breath hitched. "Reese—"

"You came back because you wanted to see me again."

"That's not—"

"Because you can't stop thinking about what almost happened between us."

"Don't." But her voice was breathless now, her pupils dilated.

"Because you want to finish what we started."

"You're insane."

"Am I?" He leaned closer, close enough to feel her breath against his lips. "Then tell me to stop."

"Stop."

"Mean it."

She stared up at him, pulse racing at her throat, and he saw the moment her resolve cracked.

"I can't," she whispered.

"Why not?"

"Because I couldn't stop thinking about you no matter how hard I tried."

The confession destroyed the last of his control. He kissed her hard, desperate, three days of wanting compressed into the meeting of mouths and tongues. She kissed him back just as fiercely, her hands fisting in his shirt, pulling him closer.

"This is crazy," she gasped against his mouth.

"Completely fucking insane," he agreed, lifting her onto the hood of the car.

"I'm leaving tomorrow."

"Then we better make tonight count."

She pulled back to look at him, something vulnerable in her expression. "What happens after?"

"I don't know." He cupped her face in his hands, thumbs stroking along her cheekbones. "But I know I'm not letting you walk away without showing you what you do to me."

DANI

He kissed her like he was trying to brand her.

Dani felt herself drowning in sensation—the heat of his mouth, the rasp of his beard against her skin, the solid weight of his body between her thighs. Her hands roamed over his chest, relearning the feel of muscle and scars, the steady rhythm of his heartbeat.

"Not here," she gasped when he broke the kiss to trail his mouth down her throat.

"Why not?"

"Because I want you naked. In a bed. Where I can take my time."

His eyes darkened. "Fuck yes."

He lifted her off the car hood, and she wrapped her legs around his waist, letting him carry her toward the cabin. His hands gripped her ass, holding her steady, and she could feel the hard length of him pressing against her core through their clothes.

"You sure about this?" he asked as he pushed through the cabin door.

"Are you having second thoughts?"

"I'm having third and fourth thoughts." He set her down beside his bed, hands still spanning her waist. "But I'm done pretending I don't want you."

"Good." She reached for the hem of his shirt. "Because I'm tired of being careful."

He let her pull the shirt over his head, then immediately started working on her clothes—jacket, thermal shirt, the sports bra underneath. His hands were everywhere, rough and gentle at the same time, mapping her body like he was memorizing every curve.

"You're beautiful," he said, voice rough with worship.

"You're overdressed."

She attacked his belt, fingers fumbling with the buckle in her haste. He helped her, kicking off boots and jeans until he stood naked before her, all hard muscle and controlled power.

And holy hell, he was magnificent.

"Your turn," he said, hooking his fingers in the waistband of her hiking pants.

She lifted her hips, letting him strip away the last barriers between them. When she was naked, he just stood there looking at her, eyes hot with appreciation.

"Second thoughts still?" she teased.

"Third and fourth thoughts about letting you leave," he said, covering her body with his.

The feel of skin against skin made them both gasp. He was hot and solid and perfect, fitting against her like they'd been made for this. When he settled between her thighs, she could feel how ready he was, thick and hard and promising.

"Condom," she breathed.

"Nightstand."

She stretched across him to reach the drawer, her breasts brushing his chest. He groaned and caught one nipple in his mouth, sucking hard enough to make her arch against him.

"Focus," she gasped, fumbling for the condom.

"I am focused." He switched to her other breast, teeth grazing the sensitive peak. "Very fucking focused."

She finally found the condom, tearing it open with shaking hands. When she reached down to roll it on, he caught her wrist.

"Let me."

"Why?"

"Because I want to watch you fall apart first."

His hand slipped between her thighs, finding her slick and ready. She cried out as he stroked her, his touch sure and deliberate, designed to drive her crazy.

"You're so wet," he said, voice rough with satisfaction. "All for me."

"Don't get cocky."

"Too late for that." He slipped one finger inside her, then another, working her with steady pressure. "You feel incredible."

"Reese—"

"What do you need?"

"You. Inside me. Now."

He positioned himself at her entrance, the head of his cock pressing against her. "Still think I'm just a caveman with a chainsaw?"

The question caught her off guard, dragging her back to their argument three days ago. The way she'd dismissed him, underestimated what he was capable of.

"No," she gasped as he pushed into her slowly. "I think you're dangerous."

"Why?" He sank deeper, stretching her, filling her completely.

"Because you make me want things I shouldn't want."

"Like what?" He started to move, setting a rhythm that made her forget how to think.

"Like this. Like you. Like staying."

"Then stay."

"I can't."

"Why not?" He thrust harder, making her arch beneath him.

"Because I'll fall for you. And you'll break my heart."

The honesty in her own voice shocked her. But it was true. She was already halfway in love with this complex, impossible man.

"What makes you think I'd break your heart?" he asked, his voice gentler now.

"Because everyone does."

He stilled above her, gray eyes searching her face. "Not everyone."

"You don't know—"

"I know you saved my career when you could have destroyed it." He cupped her face in one hand, thumb stroking across her cheek. "I know you came back when you could have stayed safe."

"That doesn't mean—"

"It means you matter to me." The words were rough, honest, devastating. "More than you should. More than is smart."

"Reese—"

"Shut up and let me love you."

He started moving again, deeper now, harder, and she lost the ability to protest. Lost everything except the feel of him inside her, the sound of her name on his lips, the growing pressure that threatened to tear her apart.

"You feel so good," he groaned against her throat. "So perfect. Like you were made for me."

"Maybe I was."

"Yeah?" He lifted her legs higher, changing the angle until she saw stars. "Then come for me. Let me feel you."

She shattered around him, crying out his name as pleasure crashed through her. He followed seconds later, his rhythm faltering as he emptied himself inside her with a broken curse.

Afterward, they lay tangled together, breathing hard, sweat cooling on their skin.

"That was—" Dani started.

"Yeah."

"We're idiots."

"Completely."

"This doesn't change anything. I still have to leave."

Reese was quiet for a long moment, his hand stroking lazy patterns on her back.

"What if you didn't?" he asked finally.

"What?"

"What if you stayed? Found work here, made a life here."

"With you?"

"With me."

The offer hung between them, tempting and impossible. Dani wanted to say yes. Wanted to throw caution aside and build something real with this man who'd shown her what it felt like to be wanted completely.

But wanting wasn't enough.

"I can't," she whispered.

"Why not?"

"Because this isn't real. It's adrenaline and proximity and really good sex."

"Is it?"

She looked up at him, seeing her own doubt reflected in his eyes. Because it didn't feel like just sex. It felt like coming home.

"I don't know," she admitted.

"Then stay and find out."

"For how long?"

"However long it takes."

The simple honesty in his voice made her chest tight. Made

her want to believe in things like second chances and happily ever after.

Made her want to stay.

"What if it doesn't work?" she asked.

"What if it does?"

Before she could answer, he was kissing her again, slow and thorough, tasting like promises and possibility.

And for the first time in years, Dani let herself believe that maybe, just maybe, some risks were worth taking.

Even if they scared her to death.

5

WRECKAGE

DANI
Dani was gone before Reese woke up.

She dressed in the gray pre-dawn light, moving like a ghost through his cabin, gathering her clothes from the floor where he'd stripped them off her. Her hands shook as she pulled on her boots, as she shouldered her pack, as she reached for the door handle.

One look back at him sleeping—hair dark against the pillow, face peaceful in a way she'd never seen—and she'd lose her nerve completely.

So she didn't look back.

She left no note. No explanation. No trace that she'd ever been there except for the lingering scent of her shampoo on his sheets.

By the time Reese found the empty bed, she was already at the airport, sitting in the departure lounge with her boarding pass clutched in white-knuckled hands.

REESE
The cold sheets told him everything.

Reese rolled over in his empty bed, reaching for warmth that wasn't there, and felt something die in his chest. The pillow still smelled like her. The bathroom still held traces of steam from her shower.

But Dani was gone.

No goodbye. No explanation. Just absence where she'd been, silence where her voice had been, cold where her body had warmed his bed.

He lay there for a long time, staring at the ceiling, letting the reality settle into his bones like poison.

She'd run. Again.

Only this time, she'd taken something with her. Something he hadn't even realized he'd been guarding until it was gone.

His phone buzzed. Text message.

Flight boards in an hour. This was a mistake. I'm sorry.

Reese stared at the words until they blurred, then deleted the message without replying.

What was there to say?

She'd made her choice.

DANI

The panic attack hit in the bathroom at Gate 23.

Dani locked herself in a stall and tried to breathe through the crushing weight in her chest, the way her hands shook, the voice in her head screaming that she was making the biggest mistake of her life.

She'd left him sleeping. Left him to wake up alone after the night they'd shared.

Left him like every other person who'd walked away when things got real.

Coward, her mind whispered. *Fucking coward.*

But staying was impossible. Staying meant admitting she'd fallen for a man she'd known for five days. Staying meant throwing away everything she'd built for something that might not last past the honeymoon phase.

Staying meant being vulnerable enough to get destroyed.

Her boarding pass crumpled in her fist. She smoothed it out, read her name printed in stark black letters, and felt sick.

Final boarding call for Flight 847 to Phoenix.

She had to move. Had to get on that plane and return to her life.

But her feet wouldn't move toward the gate.

REESE

Nash found him three days later, sitting on his porch with a half-empty bottle of whiskey and eyes that looked like winter.

"Christ, man. You look like hell."

"Feel worse."

Nash settled into the other chair without invitation, taking in the empty bottles, the unshaven jaw, the careful distance Reese was maintaining from everything that mattered.

"Want to talk about it?"

"No."

"When's the last time you ate?"

"Don't remember."

"Reese—"

"She's gone, Nash." The words came out flat, dead. "Took what she needed and left."

"The permits?"

"Everything." Reese took a pull from the bottle. "Fucking everything."

They sat in silence, watching the sun set over mountains that felt too big and too empty.

"You could go after her," Nash said finally.

"Why would I do that?"

"Because you're in love with her."

"Love's not enough." Reese's laugh was bitter. "She proved that."

"Did she? Or did she just get scared?"

"Doesn't matter. She made her choice."

Nash was quiet for a long time. "What if she comes back?"

"She won't."

"But what if she does?"

Reese looked at his friend, seeing the hope there that he couldn't afford to feel.

"Then I'll know she's only here because she feels guilty."

"And?"

"And I'll send her away."

Because some wounds were too deep to heal twice.

DANI

She lasted six days in Phoenix.

Six days of pretending she was fine, of throwing herself into the Prescott assignment, of lying awake at night thinking about gray eyes and callused hands and the way Reese had whispered her name in the dark.

On the seventh day, she cracked.

Called in sick. Drove to the airport. Bought a ticket to Denver without checking the price.

She didn't have a plan. Didn't have an excuse. Just the bone-deep certainty that she'd left something vital on that mountain.

Something she couldn't live without.

The rental car felt familiar as she drove up the winding road, past the trail marker where she'd first seen him, past the clearing where they'd almost kissed, up to the cabin that looked exactly the same but felt completely different.

His truck was there. Smoke rose from the chimney.

But when she knocked on the door, the man who answered looked like a stranger.

Hollow-eyed. Unshaven. Furious.

"What do you want?" Reese asked, his voice like gravel.

"To talk."

"We're done talking."

He started to close the door. She caught it with her palm.

"Please. Just—"

"You said everything you needed to say when you left." His eyes were winter-cold, empty of everything she'd seen there before. "Without a word. Like I was nothing."

The accusation hit like a physical blow. "That's not—"

"Isn't it?" He stepped onto the porch, and she saw how thin he'd gotten, how worn. "You got what you needed. Fixed your career. Had your fun. Now you're back because what—guilt?"

"No."

"Pity?"

"No, damn it!" The words exploded out of her. "I'm back because I can't breathe without you!"

"Bullshit."

"I'm back because leaving was the biggest mistake of my life!"

"You made your choice."

"I made the wrong choice!" She stepped closer, desperate to make him understand. "I was scared. I ran. I chose the safe thing over the right thing, and it's been killing me ever since."

Something flickered in his expression—pain, maybe, or hope quickly crushed.

"Pretty words," he said finally. "But you left once. You'll leave again."

"I won't."

"Prove it."

The challenge hung between them, loaded with hurt and doubt and the careful distance he'd wrapped around himself like armor.

"How?" she whispered.

"Stay."

"I am staying."

"For how long? Until the next time you get scared? Until someone offers you a better job? Until this gets too real again?"

The questions hit like slaps, each one designed to expose the fear she was trying to hide. Because he was right. She was terrified. Terrified of wanting him too much, of needing him, of building something real only to watch it fall apart.

"I don't know," she admitted. "I can't promise I won't get scared again. I can't promise this will be easy."

"Then what can you promise?"

"That I choose you." Her voice broke on the words. "That staying is terrifying, but leaving is impossible. That you're the only thing I've ever wanted that scared me enough to run from."

Reese stared at her for a long moment, and she saw the war in his eyes—between wanting to believe her and protecting himself from being hurt again.

"I loved you," he said quietly. "And you left me like I was nothing."

"I know."

"You broke something in me."

"I know." Tears streamed down her cheeks. "I'm sorry. I'm so fucking sorry."

"Sorry doesn't fix it."

"Then tell me what does."

He was quiet for so long she thought he might not answer. When he finally spoke, his voice was rough with exhaustion.

"I don't know if anything does."

The words hung between them like a death sentence. But he didn't go inside. Didn't shut the door.

He just stood there, looking at her like she was a puzzle he couldn't solve.

"I'll be in town," she said finally. "At the motel. For as long as it takes."

"For as long as what takes?"

"For you to decide if you can forgive me."

She turned and walked back to her car, leaving him standing on the porch. She didn't look back. Didn't beg.

Just drove away and hoped that this time, leaving was the right choice.

That giving him space to think might be the only way to earn his trust back.

But as she checked into the Pineview Motel and stared at the thin walls and scratchy sheets that would be her home for however long this took, one thought echoed in her mind:

She'd fucked up the best thing in her life.

And she had no idea how to fix it.

6

PROVING GROUND

DANI

Day three at the Pineview Motel, and Dani was losing her mind.

The walls were thin enough to hear her neighbor's TV, the shower pressure was pathetic, and the bed felt like a medieval torture device. But the worst part wasn't the accommodations.

It was the silence.

No word from Reese. No acknowledgment that she existed. She'd driven past his place twice, seen his truck in the driveway, smoke from his chimney. But he might as well have been a ghost.

She was starting to think this was a mistake. That maybe some things couldn't be fixed, some trust couldn't be rebuilt.

Then Nash Williams knocked on her door.

"You look like shit," he said without preamble.

"Good morning to you too."

"Coffee?" He held up a thermos and two cups. "We need to talk."

Five minutes later, they sat on the plastic chairs outside her room, watching the morning traffic crawl through town.

"He's worse," Nash said finally.

"What do you mean?"

"Reese. Since you showed up, he's been..." Nash searched for words. "Destructive. Reckless. Yesterday he tried to clear a widow-maker with a handheld saw instead of calling for backup."

Guilt twisted in her stomach. "Is he hurt?"

"Not yet. But he's pushing it. Like he's got a death wish."

"What do you want me to do? Leave?"

"I want you to stop sitting in this shithole feeling sorry for yourself." Nash's voice was sharp. "You want forgiveness? Earn it."

"How?"

"Trail crew's shorthanded. Storm damage assessment on the north section. Hard work, shit pay, and you'll be working directly under the most stubborn bastard in Colorado."

Dani stared at him. "You're offering me a job?"

"I'm offering you a chance." Nash stood, pocketing his cup. "Be at the equipment shed at seven tomorrow. Bring work gloves and thick skin."

"Will he even let me work with him?"

"He doesn't get a say. County contract requires two-person teams for safety." Nash's smile was grim. "But he's not gonna make it easy."

After he left, Dani sat outside her motel room and stared at the mountains. Working with Reese meant seeing him every day. Meant subjecting herself to his anger, his silence, his careful indifference.

It also meant showing him she wasn't going anywhere.

That she was willing to bleed for this.

For him.

She pulled out her phone and made two calls. First, to her

former supervisor, officially resigning from the Forest Service. Second, to the equipment store in town.

If she was going to prove herself, she needed proper gear.

REESE

Reese was checking his chainsaw when she arrived at the equipment shed.

She looked different. Work boots instead of hiking shoes. Canvas pants that had seen wear. A flannel shirt that fit like she'd owned it for years. Hair braided back, no makeup, ready for whatever the mountain could throw at her.

"Morning," she said quietly.

He didn't look up from his saw. "Nash tell you about the safety requirements?"

"Two-person teams. I know."

"Then you know this isn't a choice."

"I know."

He finally looked at her, taking in the serious expression, the careful distance she was maintaining. Good. She was learning.

"Rules," he said. "You do what I say, when I say it. No questions, no arguments. You can't keep up, you go home."

"Understood."

"This isn't a game. Trees kill people who aren't paying attention."

"I'll pay attention."

"Trail work is sixteen-hour days, minimum wage, and no guarantee you won't get hurt."

"I'm not afraid of hard work."

"We'll see."

He loaded gear into his truck—chainsaws, cables, first aid kit, emergency radio. She helped without being asked, loading her pack with precision that spoke of experience.

The north section was a disaster zone. Three massive pines

had fallen across the main trail, their root systems torn from the earth, leaving craters that would turn into erosion channels if they weren't fixed soon.

"Assessment first," Reese said, shouldering his pack. "We map the damage, then prioritize repairs."

For the next two hours, they worked in hostile silence. Reese called out measurements and GPS coordinates. Dani recorded them in a waterproof notebook, asking no questions, making no conversation.

Professional. Efficient. Exactly what he'd demanded.

Which should have been a relief.

Instead, it pissed him off.

"Tree number four," he said, standing beside a massive pine that had crushed a section of drainage channel. "Forty-two feet, eighteen-inch diameter."

"Got it." Dani made notes without looking up.

"Root damage extends twelve feet in all directions."

"Noted."

"Trail blockage complete. Estimated removal time—"

"Six hours with equipment, twelve by hand." She finally looked up. "The drainage will need complete reconstruction."

The assessment was accurate. Thorough. The kind of analysis that took years of experience to make at a glance.

"How do you know that?" he asked.

"I spent three summers on forest management crews during college." Her voice was steady, matter-of-fact. "Before I decided government work was safer than chainsaws."

"Safer."

"Stupider, as it turns out."

Something flickered in her expression—regret, maybe, or honest self-assessment. But she looked away before he could read it clearly.

"We'll start with the root system," he said. "Work our way out."

The next six hours were brutal. They dug around massive root balls, cutting through layers of earth and stone, hauling debris that weighed more than most people could lift. Dani worked without complaint, following his lead, anticipating what he needed before he asked.

She was strong. Stronger than he'd expected. Her hands didn't blister. Her pace didn't flag. And when a cable snapped and nearly took his head off, she was the one who spotted the fraying before it could whip back.

"Break," he called finally, when the sun reached its peak.

They sat on opposite sides of a fallen log, eating energy bars and drinking water. Dani's shirt was soaked with sweat, her face flushed from exertion, but she didn't look defeated.

She looked determined.

"Why are you doing this?" he asked.

"You need the help."

"Bullshit. You could work anywhere. Do anything. Why are you sitting in the dirt, digging tree roots for minimum wage?"

She was quiet for a long moment, staring at the mountains that stretched to the horizon.

"Because this matters," she said finally. "The work. The mountain. What you're trying to protect."

"And?"

"And because I want to prove I'm not the kind of person who runs when things get hard."

"You already proved you are that kind of person."

The words hit like a slap. Dani flinched but didn't look away.

"You're right," she said quietly. "I ran. I chose the easy thing over the right thing, and I hate myself for it."

"Hate's not enough."

"I know."

"So what is?"

"Staying. Working. Showing up every day until you believe I mean it."

"And if I never believe it?"

Her smile was sad but steady. "Then at least I'll know I tried."

REESE

She came back the next day.

And the next.

And the next.

Five days of working beside him in careful silence, hauling logs and mixing concrete and rebuilding the trail one stone at a time. Five days of watching her prove she wasn't the pampered government inspector he'd first thought.

She was tougher than that. Smarter. More stubborn.

And it was driving him insane.

Because every day she stayed made it harder to maintain the anger that was keeping him safe. Every competent movement, every uncomplaining hour of backbreaking work, every moment she chose to stay instead of run was eroding the walls he'd built around his heart.

On the sixth day, she saved his life.

They were working on a massive oak that had fallen across a ravine, its trunk bridging a twenty-foot drop. Reese was cutting from the top when he felt the tree shift, the weight redistributing as his saw bit through the heartwood.

"Reese!" Dani's shout cut through the whine of his chainsaw. "It's rolling!"

He looked down, saw the trunk beginning to rotate, gravity and his cut destabilizing the whole structure. In seconds, the tree would flip, taking him with it into the ravine below.

Dani was already moving, climbing onto the trunk, grabbing the back of his shirt as the oak began its deadly roll.

"Jump!"

They leaped together, hitting the ground hard as tons of wood crashed into the space where they'd been standing. Reese felt the impact drive the air from his lungs, felt Dani's body cushioning his fall as they rolled away from the debris.

For a moment, they lay tangled together in the dirt, breathing hard, hearts hammering.

"You okay?" she gasped.

"Yeah." He rolled off her, taking inventory. Bruised ribs, scraped palms, but nothing broken. "You?"

"Think so."

She sat up slowly, wincing as she moved her left shoulder. Blood seeped through her shirt where she'd scraped against a rock.

"You're hurt."

"It's nothing."

"Let me see."

She started to protest, then stopped, letting him push her shirt aside to examine the wound. It was deep enough to need stitches, but not life-threatening.

"First aid kit's in the truck," he said.

"I can—"

"Sit. Don't move."

For once, she didn't argue.

Reese cleaned the wound with water from his bottle, applied antibiotic ointment, and bandaged it with efficient movements that spoke of too much experience with field medicine.

"Thank you," he said quietly.

"For what?"

"Saving my life."

"You would have done the same."

"Would I?"

The question hung between them, loaded with everything they weren't saying. Would he have risked himself to save her? Or would his anger have made him hesitate just long enough for her to fall?

"Yes," she said with quiet certainty. "You would have."

"How do you know?"

"Because underneath all the justified fury, you're still a good man."

The simple faith in her voice cracked something open in his chest. Something he'd been protecting since the morning he'd woken up to empty sheets and silence.

"Dani—"

"Don't." She stood carefully, testing her shoulder. "Don't say anything you don't mean."

"What if I mean it?"

"Then say it tomorrow. When you've had time to think."

She gathered her tools with deliberate movements, not looking at him. But something had changed between them. Some wall had cracked.

Maybe it wasn't forgiveness.

But it was a start.

DANI

That night, Dani sat in her motel room and tried not to think about the way Reese had looked at her after she'd pulled him from the ravine.

Like maybe she was worth saving too.

Her shoulder throbbed where she'd scraped it, but the pain was nothing compared to the hope building in her chest. Dangerous hope that maybe, just maybe, she was earning her way back to him.

Her phone buzzed. Text from an unknown number.

Trail work starts at six tomorrow. Don't be late.

She stared at the message, reading between the lines. He wasn't sending her home. Wasn't cutting her loose.

He was giving her another day to prove herself.

Another chance to show him she was staying.

Dani set the phone aside and tried to sleep, but her mind kept drifting to the moment when they'd jumped together. The way he'd protected her as they fell. The careful gentleness in his hands as he'd bandaged her shoulder.

Maybe forgiveness couldn't be earned in a day.

But trust?

Trust could be built one stone at a time.

One choice at a time.

One day of showing up when it would be easier to run.

Tomorrow, she'd show up again.

And the day after that.

For as long as it took.

Because some things were worth fighting for.

Even if the fight meant bleeding on the mountain she'd learned to love.

Even if the man she loved might never forgive her for leaving in the first place.

She'd stay anyway.

And prove that this time, running wasn't an option.

7

BUILDING FOUNDATIONS

REESE

Three weeks of working beside her, and Reese was at his wits' end.

Not because Dani was incompetent—she'd proven herself ten times over, matching his pace on the trail, anticipating problems before they became disasters, bleeding right alongside him to rebuild what the storm had torn apart.

No, he was losing his mind because every day she stayed made it harder to remember why he was supposed to be angry.

Every morning she showed up at six sharp, thermos of coffee in hand, ready for whatever punishment the mountain could dish out. Every evening she drove back to that shithole motel without complaint, without asking for more than he was ready to give.

Every night he lay in his empty bed and thought about the woman sleeping twenty miles away on scratchy sheets, proving her commitment one backbreaking day at a time.

It was driving him insane.

"You're staring again," Nash said, appearing beside him with the stealth of a man who'd spent too many years reading Reese's moods.

"I'm supervising."

"You're staring at her ass while she digs that drainage channel."

Reese didn't deny it. Hard to deny something so obviously true.

"She's been here three weeks," Nash continued. "Living in that motel, working for peanuts, bleeding on your mountain. How much more proof do you need?"

"Proof of what?"

"That she's not going anywhere."

Down the hill, Dani wrestled with a boulder that outweighed her by a hundred pounds, using leverage and pure stubborn determination to move it into position. Her shirt was soaked with sweat, her face streaked with dirt, and she looked more beautiful than she had the night he'd first kissed her.

"People change their minds," Reese said.

"Some do. She hasn't."

"Yet."

Nash sighed. "What's it gonna take, man? You want her to tattoo your name on her forehead?"

"I want—" Reese stopped, the words sticking in his throat.

"What?"

I want to know she'll still be here when I wake up. I want to trust that this isn't just guilt or pity or some misguided need to fix what she broke. I want to believe that what we had was real enough to survive her running away.

"I want her off my mountain," he lied.

Nash studied his face with uncomfortable intensity. "Bullshit. You want her in your bed. In your life. In your future. You're just too scared to admit it."

"I'm not scared—"

"You're terrified. Because letting her back in means risking getting hurt again."

"She left me, Nash. Woke up next to me and walked away like I was nothing."

"And she came back. Quit her job, moved across three states, and spent three weeks proving she was wrong to leave."

"For now."

"Forever, you stubborn ass." Nash's voice turned sharp. "That woman is in love with you. Anyone with eyes can see it."

"Love's not enough."

"It is if you let it be."

Down the hill, Dani finally managed to move the boulder into place. She stood back, hands on her hips, surveying her work with the kind of satisfaction that came from solving problems with sweat and determination.

Then she looked up the hill and caught him watching. Instead of looking away, she raised her hand in a small wave. Not flirtatious. Not presumptuous. Just acknowledgment.

Like she was saying: *Still here. Still fighting. Still yours if you want me.*

Something cracked in his chest. Some carefully maintained wall developing a fracture that spread a little wider every day.

"She deserves better," he said quietly.

"She deserves to make her own choices. And she chose you."

"She chose wrong."

Nash was quiet for a long moment. When he spoke, his voice was gentler than usual.

"You know what Tyler would say if he was here?"

The mention of his dead crewmate hit like a punch to the gut. "Don't."

"He'd say you were being an idiot. That good women were rare and chances like this were rarer."

"Tyler's not here."

"No. But if he was, he'd tell you to stop punishing yourself for surviving. Stop pushing away the best thing that ever happened to you because you think you don't deserve it."

Reese closed his eyes, feeling the weight of five years' worth of guilt and three weeks' worth of want pressing against his ribs.

"What if I let her in and she leaves again?"

"What if you don't and she stays anyway?"

DANI

Dani was replacing a section of trail signage when she heard the chainsaw.

Not unusual—Reese used his saw for everything from clearing debris to cutting firewood. But this was different. Sustained cutting, the kind that meant he was working on something big.

She followed the sound through the trees, curious despite herself. They'd finished the scheduled trail work two days ago. Everything was cleared, repaired, ready for the spring hiking season.

What was he building?

She found him in a clearing she'd never seen before, about half a mile from his cabin. He'd been working for hours, judging by the neat stacks of lumber and the foundation he'd already laid.

A foundation for a cabin.

Small but solid. Good drainage, level ground, positioned to catch morning sun but sheltered from the worst weather. The kind of place someone could live year-round if they knew what they were doing.

The kind of place that said *permanent.*

Reese looked up as she approached, sweat gleaming on his bare chest, sawdust in his hair. He didn't smile, didn't speak. Just watched her take in what he was building.

"New project?" she asked, keeping her voice carefully neutral.

"Yeah."

"Client work?"

"Personal."

She walked around the foundation, noting the precision of his measurements, the quality of the materials. This wasn't rough construction. This was craftsmanship.

"It's beautiful," she said honestly. "Who's it for?"

He was quiet for so long she thought he might not answer. When he finally spoke, his voice was rough with something that might have been hope.

"Someone who needs a place to stay."

"Anyone I know?"

"Depends." He set down his saw, facing her across the skeleton of what would become walls. "You planning to keep living in that motel?"

The question hit like a physical blow. Dani stared at him, hardly daring to understand what he was offering.

"Reese—"

"It's got good bones. Solid foundation. Built to last." His gray eyes held hers. "But it needs someone who's not going to run when things get complicated."

"Are you asking me to move in with you?"

"I'm asking if you want your own place. On the mountain. Close enough to work the trails, far enough to have space."

Her own place. Not his place that he was sharing. *Her* place that he'd built with his hands because he believed she might stay.

"Why?" she whispered.

"Because you've been sleeping on a mattress that I'm sure feels like a medieval torture device for three weeks. Because you've proven you're not going anywhere. Because—" He stopped, jaw working like the words were stuck.

"Because what?"

"Because I miss you."

The simple admission cracked her heart wide open. She wanted to cross the distance between them, wanted to throw herself into his arms and promise she'd never leave again.

But something in his posture stopped her. He was offering her a cabin, not forgiveness. Space, not his heart.

"What are we doing here, Reese?" she asked quietly.

"I don't know."

"Are we friends? Coworkers? Something more?"

"I don't know that either."

"What do you know?"

He was quiet for a long time, staring at the foundation he'd built for her. When he looked up, his eyes were raw with honesty.

"I know you left me once and it nearly killed me. I know I can't go through that again."

"I won't—"

"You can't promise that. No one can."

"Then what are you offering?"

"A place to stay. Work that matters. A chance to figure out what this is without pressure."

"And if we figure out it's nothing?"

"Then you've got a cabin on the mountain and I've got the best trail partner I've ever worked with."

"And if we figure out it's everything?"

Something flickered in his expression—want, hope, fear in equal measure.

"Then we figure out what everything looks like."

It wasn't a declaration of love. It wasn't even forgiveness. But it was more than she'd dared hope for three weeks ago.

It was a chance.

"How long to finish it?" she asked.

"Two weeks. Maybe three."

"I'll help."

"You don't have to—"

"I want to." She stepped closer, close enough to see the flecks of gold in his gray eyes. "I want to build something with you."

"Even if you don't know what it is yet?"

"Especially then."

For the first time in three weeks, Reese almost smiled.

"Better get started then," he said, picking up his saw. "Daylight's burning."

REESE

They worked together for two weeks, building her cabin from the ground up.

Not side by side—that would have been too much, too fast. But in careful coordination, Reese framing the walls while Dani installed insulation, him running electrical while she painted, both of them pretending this was just another trail project.

Pretending it didn't feel like building a future.

On the last day, as Dani hung curtains in windows he'd cut by hand, Reese stood on the porch and tried to name what he was feeling.

Not forgiveness—that would take longer, maybe years. Not trust—that had to be earned day by day, choice by choice.

But hope. Definitely hope.

"What do you think?" Dani appeared in the doorway, hair tied back with a paint-stained bandana, face bright with accomplishment.

"It's perfect."

"Really?"

"Really." He looked at the woman he'd built this for, this stubborn, brilliant, impossible woman who'd stayed when leaving would have been easier. "You ready to move in?"

"Tomorrow," she said. "Tonight I've got one more night at the Pineview."

"Why?"

"Because I want to wake up here for the first time knowing it's really mine."

The simple honesty in her voice made his chest tight. "Dani—"

"Thank you," she said quietly. "For building this. For giving me another chance. For letting me prove I'm not the kind of person who runs."

"You proved that weeks ago."

"Did I?"

"You're standing here, aren't you? On a mountain, in the middle of nowhere, talking to a man who's been an ass to you for weeks on end."

"You haven't been an ass. You've been careful."

"Is there a difference?"

"Sometimes careful is the only way to survive."

She stepped onto the porch beside him, not touching but close enough that he could feel her warmth. They stood in comfortable silence, watching the sun set over mountains that belonged to both of them now.

"Reese?" she said finally.

"Yeah?"

"What happens tomorrow?"

"Tomorrow you move into your cabin. We keep working the trails. We figure out what this is one day at a time."

"And tonight?"

He looked at her, seeing the question in her eyes, the want she wasn't trying to hide.

"Tonight you sleep in your own bed," he said. "And I sleep in mine."

"Because?"

"Because when I come to you again—if I come to you—I want it to be because I choose to. Not because I'm lonely or horny or tired of being angry."

"And how will you know?"

"I'll know."

She nodded, understanding flickering in her expression. "And until then?"

"Until then, we build trails. We figure out how to be partners before we figure out how to be anything else."

"That could take a while."

"Good things usually do."

DANI

Six months later, Dani woke in her own bed, in her own cabin, to the sound of Reese splitting wood on his porch half a mile away.

They'd found their rhythm over the winter. Trail work during the day, separate cabins at night. Careful friendship that sometimes flared into something deeper before they both pulled back.

It was slow. Frustrating. Sometimes maddening.

It was also real in a way that nothing else in her life had ever been.

She made coffee and stepped onto her porch, breathing in mountain air that tasted like pine and possibility. In the distance, she could see smoke rising from Reese's chimney, could picture him moving around his kitchen with the efficient grace she'd learned to love.

Her radio crackled. "Trail team one, this is base. You copy?"

Dani picked up the handset. "Trail team one. Go ahead, base."

"We've got a medical emergency on the north section. Hiker with a possible broken ankle. Can you respond?"

"Copy that. En route."

She was pulling on her boots when she heard Reese's truck in her driveway. He appeared in her doorway without knocking, medical kit already slung over his shoulder.

"Heard the call," he said. "Ready?"

"Always."

They worked together like they'd been born to it, Dani handling triage while Reese coordinated with the helicopter crew. The hiker—a college kid who'd bitten off more than he could chew—would be fine, but it was a complicated extraction from difficult terrain.

By the time they got back to the cabin, it was nearly dark.

"Good work today," Reese said as they unloaded gear from his truck.

"You too." She paused, keys in her hand. "You want to come in? I've got actual food, not just emergency rations."

It wasn't the first time she'd asked. It wasn't the first time he'd said no.

But tonight, something was different in his expression.

"Yeah," he said quietly. "I'd like that."

They ate dinner on her porch, watching stars appear over mountains that had become home. The conversation was easy, comfortable, punctuated by silences that didn't need filling.

"Dani," Reese said as she gathered their empty plates.

"Yeah?"

"I choose you."

The words were simple, quiet, devastating in their certainty.

"Are you sure?"

"I've been sure for months. Just took me this long to trust it."

She set the plates aside and moved to sit beside him on the porch swing he'd built for her last month.

"What changed your mind?"

"You did. Every day, every choice, every time you stayed when leaving would have been easier." He cupped her face in his hands, thumbs stroking across her cheekbones. "I love you. And I'm done pretending I don't."

"I love you too," she whispered. "I never stopped."

When he kissed her, it was different from that first desperate night in his cabin. This was sure, steady, built on months of trust carefully rebuilt.

This was forever.

"So what happens now?" she asked against his lips.

"Now we stop sleeping in separate cabins like idiots."

"Your place or mine?"

"Ours," he said, kissing her again. "We build ours."

Down the mountain, at the main trail headquarters, Frankie Martinez was working late again.

The quiet crew member who fixed everything and said nothing was elbow-deep in a generator repair when Lena Hartwell knocked on the workshop door.

"You know it's past midnight, right?" the trail medic asked, leaning against the doorframe.

Frankie looked up, taking in her soft smile, the way her scrubs clung to her lush curves, the warmth in her eyes that made his chest tight.

"Generator won't fix itself," he said, looking away before he did something stupid.

Like tell her he'd been in love with her for two years.

Like admitting that he stayed late just hoping she'd stop by after her shift at the clinic.

"No," Lena said, stepping into the workshop. "But it'll still be broken tomorrow. You need sleep."

"I'm fine."

"When's the last time you ate something that wasn't from a vending machine?"

Frankie shrugged. Food was fuel. Sleep was time wasted. Work was the only thing that kept his hands busy and his mind off things he couldn't have.

Things like the beautiful medic who looked at him like she could see straight through to his soul.

"Frankie," Lena said, her voice gentle. "Look at me."

Against his better judgment, he did.

And saw something in her expression that made his heart slam against his ribs.

Want. Interest. The kind of heat that had nothing to do with friendship.

"What?" he asked roughly.

"Nothing," she said, but she didn't look away. "Just... you matter, you know? To the crew. To me."

Before he could respond, she was gone, leaving him alone with his broken generator and the sudden, impossible hope that maybe he wasn't as invisible as he'd thought.

Maybe some risks were worth taking.

Even for a man who'd spent his whole life in the shadows.

THE END

IRRESISTIBLE MOUNTAIN MAN

A TOUCH-STARVED MOUNTAIN MAN & CURVY MEDIC STEAMY WORKPLACE ROMANCE

1

TENSION BENEATH THE SURFACE

FRANKIE

The saw bit into Frankie's thumb before he could stop it.

"Fuck." He dropped the tool and stepped back, watching blood well up through the split skin. Not deep enough for stitches, but messy enough to need attention.

Through the workshop window, he spotted Lena's pickup pulling up to the medical trailer. Perfect timing, if you believed in that sort of thing. He didn't. But he also wasn't stupid enough to let a cut get infected when the best medic on the mountain was fifty yards away.

He wrapped his thumb in a shop rag and headed across the compound.

The medical trailer was regulation-issued white with red crosses on the sides, but Lena had made it her own. Lavender plants lined the steps. String lights hung from the awning. A hand-painted sign read "No Dying Allowed" in cheerful purple letters.

Everything about it was warm, inviting, and completely at odds with the sterile facilities he'd grown up around.

Everything about it was Lena.

He knocked once and pushed inside without waiting for permission. She looked up from restocking supplies, and her face lit up with the kind of smile that made his chest tight.

"Frankie! What brings you to my domain?" Her gaze dropped to the bloody rag around his thumb. "Besides the obvious."

"Saw slipped." He held up his hand. "Nothing major."

"Let me be the judge of that." She gestured toward the examination table. "Sit."

He perched on the edge of the table, hyperaware of how small the trailer felt with both of them in it. Lena moved around the space with practiced efficiency, gathering supplies, but he couldn't focus on anything except the way her scrubs hugged her curves.

She had the kind of body that made men forget their own names. Soft in all the right places, with hips that swayed when she walked and a chest that tested the limits of professional fabric. But it was her eyes that undid him—warm brown, direct, like she could see straight through to his soul.

"This might sting," she warned, unwrapping the rag.

Her fingers were gentle as she examined the cut, but they might as well have been brands for how they affected him. She smelled like lavender and antiseptic, a combination that shouldn't work but somehow did.

"You're lucky," she said, dabbing at the wound with gauze. "Clean cut, no debris. How'd it happen?"

"Wasn't paying attention."

She glanced up, brown eyes curious. "That's not like you. You're usually the most careful person on the crew."

He was. Had to be. Growing up in foster care taught you to watch everything, trust nothing, and keep your head down. But watching Lena patch up Sawyer's split lip after a bar fight last week had scrambled his brain for days.

"Just tired," he said.

"When's the last time you slept more than four hours?"

He shrugged. Sleep was time wasted when he could be working. Building. Fixing things that made sense, unlike the mess in his head whenever she was around.

"Frankie." Her voice went soft, concerned. "Look at me."

Against his better judgment, he did.

Her face was closer than before, close enough that he could see the gold flecks in her brown eyes. Close enough to count the freckles scattered across her nose. Close enough to wonder if her lips were as soft as they looked.

"Your jaw's tight," she murmured, fingers still working on his thumb. "You're holding tension in your shoulders."

The observation hit him like a physical blow. She'd been watching him. Paying attention to more than just his injuries.

"I'm fine," he managed.

"You're not." She secured the bandage with careful precision. "But you don't have to be. Not all the time."

Her hands stilled on his, and for a moment, the air between them shifted. Thickened. He felt her pulse jump under his thumb where it rested against her wrist.

She felt it too. He could see it in the way her breath caught, the way her eyes darkened.

Then she stepped back, breaking the connection.

"Keep it dry for twenty-four hours," she said, her voice slightly unsteady. "Change the bandage tomorrow. If it starts to look infected—"

"I'll come back." The words came out rougher than intended.

"Good." She busied herself cleaning up supplies, not meeting his eyes. "And Frankie? Get some sleep. That's an order."

He slid off the table, hyperaware of the space between them. "Yes, ma'am."

He was almost to the door when she called his name.

"Frankie?"

He turned back.

"Be careful tomorrow. I know Nash has you working the north ridge. That section's unstable after the storm."

She'd been paying attention to his assignments. Knew where he'd be working. Cared enough to worry about his safety.

"I'm always careful," he said.

"I know. But be extra careful. For me."

The words hung between them, loaded with meaning neither of them was ready to name. He nodded once and left before he did something stupid.

Like tell her he'd been careful his whole life, and it had gotten him exactly nowhere.

Like admit that maybe being reckless—with her—might be worth the risk.

LENA

Lena's hands shook as she finished putting away the medical supplies.

She'd been patching up crew members for two years. Cuts, scrapes, burns, the occasional broken bone. It was routine work, mechanical, something she could do in her sleep.

But touching Frankie Martinez had been anything but routine.

She'd felt the tension in his shoulders, seen the way his jaw had clenched when she'd moved closer. Had noticed how his breathing had changed when she'd touched his wrist.

And God, the way he'd looked at her when she'd asked him to be careful. Like her words mattered. Like she mattered.

She sank into her desk chair and pressed her palms to her

cheeks, trying to cool the heat that had nothing to do with the trailer's poor ventilation.

This was dangerous territory. The last time she'd let herself get involved with someone from work, it had ended with her reputation in tatters and a transfer request that saved her career but cost her everything else. Dr. Marcus Webb had been charming, established, and married—three facts she'd learned in the wrong order.

The fallout had been swift and brutal. Whispers in the hospital corridors. Assumptions about how she'd earned her position. A promising career in emergency medicine was derailed by one stupid, naive mistake.

She'd sworn then that she'd never mix work and personal life again. Had taken the trail crew position partly because it seemed safer—a small, professional team where everyone kept their distance.

But Frankie was different. Quiet, competent, reliable Frankie, who fixed everything and never asked for anything in return. Who looked at her like she was something precious instead of something broken.

She'd been watching him for months, if she was honest. She had found excuses to be near the workshop when he was working, had memorized his schedule so she could time her medical rounds to coincide with his breaks. She had told herself it was professional concern, that she worried about all the crew members equally.

But it wasn't professional concern that made her pulse race when he smiled. It wasn't medical interest that made her want to smooth the lines of exhaustion from his face.

It was want. Pure, simple, terrifying want.

And wanting someone on the crew—wanting Frankie—was the fastest way to destroy everything she'd rebuilt.

Her phone buzzed with a text from Nash: *Crew meeting tomorrow at 0800. New assignments.*

She stared at the message, knowing that whatever assignments came down would determine who worked where, who got paired with whom. Maybe she'd get assigned to the opposite end of the mountain and have time to get her head straight.

Or maybe she'd get paired with Frankie for medical rounds and finally have to face what was building between them.

Her phone buzzed again. This time it was a text from an unknown number: *Thank you for patching me up. Sleep well. - F*

She stared at the message, heart hammering. He'd gotten her number from the crew contact list. Had taken the time to text her and let her know he was thinking about her.

She typed and deleted a dozen responses before settling on: *Anytime. Sweet dreams.*

Then she turned off the lights and headed home, already counting the hours until she'd see him again—and terrified of what that meant.

FRANKIE

Two hours later, Frankie sat in his workshop, staring at a piece of pine that had somehow appeared in his hands.

He couldn't remember picking it up. Couldn't remember starting to carve. But his knife was moving, shaving away thin curls of wood, and a shape was emerging from the grain.

His hands were skilled at their craft, even if his mind wandered off. They'd been carving since he was eight, since his first foster father had shown him how to whittle to keep his hands busy and his mouth shut.

The wood was revealing itself slowly. A small cross, medical and clean, with delicate curves that somehow reminded him of lavender plants and warm brown eyes.

"You're brooding again."

Frankie looked up to find Nash leaning against the doorframe, coffee in hand and a knowing smirk on his face. He quickly closed his knife and set the carving aside.

"Just working," Frankie said.

"Uh-huh." Nash stepped into the workshop, his gaze flickering to the half-finished carving before settling on Frankie's face. "Lena patch you up?"

"Cut's fine."

"I wasn't asking about the cut." Nash's grin widened. "I was asking about Lena."

Heat crawled up Frankie's neck. "She's crew."

"So?"

"So it's complicated."

"Only if you make it complicated." Nash moved closer, his voice dropping to the tone he used when he was being serious instead of annoying. "Life's short, Frankie. Trust me on that. And that woman looks at you like you hung the moon."

Frankie picked up the carving again, thumb tracing the smooth wood. "What if I'm wrong?"

"What if you're right?"

The question hung between them, loaded with possibility and terror in equal measure.

Nash clapped him on the shoulder. "Crew meeting tomorrow at eight. New assignments are coming down. Maybe you'll get lucky."

After Nash left, Frankie held up the carving, studying it in the workshop light. Without conscious thought, his hands had shaped something that belonged to her. Something that said what he couldn't.

Maybe some risks were worth taking after all.

2

PRESSURE COOKER

LENA

The 0800 crew meeting was held in the main conference room, which was essentially the dining hall with folding chairs arranged in a rough circle. Lena arrived early, coffee in hand, and chose a seat near the door where she could observe without being obvious about it.

She'd barely slept. Every time she'd closed her eyes, she'd seen Frankie's face when she'd asked him to be careful *for her*. The way his breath had caught. The way his eyes had darkened.

The way he'd looked at her like she was something worth protecting.

Nash walked in at exactly eight, flanked by Emily, the crew's logistics coordinator, and Josh, one of the senior trail builders. Behind them came the rest of the team—Sawyer with his perpetual smirk, Micah looking like he'd rather be anywhere else, and finally Frankie.

He spotted her immediately, their eyes meeting across the

room for a brief, electric moment before he looked away and took a seat on the opposite side of the circle. Professional distance. Smart.

So why did it make her chest ache?

"All right, people," Nash said, settling into his chair with the easy authority of a man born to lead. "We've got three major projects coming down from the Forest Service, and they all need to be completed before the snow hits."

He gestured to Emily, who stood and consulted her tablet. "North ridge trail reconstruction—that's a two-week job, minimum. East sector bridge repairs—one week if the weather holds. And we've got a new request for medical assessments on all remote sites."

Lena's pulse quickened. Medical assessments meant overnight stays at various outposts, checking on the safety and preparedness of isolated work sites. It was exactly the kind of assignment that would put her in close quarters with crew members.

"Assignments," Nash continued. "Sawyer and Micah, you've got the bridge work. Josh and Reese, North Ridge. Emily, you're coordinating supply runs from base camp."

He paused, his gaze moving between Lena and Frankie with what she swore was deliberate intent.

"Lena, I need you on medical assessments for the remote sites. You'll be working with Frankie—he knows the locations, the equipment, and he can handle any structural issues you might find. We've got five sites that need overnight evaluations." Her heart slammed against her ribs. Five sites. Two weeks minimum, maybe more. Just her and Frankie, working isolated outposts, staying overnight in mountain shelters barely big enough for two people. "You'll start with Lookout Ridge," Nash continued, "then work your way through the eastern sector. Full safety and equipment assessments at each location."

She risked a glance at him and found him staring at his hands, jaw tight, every line of his body screaming tension.

"Any questions?" Nash asked.

Silence.

"Good. Pack for extended field work, you'll head out this afternoon."

As the meeting broke up, Lena found herself surrounded by the usual post-assignment chatter. But her focus was entirely on Frankie, who was making a beeline for the door like the room was on fire.

"Lena." Emily appeared at her elbow, tablet in hand, and a knowing smile on her face. "I've got your supply list for the medical assessments. Fair warning—some of these sites haven't been checked in months. You might find more than structural issues."

"What do you mean?"

"Let's just say the isolation can get to people. Keep an eye on your partner." Emily's smile widened. "Though something tells me that won't be a hardship."

Heat flooded Lena's cheeks. "It's a professional assignment."

"Of course it is." Emily's tone was perfectly innocent. "I'm just saying, Frankie's been wound tighter than a drum lately. Maybe some time away from base camp will do him good."

Before Lena could respond, Emily was gone, leaving her standing in the empty conference room with a racing heart and the sudden, terrifying certainty that the next few weeks would change everything.

FRANKIE

Three hours later, Frankie loaded the last of their gear into his truck and tried not to think about the sleeping arrangements at Lookout Ridge.

The outpost was a twelve-by-sixteen cabin with basic amenities—wood stove, two-burner camp kitchen, and one bed. One. Single. Bed.

He'd volunteered to sleep on the floor before they'd even discussed it, but Lena had waved him off with a laugh and something about being adults who could share space without making it weird.

If only she knew how weird he was planning to make it in his head.

"Ready?" she asked, appearing beside the truck with her medical kit and overnight bag. She'd changed from her usual scrubs into hiking gear—cargo pants that hugged her curves and a fitted thermal that left nothing to his imagination.

He was so fucked.

"Ready," he managed.

The drive to Lookout Ridge took two hours on winding forest roads that grew progressively narrower and more treacherous. Lena spent most of the trip reviewing medical protocols on her tablet, occasionally looking up to comment on the scenery or ask questions about their destination.

Professional. Friendly. Completely unaware that every casual comment was setting his nerves on fire.

"So what exactly are we looking for?" she asked as they began the final ascent.

"Structural integrity, equipment functionality, emergency preparedness." He kept his eyes on the road. "Making sure the site can support extended stays without anyone dying."

"Cheerful."

"These places are isolated for a reason. If something goes wrong, help is hours away at best."

"Is that why you volunteered for this assignment? Because you're good in emergencies?"

The question caught him off guard. He glanced at her, trying to read her expression, but she was looking out the window at the dense forest passing by.

"Nash assigned me," he said.

"Nash assigns lots of people to lots of things. But he paired us specifically." She turned to face him, and her directness made his chest tight. "I'm wondering why."

Because Nash was a meddling bastard who'd clearly noticed Frankie's pathetic attraction to the crew medic. Because two years of careful distance had apparently been as subtle as a forest fire. Because his boss had decided that what Frankie needed was a few weeks alone with the woman who'd been driving him crazy since the day she'd arrived.

"I know the sites," he said instead.

"So does Josh. So does Sawyer."

"They're busy with other assignments."

"Mm-hmm." She didn't sound convinced, but she let it drop, turning her attention back to her tablet.

The Lookout Ridge outpost sat on a bluff overlooking the Cascade Valley, a small log cabin surrounded by towering pines and granite outcroppings. It was beautiful, isolated, and the first of five sites they'd be evaluating over the next two weeks. Exactly the kind of place where a man could lose his mind thinking about the woman who'd be sharing his space for the foreseeable future.

"Wow," Lena breathed as they pulled up to the cabin. "It's gorgeous."

"Good views," he agreed, unloading their gear. "Sometimes too good. Easy to get distracted."

She shot him a look. "Speaking from experience?"

"Speaking from common sense."

Inside, the cabin was exactly as he'd remembered—functional, sparse, and dominated by the single bed that seemed to take up half the main room. Lena set her bags down and began a methodical inspection of the medical supplies while Frankie checked the structural elements.

They worked in comfortable silence for the first hour, each focused on their respective tasks. But as the afternoon wore on, the space seemed to shrink around them. Every time she moved, he was aware of it. Every time she spoke, he found himself listening not just to her words but to the warm timbre of her voice.

"Frankie," she called from the kitchen area. "Can you check this water heater? The pilot light won't stay lit."

He crossed to where she was crouched beside the small unit, her hair falling forward to hide her face as she peered at the controls. The scent of her shampoo—something floral and clean—hit him like a physical blow.

"Safety's probably dirty," he said, kneeling beside her. "Hand me that screwdriver."

Their fingers brushed as she passed him the tool, and the brief contact sent electricity shooting up his arm. She felt it too—he saw it in the way her breath caught, the way she didn't immediately pull her hand away.

"Got it," he said, his voice rougher than it should have been.

The pilot light caught and held, a steady, warm blue flame. But neither of them moved. They knelt there in the small kitchen, close enough that he could count her freckles, close enough to see the gold flecks in her brown eyes.

"Thank you," she said softly.

"No problem."

The moment stretched between them, loaded with possibility and danger in equal measure. Then Lena cleared her throat and stood, breaking the spell.

"I should finish the medical inventory," she said.

"Right. And I need to check the roof."

But as he headed for the door, he could feel her watching him, and the weight of her gaze followed him outside into the cooling mountain air.

LENA

By sunset, they'd completed their respective inspections and compiled a comprehensive report on the outpost's readiness. The cabin was in good shape—structurally sound, well-stocked, and equipped to handle extended stays even in winter conditions.

All of which meant they had no reason to delay the overnight stay that was part of the assessment protocol.

Lena stood on the cabin's small porch, watching the sun disappear behind the western peaks and trying to convince herself that sharing a bed with Frankie Martinez was no big deal. They were both adults. Both professionals. Both capable of maintaining appropriate boundaries.

The fact that she'd been fantasizing about crossing those boundaries for months was irrelevant.

Behind her, she could hear Frankie moving around the cabin —starting a fire, checking windows, doing the sort of methodical safety checks that she'd learned to associate with his careful, competent presence. He approached everything with the same quiet intensity, whether he was repairing equipment or bandaging a wound, or simply existing in a space.

It was that intensity that had first caught her attention. The way he focused completely on whatever task was in front of him, like the rest of the world had temporarily ceased to exist. She'd found herself watching him work, studying the way his hands moved with sure precision, the way his jaw tightened when he was concentrating.

The way he looked at her sometimes, when he thought she wasn't paying attention.

"Getting cold out there," he said from the doorway.

She turned to find him silhouetted against the warm light spilling from inside the cabin. He'd removed his outer layers, leaving him in dark jeans and a long-sleeved thermal that clung to his broad shoulders and chest. The fire he'd built cast flickering shadows across his face, highlighting the strong line of his jaw, the intensity in his dark eyes.

"Yeah," she said, her voice slightly breathless. "I should come in."

But she didn't move. Instead, she found herself studying his face, searching for some sign of what he was thinking. What he was feeling.

"Lena," he said, her name rough in his throat.

"Yeah?"

For a moment, she thought he might say something important. Something that would crack open the careful distance they'd been maintaining. But then his expression shifted and he stepped aside to let her pass.

"Dinner's ready," he said.

Inside, the cabin felt smaller than it had during the day. The fire filled the space with warm, dancing light, and the single bed seemed to loom larger than ever. They ate the simple meal he'd prepared—canned chili heated over the camp stove, bread that was only slightly stale—in the kind of charged silence that made every casual comment feel loaded with meaning.

"This is good," she said, gesturing with her spoon. "You're a better cook than I expected."

"Trail food isn't exactly gourmet."

"No, but you put actual effort into it. Most people would just heat and eat."

He shrugged, uncomfortable with the compliment. "No point in eating if it tastes like shit."

She smiled. "Spoken like a man who's spent time being really hungry."

The observation was more perceptive than he'd expected, and for a moment his careful guard slipped. "Foster care teaches you to appreciate decent food when you can get it."

The admission hung between them, more personal than anything he'd ever shared with her. Lena set down her spoon and looked at him directly.

"How old were you when you went into the system?"

"Seven." The word came out clipped, defensive. "Look, we don't need to—"

"I'm not prying," she said gently. "I'm just... interested in you. As a person."

Interested in you. The words hit him like a physical blow. When was the last time someone had said that to him? When was the last time someone had looked at him like he was worth knowing?

"It was a long time ago," he said finally.

"But it shaped you."

"Everything shapes you."

"True. But some things shape you more than others." She leaned forward slightly, her eyes never leaving his face. "You're careful. Precise. You think three steps ahead in every situation. That doesn't happen by accident."

He was quiet for a moment, torn between the instinct to deflect and the dangerous desire to let her see him. Really see him.

"You learn to watch," he said finally. "To anticipate problems before they happen. It's safer that way."

"Safer for who?"

"Everyone."

The simple honesty in his voice made her chest ache. "That sounds lonely."

"It's practical."

"It can be both."

Outside, the wind picked up, rattling the windows and sending sparks up the chimney. The storm that had been threatening all day was finally arriving, and the first fat raindrops began to spatter against the glass.

"Looks like we're staying put until morning," Frankie said, grateful for the distraction.

"Good thing we're prepared."

She stood to clear their dishes, and as she reached across the table, her shoulder brushed against his. The contact was brief, innocent, but it sent heat racing through his system like wildfire.

She felt it too. He saw it in the way she went still, the way her breathing changed. For a moment, they were frozen there—her leaning across the table, him trapped between her warmth and the solid wood at his back.

"Lena," he said, her name barely a whisper.

She straightened slowly, dishes forgotten, and turned to face him. The space between them felt electric, charged with two years of careful distance and growing attraction.

"What are we doing, Frankie?" she asked softly.

The question hung in the air between them, loaded with possibility and danger and the kind of honesty that could change everything.

"I don't know," he admitted. "But I can't stop thinking about yesterday. About the way you looked at me in the medical trailer."

"How did I look at you?"

"Like maybe I wasn't invisible after all."

The raw vulnerability in his voice cracked something open in her chest. This strong, competent man who fixed everything and asked for nothing—he thought he was invisible. The idea was so ridiculous that it was heartbreaking.

"Frankie," she said, stepping closer. "You have never been invisible to me. Not once."

And then, before either of them could think better of it, she reached up and cupped his face in her hands, her thumbs tracing the sharp line of his cheekbones.

"Not once," she repeated, and pulled him down to kiss her.

3

CLOSE QUARTERS

FRANKIE

The kiss lasted exactly three seconds.

Three seconds of Lena's soft mouth against his, her hands warm on his face, her body close enough that he could feel her heart hammering against his chest. Three seconds of pure, perfect heat that burned through two years of careful restraint like it was tissue paper.

Then reality crashed in.

Frankie pulled back so fast he nearly knocked over his chair, putting space between them like his life depended on it. Because maybe it did. Maybe this was exactly the kind of mistake that destroyed everything good in his world.

"Fuck," he breathed. "Lena, I—"

"Don't." Her voice was steady, but her cheeks were flushed, her breathing uneven. "Don't apologize. Not for that."

"We can't." The words came out harsher than he'd intended. "We work together. We—"

"We're adults."

"You're crew."

"So are you."

"It's different." He ran a hand through his hair, pacing to the window where rain was starting to streak the glass. "You don't understand what this could—"

"What? What could it do, Frankie?" She stood, moving closer, and he forced himself not to back away. "Ruin your reputation? Make people talk? Or are you worried it'll be messy?"

"All of it." The honesty came out raw, unfiltered. "I don't do messy, Lena. I don't do complicated. I fix things, I keep my head down, and I don't rock boats."

"And you think I'm a boat-rocker?"

He looked at her then—really looked. At the way her hair caught the firelight, the stubborn set to her jaw, the heat still simmering in her brown eyes. She was beautiful, competent, everything he'd ever wanted and everything he couldn't risk.

"I think you're dangerous," he said quietly.

Something flickered across her face. Hurt, maybe, or disappointment. But when she spoke, her voice was calm.

"Dangerous to who?"

"To me."

The admission hung between them, honest and terrifying. Outside, the storm was intensifying, rain hammering the windows with increasing force. The sound filled the silence as they stared at each other across the small space.

"The tent," Lena said suddenly.

"What?"

"We were supposed to set up the emergency tent. Part of the assessment protocol." She gestured toward their packs. "Test the shelter systems in actual field conditions."

Frankie blinked, trying to shift gears from the emotional minefield they'd been navigating to the practical matter at hand. Right. The tent. Part of their job.

"Storm's too strong," he said. "We'll get soaked trying to set it up."

"The protocol doesn't care about comfort. It cares about whether the equipment works when lives depend on it."

She was right, and they both knew it. But the thought of spending the night in a two-person tent with Lena, after what had just happened between them, made his chest tight with something that had nothing to do with professional concern.

"We could wait until morning," he suggested.

"We could. But that wouldn't be following protocol, would it?" She tilted her head, studying his face. "You always follow protocol, Frankie. It's one of the things I—" She stopped herself, color rising in her cheeks.

"One of the things you what?"

"One of the things I've noticed about you." Her voice was carefully neutral. "You're thorough. Precise. You don't cut corners."

Don't cut corners. Right. Even when cutting corners would save him from a night of exquisite torture in close quarters with the woman who'd just kissed him senseless.

"Fine," he said. "We'll set up the tent."

LENA

Twenty minutes later, Lena was questioning every decision that had led to this moment.

The emergency tent was designed for survival, not comfort. Two-person capacity in the same way that a phone booth could technically hold two people if they really, really wanted to be close. The setup had gone smoothly despite the rain—Frankie was nothing if not competent—but now they sat inside the cramped space, listening to water drum against the rainfly, and the proximity was almost unbearable.

Almost.

Because, despite everything rational and professional telling her to maintain distance, Lena couldn't stop stealing glances at him. The way his wet hair had dried into unruly waves. The way his thermal shirt clung to his broad shoulders. The way he was very carefully not looking at her while they tested the camp stove and emergency supplies.

"Temperature's holding steady," she said, checking the thermometer. "Ventilation is adequate. No leaks in the fly."

"Ground sheet's dry," he reported, not meeting her eyes. "Sleeping system setup is straightforward."

They spoke in the clipped, professional tones of people determined to ignore the elephant in the tent. Or in this case, the kiss that had changed everything and the sleeping bags that were currently spread out side by side on the tent floor.

"We should test the full overnight scenario," Lena said, because apparently she was a glutton for punishment. "Make sure the shelter maintains thermal efficiency through an entire sleep cycle."

Frankie's jaw tightened. "That's not necessary."

"It's in the protocol."

"The protocol doesn't account for—" He stopped himself.

"For what?"

"For the fact that I've been trying not to think about what you look like when you sleep for the past two years."

The words hit her like a physical blow. Raw, honest, devastating in their vulnerability. She stared at him, watching as his hands clenched into fists at his sides and his breathing became shallow.

"Two years?" she asked softly.

"Since the day you arrived at base camp. Since you smiled at me like I was worth your time instead of just another broken thing to fix."

"Frankie—"

"I know how this looks," he continued, the words spilling out like he couldn't stop them. "The weird loner who never talks suddenly confessing feelings to the woman everyone likes. I know how pathetic—"

"Stop." She moved closer, close enough to touch his face again, to make him look at her. "You are not pathetic. You are not weird. And you are definitely not just another broken thing."

His eyes were dark, troubled, full of doubts she wanted to erase with her mouth.

"You don't know what you're getting into," he said.

"Then tell me."

The challenge hung between them, loaded with possibility and risk. Outside, thunder rolled across the mountains, and the tent swayed gently in the wind. They were alone, isolated, surrounded by nothing but wilderness and weather.

And despite every rational reason to maintain professional distance, Lena found herself leaning closer.

"Tell me what I'm getting into, Frankie."

FRANKIE

She was close enough to kiss again.

The thought hit him like lightning, followed immediately by the memory of how she'd tasted—warm, sweet, with just a hint of the coffee they'd shared after dinner. How her mouth had been soft and sure under his, like she'd been thinking about kissing him for as long as he'd been thinking about kissing her.

"You're getting into a man who doesn't know how to be close to people," he said, his voice rough. "Who grew up in group homes and foster care and learned that wanting things was the fastest way to lose them."

"That's not—"

"You're getting into someone who works alone because it's safer. Who fixes things because broken objects don't leave. Who's been watching you for two years and telling himself it was hopeless because women like you don't notice men like me."

She was quiet for a moment, studying his face in the dim light filtering through the tent walls. When she spoke, her voice was soft.

"What kind of woman am I, Frankie?"

"Smart. Competent. Beautiful." Each word came out like a confession. "The kind who could have anyone. The kind who deserves better than someone who's held together with duct tape and silence."

"And what kind of man are you?"

The question caught him off guard. "I just told you—"

"No, you told me what you think you lack. I'm asking what you are."

He stared at her, lost. "I don't understand."

"You're the man who notices when people are hurt before they even know it themselves. Who stays late to make sure the equipment won't fail when lives depend on it. Who carves beautiful things with his hands because he sees potential in everything, even broken wood."

His breath caught. "You've seen my carvings?"

"I've seen the way you look at them. Like they matter. Like they're worth your time and attention and care." She moved closer, close enough that he could feel her warmth. "That's the kind of man you are, Frankie. The kind who makes things beautiful. The kind who's worth knowing."

The words cracked something open in his chest. Something he'd been protecting for so long he'd forgotten what it felt like to be without it.

"Lena," he said, her name barely a whisper.

"Yeah?"

"I want to kiss you again."

"Then why aren't you?"

The question hung between them for a heartbeat. Then Frankie was moving, cupping her face in his hands, pulling her against him with all the desperate hunger of a man who'd been starving for touch.

This kiss was different from the first. Deeper, hungrier, full of two years of careful watching and wanting. She opened for him immediately, her hands fisting in his shirt, her body molding against his in the confined space of the tent.

When they broke apart, both breathing hard, her eyes were dark with want.

"We're going to have to sleep in here tonight," she said.

"Yeah."

"Together."

"Yeah."

"In very close quarters."

"Lena." His voice was strained. "Are you trying to kill me?"

She smiled then, the first real smile she'd given him since they'd entered the tent. "I'm trying to follow protocol. The protocol says we test the full overnight scenario."

"The protocol doesn't know what it's asking."

"Maybe not." She settled back against her sleeping bag, but her eyes never left his face. "But I do."

4

CRACK AND COLLAPSE

FRANKIE

The moment they couldn't hold back anymore came at 2:47 AM.

Frankie knew the exact time because he'd been staring at his watch for the past hour, listening to Lena breathe in the sleeping bag beside him, trying to convince himself he could survive until dawn without touching her.

He couldn't.

The tent was too small, her presence too overwhelming, the memory of that kiss too vivid. Every time she shifted in her sleep, her body brushed against his. Every soft sound she made sent heat racing through his system like wildfire.

When she rolled over in her sleep and her hand landed on his chest, he nearly came out of his skin.

"Lena," he whispered.

Her eyes opened immediately, alert despite the hour. "What's wrong?"

"I can't—" He stopped, swallowed hard. "I can't stop thinking about kissing you."

She was quiet for a moment, studying his face in the dim light filtering through the tent walls. When she spoke, her voice was soft.

"Then do it again."

The words shattered his last shred of restraint. He rolled toward her, cupping her face in his hands, pulling her mouth to his with all the desperate hunger of a man who'd been starving for touch.

This kiss was different from the others. Deeper, hungrier, full of need that had been building for two years. She opened for him immediately, her hands fisting in his thermal shirt, her body molding against his in the confined space.

When they broke apart, both breathing hard, her eyes were dark with want.

"Frankie," she said, his name barely a whisper.

"Yeah?"

"I want you."

The simple honesty in her voice nearly undid him. "Lena, if we do this—"

"We're doing this." She silenced his protests with another kiss, this one even more demanding than the last. "I've wanted you for months. I'm tired of pretending I don't."

Her confession hit him like lightning. "Months?"

"Since you fixed the generator in my trailer during that storm last spring. You worked for six hours straight to make sure I had power. You never even asked for a thank you."

He remembered that night. Remembered the way she'd brought him coffee, the way she'd smiled when the lights came back on, the way he'd driven home afterward, telling himself not to read too much into her gratitude.

"I was just doing my job," he said.

"No, you were taking care of me. The way you always do. The way you take care of everyone." Her hands slid under his shirt, palms warm against his skin. "When do you let someone take care of you?"

The question caught him off guard. "I don't need—"

"Everyone needs." She pushed up on her elbow, looking down at him. "Let me."

Before he could respond, she was kissing him again, her mouth soft and sure against his. Her hands explored the planes of his chest, tracing scars he'd forgotten he had, touching him like he was something precious instead of something broken.

"Lena," he said against her lips.

"I'm right here."

She was. She was right there, warm and willing in his arms, looking at him like he was worth wanting. The thought was intoxicating and terrifying in equal measure.

"I don't know how to do this," he admitted.

"Do what?"

"Be close to someone. Be wanted." The words came out raw, honest. "I don't know how to be good at this."

Her expression softened. "You think you're not good at this?"

"I know I'm not."

"Frankie." She cupped his face in her hands, forcing him to meet her eyes. "You've been driving me crazy for months with how good you are at this. The way you listen when I talk. The way you remember things that matter to me. The way you look at me like I'm the most interesting thing in the room."

"You are."

The admission came out without his permission, honest and unfiltered. Her breath caught.

"See?" she said softly. "You're already better at this than you think."

She kissed him then, slow and sweet, her hands tangling in his hair. He lost himself in the taste of her, the feel of her body against his, the way she made soft sounds of pleasure when he touched her.

LENA

She'd been fantasizing about this moment for months, but the reality was better than anything she'd imagined.

Frankie's hands were everywhere—careful, reverent, like he was memorizing every inch of her skin. When he pushed her thermal shirt up and over her head, his gaze was so intense it made her shiver.

"You're beautiful," he said, voice rough with want.

"So are you."

She meant it. In the dim light, he was all sharp angles and lean muscle, scars that told stories she wanted to hear, hands that knew how to build and fix and create. He was gorgeous in the way that working men were gorgeous—functional, strong, real.

When he bent his head to kiss her throat, she arched against him, need building low in her belly.

"More," she whispered.

He obliged, his mouth trailing lower, leaving a path of heat across her collarbone, down to the valley between her breasts. When he took one nipple into his mouth, she gasped, her back arching off the sleeping bag.

"Fuck, Frankie."

The curse seemed to flip a switch in him. His control slipped, and suddenly his hands were less careful, more demanding. He pressed her back against the sleeping bag, his body covering hers, his mouth claiming her with a hunger that made her head spin.

"Tell me what you want," he said against her skin.

"You. All of you."

He looked up at her then, something vulnerable flickering in his dark eyes. "Are you sure?"

Instead of answering with words, she reached for the waistband of his pants, tugging them down over his hips. He was hard, ready, and when she wrapped her hand around him, he groaned like she was killing him.

"Lena," he said, her name breaking on his lips.

"I'm sure," she said, guiding him to her. "I've never been more sure of anything."

FRANKIE

When he entered her, everything else disappeared.

The storm outside, the cramped tent, the voice in his head that insisted he didn't deserve this—all of it faded until there was nothing but Lena, warm and tight around him, looking up at him like he was everything she'd ever wanted.

"God," he breathed.

She wrapped her legs around his hips, pulling him deeper, and the sensation nearly shattered what was left of his control.

"Move," she whispered.

He did, slowly at first, then with increasing urgency as she met him thrust for thrust. She was everything—soft where he was hard, gentle where he was rough, open where he was closed off. She undid him completely, breaking down walls he'd spent decades building.

"You feel so good," she gasped, her nails digging into his shoulders.

"So do you. So fucking good."

The words came out broken, desperate. He'd never been good with words, but she seemed to understand anyway. Her hands tangled in his hair, pulling his mouth down to hers for a kiss that was all heat and need.

When she came, it was with his name on her lips and her body clenching tight around him. The sensation sent him over the edge, and he followed her into oblivion with a groan that seemed to come from his soul.

Afterward, they lay tangled together in the narrow sleeping bag, hearts hammering, skin slick with sweat. The storm outside had gentled to a steady patter of rain against the tent walls.

"That was," Lena started, then stopped.

"Yeah," Frankie agreed.

She turned in his arms, pressing her face against his chest. "What happens now?"

The question he'd been dreading. Because now came the complications, the crew dynamics, the thousand ways this could go wrong and destroy everything good in his life.

But looking down at her, feeling the way she fit perfectly against him, he couldn't bring himself to care about any of that.

"Now we figure it out," he said.

"Together?"

"If you want to."

She lifted her head to look at him. "I want to. But Frankie, I need you to know something."

"What?"

"This isn't just sex for me. This isn't just scratching an itch or satisfying curiosity. This is—" She paused, searching for words. "This matters."

The vulnerability in her voice cracked something open in his chest. "It matters to me too."

"Good." She settled back against his chest. "Because I'm not done with you yet."

Despite everything—the complications, the unknowns, the voice in his head insisting this was too good to last—Frankie smiled.

For the first time in his life, he was exactly where he wanted to be.

LENA

She woke to the sound of rain and the feeling of Frankie's absence.

The sleeping bag beside her was cold, and when she sat up, she saw him silhouetted against the tent entrance, fully dressed, staring out at the storm.

"Hey," she said softly.

He turned, and something in his expression made her stomach drop. The walls were back up, the careful distance restored. It was like the man who'd made love to her with desperate tenderness had never existed.

The radio crackled to life before either of them could say more. Nash's voice cut through the static: "All teams, return to base immediately. Weather system moving in faster than predicted. Road conditions deteriorating. Repeat—all field teams return to base." Frankie reached for the handset. "Base, this is Lookout Ridge. Copy the recall."

"Confirmed. Pack it up and get out of there. The other four sites will have to wait until after the storm passes." Lena felt something sink in her chest. Four more sites meant four more chances to figure this out. Now they were heading back to base camp with everything unresolved.

"Storm's letting up," he said. "We should pack up soon."

"Frankie." She reached for her clothes, suddenly feeling exposed. "What's wrong?"

"Nothing's wrong."

"Don't lie to me. Not after last night."

He was quiet for a moment, his jaw working like he was trying to find words. When he spoke, his voice was carefully neutral.

"Last night was—"

"A mistake?"

"Complicated."

The word hit her like a slap. She finished getting dressed in silence, watching him avoid her eyes, seeing the way he held himself apart from her, even in the small space.

"So what now?" she asked finally. "We pretend it didn't happen?"

"We go back to base camp. We do our jobs. We don't make this harder than it has to be."

"Harder for who?"

"For everyone."

She stared at him, trying to understand how he could shut down so completely after the connection they'd shared. How he could make love to her like she was everything, and then talk about her like she was a complication to be managed.

"I see," she said quietly.

Something flickered in his eyes—regret, maybe, or pain—but he didn't take it back. Didn't reach for her. Didn't do anything to bridge the sudden chasm between them.

Fine. If he wanted to pretend last night meant nothing, she could play that game.

But as she packed her gear and prepared to leave the tent—and everything that had happened inside it—behind, Lena couldn't shake the feeling that she'd just lost something important.

Something she might never get back. Something she'd finally reached for. Something he'd made her believe she could have.

5

DISTANCE HURTS WORSE

LENA
Two hours of silence. Two hours of not knowing if he regretted everything—or nothing.

Lena sat in the passenger seat of Frankie's truck, separated by more than just the center console. He kept his eyes on the road, hands gripping the wheel like it was the only thing keeping him grounded. Every attempt she made at conversation was met with monosyllabic responses or complete silence.

By the time they pulled into headquarters, Lena felt like she was suffocating on everything left unsaid.

"I'll file the assessment report," she said as they unloaded their gear.

"Fine."

"The tent performed well. We should recommend it for field use."

"Whatever you think."

She wanted to shake him. Wanted to grab his face and force

him to look at her, to acknowledge what had happened between them, to stop pretending she was invisible again.

Instead, she shouldered her medical kit and walked toward the main building, leaving him standing by his truck like a man made of stone.

Nash appeared in the doorway as she approached, coffee in hand, and his usual knowing expression.

"How'd the assessment go?" he asked.

"Equipment checks out. Site's operational." She kept her voice professional, but something in her tone must have given her away because Nash's expression sharpened.

"Everything else okay?"

"Why wouldn't it be?"

"Because you look like someone who's been hit by a truck, and Frankie looks like the truck." Nash's gaze flicked over her shoulder to where Frankie was methodically organizing his gear with unnecessary precision. "Want to talk about it?"

"No."

"Uh-huh." Nash stepped aside to let her pass. "Conference room in ten. New assignments."

Lena's stomach dropped. "New assignments?"

"Forest Service wants to accelerate the timeline. We're splitting into smaller teams to cover more ground." Nash's expression was carefully neutral. "You'll be working the eastern sector. Frankie's heading west."

Opposite sides of the mountain. Maximum distance. No chance of accidental encounters or shared assignments.

"For how long?" she asked.

"Rest of the season. Maybe longer, depending on funding."

She nodded, not trusting her voice. Nash watched her for a moment longer, then clapped her gently on the shoulder.

"For what it's worth," he said quietly, "some things are worth fighting for."

FRANKIE

Ten minutes later, Frankie sat in the conference room surrounded by his crewmates and tried to focus on Nash's words instead of the way Lena had looked when she'd walked away from his truck.

Hurt. Disappointed. Like he'd proven every low opinion she'd ever had about him.

Which maybe he had.

"Eastern sector's been hit hard by the storms," Nash was saying. "Trail damage, bridge washouts, multiple access points compromised. It's a big job."

"How big?" Lena asked. Her voice was steady, professional. Like nothing had changed.

"Three weeks, minimum. Maybe a month if the weather doesn't cooperate." Nash consulted his tablet. "You'll be working with Josh and the new intern. Base camp at Miller's Creek."

Frankie felt something cold settle in his chest. Miller's Creek was a day's drive from anywhere, completely isolated. She'd be gone for weeks, maybe longer, working with Josh, who was competent and reliable and everything Frankie wasn't.

"What about the west sector?" someone asked.

"Frankie's taking point on the fire access roads. Solo assignment, mostly. Some of the terrain's too rough for teams."

Solo. Of course. Nash was sending him back to what he did best—working alone, fixing things that couldn't hurt him, avoiding complications.

The meeting continued, but Frankie barely heard the rest. He was too busy watching Lena take notes, her pen moving with sharp, precise strokes across the paper. She didn't look at him once.

When Nash dismissed them, she was the first one out the door.

Frankie lingered, pretending to organize his notes while the others filtered out. When the room was empty except for him and Nash, his boss leaned back in his chair and studied him with knowing eyes.

"You want to tell me what happened up there?" Nash asked.

"Equipment worked fine. Site's good to go."

"That's not what I'm asking about."

Frankie met his gaze. "Nothing to tell."

"Bullshit." Nash's voice was mild, but steel lay underneath. "I've seen you and Lena dance around each other for two years. I finally give you both a chance to figure it out, and you come back looking like someone shot your dog."

"Maybe some things are better left alone."

"Maybe. Or maybe you're a chickenshit who's too scared to fight for something good."

The words hit like a physical blow. Frankie stood, his chair scraping against the floor.

"I'm not scared."

"No? I just put a whole mountain between the two of you and you're not fighting me on it. If anything, you look like you're planning to disappear into the woods until whatever happened at the cabin blows over."

Because she was better off without him. Because he'd proven last night that he couldn't handle intimacy without making it complicated. Because the smart thing—the safe thing—was to let her go before he hurt her worse.

"Some people aren't built for close relationships," he said instead.

Nash was quiet for a long moment. When he spoke, his voice was gentler.

"That's fear talking, hermano. And fear makes good men do stupid things."

After Nash left, Frankie sat alone in the empty conference room, staring at the assignment board where their names were listed under different sectors. Different worlds.

It was better this way. Cleaner. No complications, no hurt feelings, no risk of destroying the best thing that had ever happened to him.

So why did it feel like he was dying inside?

LENA

Three days later, Lena was knee-deep in trail assessments and trying very hard not to think about Frankie Martinez.

She was failing spectacularly.

Miller's Creek base camp was everything Nash had promised —isolated, well-equipped, and staffed with competent people who treated her with professional respect. Josh was an excellent team leader, and the new intern, Marcus, was eager to learn and quick to help.

Marcus had a habit of narrating his work like a nature documentary. "And here we see the trail marker in its natural habitat," he'd say while hammering stakes, "completely unaware that it's about to become someone's lifeline." It should have been annoying, but somehow his earnest enthusiasm made even the most mundane tasks feel important.

The dynamic should have been perfect.

Instead, she found herself staring at her radio every evening, wondering if Frankie was checking in from the west sector. Wondering if he was sleeping. Wondering if he was thinking about her at all.

"You okay, Lena?" Josh asked on the fourth night as they sat around the camp stove, eating dinner and reviewing the next day's route.

"Fine. Just tired."

"You sure? You've been kind of... distant since you got here."

She looked up to find both Josh and Marcus watching her with concern. Great. She was being obvious.

"Just adjusting to the new assignment," she said. "Different routine, different people."

"Is it the people?" Marcus asked, his documentary voice replaced by genuine worry. "Because if we're doing something wrong—"

"No, you're both great. Really." She forced a smile. "I'm just not used to working this far from base camp."

It wasn't exactly a lie. She wasn't used to being separated from Frankie by hundreds of miles of wilderness. She wasn't used to waking up without the possibility of seeing him at breakfast, or catching glimpses of him in the workshop, or finding excuses to bring him coffee when he was working late.

She missed him. Missed him with an intensity that scared her, because it proved that what had happened between them had been real. At least for her.

Her radio crackled. "Miller's Creek base, this is HQ. Radio check."

Josh reached for the handset, but Lena was faster. "HQ, this is Miller's Creek. We copy."

"Status report?"

"All good here. Team's healthy, weather's holding, progress on schedule."

"Copy that. Any supply needs?"

"We're good for now."

"Roger. HQ out."

She set the radio aside, trying to ignore the disappointment that it had been Emily's voice and not Nash's. Not that it mattered. Nash wouldn't mention Frankie even if she asked.

"You want to tell us what's really going on?" Josh asked quietly.

Lena looked at him—really looked. He was younger than Nash, maybe early thirties, with the kind of steady, reliable presence that made him a natural leader. There was no judgment in his expression, just genuine concern.

"It's complicated," she said finally.

"Most things worth caring about are."

The simple observation cracked something open in her chest. Before she could stop herself, the words were spilling out.

"There's someone at base camp. Was someone. I don't know what he is now." She laughed, but it sounded bitter even to her own ears. "We worked together for two years. I thought... I hoped there was something there. And then finally, finally, we had a moment. A real moment. And it was everything I'd imagined it would be."

"But?" Marcus prompted gently.

"But the next morning, he acted like it had never happened. Like I was a mistake he needed to manage instead of a person he'd just—" She stopped herself before she said too much.

"Been there," Josh said quietly. "Sometimes people get scared when something real happens. Especially if they're not used to real."

"Or maybe it wasn't real for him. Maybe it was just proximity and opportunity, and I read too much into it."

"Did it feel like just proximity?"

She thought about the way Frankie had looked at her in the tent, the way he'd touched her like she was something precious, the way he'd said her name like a prayer.

"No," she whispered. "It felt like everything."

"Then maybe you should fight for it."

"How do you fight for someone who won't even look at you?"

Josh smiled. "You make them look."

FRANKIE

A week into his solo assignment, Frankie was carving again.

He hadn't meant to start. Had planned to focus on the fire roads, the bridge repairs, the endless practical tasks that kept his hands busy and his mind occupied. But every evening, when the work was done and the silence of the woods pressed in around him, he found himself reaching for his knife.

Tonight's piece was different from his usual work. Not a simple utilitarian object or abstract design, but something specific. Something that had been taking shape in his mind since the night in the tent.

A medical cross, delicate and precise, with flowing lines that somehow reminded him of lavender plants and warm brown eyes. At the base, he'd carved a small L, barely visible unless you knew to look for it.

For Lena.

He held it up to the firelight, examining the grain, the balance, the way it felt in his palm. It was some of his best work—clean lines, perfect proportions, finished to a satin smoothness that begged to be touched.

She'd never see it. He'd never have the courage to give it to her. But carving it felt like a prayer, like a way of keeping her close even when she was hundreds of miles away.

His radio crackled. "West sector, this is HQ. Radio check."

Frankie reached for the handset, his pulse quickening. "HQ, this is West sector. I copy."

"Status report?"

Nash's voice. Not Lena's. Of course not. She was at Miller's Creek, probably sitting around a campfire with Josh and the intern, laughing at something Frankie would never be part of.

"Roads are clear through sector seven," he reported. "Bridge at

Devil's Canyon needs new supports, but it's passable. Weather's been good."

"Any supply needs?"

"I'm good."

"You eating enough? Getting enough sleep?"

Frankie frowned. Nash didn't usually ask personal questions during radio checks. "I'm fine."

"Uh-huh. You know, we've got some flexibility in the schedule if you want to rotate back to base camp for a few days."

The offer was tempting. Too tempting. Which was exactly why he couldn't take it.

"I'm good here," he said. "Plenty of work to keep me busy."

"Copy that." Nash paused. "Frankie?"

"Yeah?"

"Some mistakes are worth making twice."

The transmission ended, leaving Frankie alone with the crackling fire and the weight of Nash's words. He looked down at the carving in his hands, at the small L that marked it as belonging to someone he'd pushed away out of fear.

Maybe Nash was right. Maybe some mistakes were worth making twice.

But first, he had to find the courage to make them right the first time.

The piece of wood seemed to burn in his palm, warm and smooth and full of possibility. Like a bridge across the distance he'd created. Like a way home.

If he was brave enough to cross it.

6

BREAKPOINT

LENA

Two weeks into the Miller's Creek assignment, Lena found something that made her hands shake.

She was doing inventory in the supply shed, cataloging medical equipment and checking expiration dates, when she discovered a box tucked behind the emergency blankets. At first glance, it looked like standard storage—the kind of forgotten supplies that accumulated in remote outposts over the years.

But when she opened it, her breath caught.

Wood carvings. Dozens of them.

A small bird, wings spread in flight. A mountain peak, detailed down to the tree line. A compass rose with perfect symmetry. Each piece was unsigned but unmistakable—she'd know Frankie's work anywhere. The same precision, the same careful attention to detail, the same way of finding beauty in simple shapes.

At the bottom of the box, wrapped in an old shop rag, she found a medical cross.

Delicate. Perfect. With flowing lines that somehow reminded

her of lavender plants and warm summer evenings. At the base, barely visible unless you knew to look for it, was carved a small L.

Her hands trembled as she lifted it to the light streaming through the shed window. It was beautiful—maybe the most beautiful thing she'd ever seen. And he'd made it for her. Had carved her initial into wood like a promise, like a prayer.

Like she mattered.

"Lena?" Marcus's voice came from outside the shed. "You find those gauze pads?"

"Just a minute," she called back, her voice unsteady.

She wrapped the carving carefully and tucked it into her pocket, then finished the inventory with mechanical precision. But her mind was spinning, heart hammering against her ribs.

He'd made this for her. Before their night together, or after? Had he been carrying it around, afraid to give it to her? Had he left it here, hoping she'd find it?

The questions burned through her as she rejoined Josh and Marcus for the afternoon's trail work. But underneath the confusion was something else. Something that felt dangerously like hope.

How do you fight for someone who won't even look at you?
You make them look.

Josh's words echoed in her mind as they worked, and by the time they made camp that evening, Lena had made a decision.

"Josh," she said as they sat around the camp stove after dinner. "I need a favor."

"Name it."

"I need a ride across the ridge."

FRANKIE

Frankie was splitting wood when he heard the truck.

He'd been at it for an hour, working off the restless energy that seemed to plague him these days. The repetitive motion helped—

ax up, ax down, wood splitting clean along the grain. Simple. Predictable. Unlike everything else in his life since that night in the tent.

The sound of an engine echoing off the canyon walls made him pause, ax frozen at the top of its arc. No one was supposed to be coming out here. His supply run wasn't scheduled for another week, and Nash had been clear about the solo nature of this assignment.

A familiar pickup truck rounded the bend and pulled up to his temporary camp. Josh climbed out of the driver's seat, but it was the passenger door that made Frankie's heart stop.

Lena.

She stood beside the truck, wearing her usual hiking gear, medical kit slung across her shoulder. Her dark hair was pulled back in a practical ponytail, and her brown eyes were fixed on him with an intensity that made his chest tight.

"Afternoon, Frankie," Josh said easily. "Hope you don't mind the company. Lena had some questions about the medical protocols for solo assignments."

It was a transparent excuse, and they all knew it. But Frankie found himself nodding anyway, setting down the ax with careful precision.

"Josh," Lena said without taking her eyes off Frankie. "Could you give us a few minutes?"

"Sure thing. I'll check the water levels at the creek." Josh tipped his hat and walked away, leaving them alone in the clearing.

The silence stretched between them, loaded with everything they hadn't said. Lena reached into her pocket and pulled out something wrapped in cloth.

"I found this," she said, unwrapping the medical cross he'd carved.

His heart slammed against his ribs. "Where?"

"Supply shed at Miller's Creek. There was a whole box of your work." She held up the carving, turning it so that the afternoon light caught the small "L" at the base. "Were you ever going to give this to me?"

He couldn't speak. Couldn't breathe. Couldn't do anything but stare at the piece of wood that had somehow become a confession he wasn't ready to make.

"Frankie," she said, stepping closer. "Look at me."

Against every instinct screaming at him to run, he did.

Her eyes were bright with unshed tears, but there was steel underneath. Determination. The kind of strength that had carried her through medical school, through whatever had brought her to the mountains, through two weeks of his silence.

"This is beautiful," she said, holding up the carving. "It's the most beautiful thing anyone's ever made for me. And if you think I'm going to let you hide behind your fear and throw away what we have, you're wrong."

"Lena—"

"I'm not done." Her voice was steady, but he could see the tremor in her hands. "You said I was dangerous. You were right. I am dangerous—to your carefully controlled world, to your plan to stay safe by staying alone, to every excuse you've been telling your-self about why you don't deserve to be happy."

She moved closer, close enough that he could smell her sham-poo, could see the gold flecks in her eyes.

"But you know what's more dangerous?" she continued. "Pre-tending that night didn't mean anything. Pretending you don't care. Pretending you can just carve my name into wood and hide it away like some secret you're ashamed of."

"I'm not ashamed—"

"Then prove it."

The challenge hung between them, simple and devastating.

She was asking him to choose—safety or her, control or chaos, the careful distance he'd maintained his whole life or the terrifying possibility of letting someone in.

"What do you want from me?" he asked, his voice rough.

"I want you to fight for us. I want you to stop running. I want you to admit that what happened between us was real and important and worth the risk." She stepped closer still, until she was almost touching him. "I want you to trust me enough to let me love you."

The words hit him like a physical blow. Love. She was talking about love, and he didn't know how to handle that. Didn't know how to be the kind of man who deserved that kind of gift.

"I don't know how," he whispered.

"Then learn. With me." She reached out and took his hand, her fingers warm and sure around his. "I'm not going anywhere, Frankie. I'm not giving up on us. But I need to know you're willing to try."

He looked down at their joined hands, at the carving she still held in her other palm, at the evidence of his feelings laid bare. For so long, he'd convinced himself that wanting her was hopeless. That she could never see anything in a man like him.

But she was here. She'd driven across the mountain to find him, to call him out on his cowardice, to offer him something he'd never dared to hope for.

"I've been in love with you for two years," he said, the words coming out broken and honest. "Since the day you smiled at me like I was worth your time. I carved that for you because I couldn't figure out how to tell you, and I was too scared you'd laugh or feel sorry for me or—"

She silenced him with a kiss.

Soft at first, then deeper, full of relief and promise and everything he'd been too afraid to ask for. When they broke apart, both breathing hard, she rested her forehead against his.

"You're not getting rid of me that easily," she said.

"Good," he said, and meant it. "Because I don't know how to let you go."

LENA

The kiss was everything she'd hoped for and more.

Not desperate like their first kiss, or hungry like the ones in the tent. This was sure, steady, full of promise and possibility. This was Frankie choosing her, choosing them, choosing to be brave.

When they broke apart, his hands were shaking.

"What happens now?" he asked.

"Now we figure it out. Together." She smiled, the first real smile she'd felt in weeks. "But first, you're going to show me what else is in that box of carvings. And then we're going to have a very long conversation about communication and trust and why hiding your feelings in wood instead of sharing them with words is not an acceptable relationship strategy."

He laughed—actually laughed—and the sound sent warmth flooding through her chest.

"Yes, ma'am."

"And Frankie?"

"Yeah?"

"I love you too. In case that wasn't clear."

He kissed her again, deeper this time, his hands tangling in her hair. When Josh's voice echoed across the clearing—"Creek's looking good! You ready to head back?"—they were both breathless and grinning.

"I should go," Lena said, but she didn't step out of his arms.

"Should you?"

"People will talk."

"Let them."

The simple confidence in his voice made her heart race. This was Frankie without the walls, without the fear. This was the man she'd fallen in love with—strong, capable, and finally, finally ready to let himself be loved in return.

"Besides," he added, pressing a kiss to her temple, "Nash has been plotting to get us together for months. I think he'll be relieved he can stop with the subtle matchmaking."

"Subtle?" Lena laughed. "Pairing us for overnight assignments was about as subtle as a forest fire."

"Nash doesn't do subtle."

"Good thing we don't need it anymore."

She pulled back to look at him, memorizing the way he looked in the afternoon light—relaxed, happy, his guard finally down.

"I have to finish this assignment," she said. "Two more weeks at Miller's Creek."

"I know."

"But after that—"

"After that, we figure out what comes next. Together."

He said the word like a promise, and Lena felt something settle in her chest. Something that had been restless and uncertain for weeks.

"Together," she agreed.

Josh appeared at the edge of the clearing, diplomatically studying the sky. "Storm's coming in from the west. We should probably get moving if we want to beat it back to Miller's Creek."

Lena looked at Frankie, suddenly reluctant to leave. Two weeks felt like a lifetime.

"I'll be here when you get back," he said, reading her expression. "Not going anywhere."

"Promise?"

"Promise."

She kissed him once more, quick and sure, then stepped back. "Two weeks."

"Two weeks."

As Josh's truck disappeared around the bend, taking her away from him again, Lena clutched the wooden cross and smiled.

For the first time in months, she knew exactly where she belonged.

And in two weeks, she'd be home.

7

STAY

LENA

Two weeks later, Lena knocked on the door of Frankie's workshop at exactly 11:47 PM.

She'd driven straight through from Miller's Creek, assignment complete, paperwork filed, Josh and Marcus safely delivered back to base camp. She should have been exhausted. Should have gone to her own quarters, unpacked, and gotten some sleep.

Instead, she'd seen the light on in his workshop and felt her heart start racing.

"It's open," came his voice from inside.

She pushed through the door and found him exactly where she'd expected—bent over his workbench, surrounded by wood shavings and the warm scent of cedar. He looked up when she entered, and the smile that spread across his face made her forget how to breathe.

"You're back," he said.

"I'm back."

He set down his tools and crossed to her in three strides,

pulling her into his arms like she was something precious he'd thought he'd lost. The kiss was soft, sure, full of two weeks of missing her.

"How was Miller's Creek?" he asked against her lips.

"Long. Productive. Successful." She pulled back to look at him. "But I missed you every single day."

"Good," he said, and kissed her again. "Because I carved you something."

He led her to his workbench, where a small wooden plaque sat beside his tools. The craftsmanship was exquisite—smooth lines, perfect lettering, finished to a warm honey glow.

It read: *"Come Home Safe."*

"For your tent," he explained, suddenly shy. "So you'll always have something to come back to."

Lena's throat tightened. "Frankie..."

"I know it's presumptuous. I know we haven't talked about what happens next, or where this goes, or—"

She silenced him with a kiss, pouring two weeks of longing and love into the contact. When they broke apart, both breathing hard, she rested her forehead against his.

"I love it," she said. "I love you. And yes, before you ask—I'm staying. Here, with you, for as long as you'll have me."

"Forever," he said without hesitation. "I want forever."

"Then you've got it."

The promise hung between them, simple and true. Outside, the mountain wind rattled the workshop windows, but inside, surrounded by the evidence of his craft and the warmth of his arms, Lena had never felt more at home.

"So," she said, tracing the letters on the plaque with one finger. "What do we do now?"

"Now?" Frankie's smile was soft, content. "Now I fix the cut on your thumb."

She looked down, surprised. She'd scraped it on a rough piece of equipment earlier that day and hadn't even noticed it was still bleeding.

"How did you—?"

"I've been watching you for two years, remember? I notice everything." He guided her to sit on his workbench, then gathered supplies from the first aid kit he kept in his tool cabinet. "This might sting."

"I'm not worried," she said, watching him clean the small wound with the same careful precision he brought to everything. "I trust you."

The words meant more than just the bandage he was applying. They were talking about the future, about building something together, about all the ways they could take care of each other.

"There," he said, securing the adhesive. "Good as new."

"Thank you." She caught his hands in hers, studying the calluses and scars that told the story of his work, his life. "For patching me up. For carving me beautiful things. For being brave enough to fight for us."

"You fought too," he pointed out. "You came across the mountain to find me."

"Best decision I ever made."

He lifted their joined hands and pressed a kiss to her knuckles. "You matter, you know. To the crew. To me."

The words were an echo of that first night in the medical trailer, when she'd tried to show him he wasn't invisible. Now he was returning the gift, reminding her that she was seen, valued, and loved.

"I know," she said. "Finally."

FRANKIE

Three hours later, they were still in his workshop.

Not because they needed to be, but because neither of them

wanted to break the spell of being together again. Lena sat on his workbench, legs swinging, watching him show her the pieces he'd been working on during their separation.

"This one's for Nash," he said, holding up a compass rose. "His old one broke last month."

"And this?" She picked up a delicate wooden bird, wings spread in flight.

"That's for you. I was going to give it to you for Christmas, but..." He shrugged, suddenly uncertain. "Maybe it's too much. Too soon."

"Frankie Martinez," she said, hopping down from the bench to stand in front of him. "Nothing you make for me will ever be too much. Do you understand?"

He nodded, throat tight with emotion he was still learning to express.

"Good. Now show me what else you've been hiding in here."

He showed her everything—the half-finished projects, the pieces he'd carved and then abandoned, the small mountain of wood shavings that represented hours of thinking about her while his hands stayed busy.

"You're incredible," she said when he'd finished the tour. "I had no idea you'd made so much."

"It's just wood."

"No, it's not." She picked up the bird again, running her thumb along its smooth surface. "It's love. All of it. Every piece is you showing love the only way you knew how."

The observation hit him like a revelation. She was right. Every carving, every careful hour spent shaping wood into something beautiful—it had all been practice for this moment. For having someone who saw the love in his work, who understood what he was trying to say.

"I love you," he said, the words coming easier now. "I'm going to keep saying it until you get tired of hearing it."

"Never," she said fiercely. "Say it as much as you want. I'll never get tired of it."

A knock on the workshop door interrupted them. Nash's voice came through the wood, amused and knowing.

"You two planning to come up for air anytime soon? Or should I just leave the weekly supply reports on the porch?"

Lena laughed, color flooding her cheeks. "We should probably—"

"Go," Frankie agreed. "Before he starts making jokes about workshop safety protocols."

But as they gathered their things and prepared to face the world as a couple, Frankie felt something settle in his chest. Something that had been restless and uncertain his whole life, finally found its place.

They walked out of the workshop hand in hand, and for the first time in his life, Frankie Martinez wasn't invisible.

He was home.

NASH

Nash was waiting on the porch of the main building, coffee in hand and a satisfied smirk on his face.

"Morning, you two," he said as they approached. "Good to see you back, Lena. How was Miller's Creek?"

"Productive," she said, not letting go of Frankie's hand. "All sites are operational and up to code."

"Excellent. And Frankie, how were the fire roads?"

"Clear. Bridge repairs are holding."

Nash nodded approvingly, then his expression turned serious. "I hate to interrupt whatever reunion you've got planned, but we've got a situation developing."

Frankie tensed. "What kind of situation?"

"The kind that involves a certain trail crew member who's been AWOL for the past month." Nash's expression darkened. "Beckett Williams finally decided to resurface. Apparently, he's been holed up in some cabin in Colorado, drinking himself stupid and ignoring every attempt at contact."

Lena frowned. "Beckett? I thought he was on extended leave after the incident."

"Yeah, he fell off the face of the earth. His family's been calling every day, demanding answers. The Forest Service is starting to ask questions." Nash sighed. "Problem is, his leave officially ends next week, and he's scheduled to lead a major survey project in the eastern sector."

"So send someone else," Frankie suggested.

"Can't. Contract specifically requests him by name. Apparently, he's the only one certified for the type of survey they need." Nash paused. "Plus, there's another complication."

"Which is?"

"The site coordinator they're sending is Riley Chen."

Frankie went still. Even Lena, who'd only been with the crew for two years, recognized the name. Riley Chen—the environmental scientist who'd been engaged to Beckett Williams five years ago. Who'd disappeared after her basically left her at the altar.

"Shit," Frankie said.

"My thoughts exactly." Nash finished his coffee and set the mug aside. "Riley arrives tomorrow. Beckett's supposed to be back by Monday. This is either going to be the most awkward professional reunion in history, or it's going to be a complete disaster."

"What do you need from us?" Lena asked.

"Nothing right now. Just wanted to give you a heads up. Things are about to get interesting around here." Nash stood, pausing at the door. "Oh, and Frankie? Next time you two decide to have a heart-to-heart in the workshop, maybe close the blinds. Half the crew saw you kissing through the window."

He disappeared inside, leaving them alone on the porch.

"Well," Lena said after a moment. "That's going to be complicated."

"Beckett and Riley? Yeah. They have history."

"Bad history?"

Frankie thought about his friend—brilliant, driven, completely destroyed after he got cold feet before the wedding. Beckett had never recovered, never dated anyone else, never stopped beating himself up about how things ended.

And now she was coming back.

"The worst kind," he said.

Lena squeezed his hand. "Think they'll be okay?"

Frankie looked toward the eastern sector, where in a few days, two people who had once loved each other enough to plan a life together would have to work side by side, pretending the past didn't matter.

"I hope so," he said. "But knowing Beckett? This is going to get messy fast."

As they walked toward Lena's quarters, hands still joined, Frankie couldn't help but feel grateful for his own second chance. Not everyone got the opportunity to fight for love twice.

He just hoped his friend would be brave enough to take his.

THE END

RELENTLESS MOUNTAIN MAN

A SECOND CHANCE MOUNTAIN MAN
ROMANCE WITH EMOTIONAL GROVEL
AND HEAT

1

COLLISION COURSE

RILEY

The Bitterroot Ridge base camp looked exactly the same as it had five years ago. Same weathered cabins, same equipment shed, same view of the jagged peaks that used to make my chest tight with possibility instead of dread.

I pulled my truck into the gravel lot and killed the engine, hands still gripping the wheel. The contract in my passenger seat was signed, sealed, and about to deliver me straight into hell. Three months of topographical surveying for the Forest Service. Three months of decent pay and mountain air and pretending I hadn't spent five years avoiding this exact place.

The front door of the main cabin swung open. Nash stepped out, coffee mug in hand, looking older but just as solid as ever. Trail boss. Voice of reason. The man who'd tried to talk Beckett out of leaving me at the altar.

I climbed out of the truck and grabbed my gear bag. Nash's face split into a grin that didn't quite reach his eyes.

"Riley fucking Chen," he said, walking over. "Thought you swore off mountains."

"I swore off a lot of things." I shouldered the bag. "Turns out I'm bad at keeping promises."

He laughed, but it had an edge. "Come on. Let me show you the crew."

The main cabin buzzed with pre-assignment energy. Maps spread across tables, gear being sorted, voices mixing in the organized chaos, I remembered. Faces I recognized—Sawyer with his easy grin, Frankie quiet in the corner, a few new guys I didn't know.

Nash cleared his throat. "Listen up. This is Riley Chen, our surveyor for the Cascade Ridge project. She'll be working point on terrain mapping."

A few nods, some curious looks. Normal crew dynamics. I started to relax.

"She'll be partnered with Beckett for field leadership."

The room went dead quiet.

My blood turned to ice. "What?"

"He's the most experienced with that section," Nash said carefully. "Knows every trail, every hazard point."

"Find someone else."

"Riley—"

"I said, find someone else." My voice came out steady, professional. Inside, I was screaming.

The cabin door opened behind me. I didn't need to turn around. The air changed—thicker, charged with the kind of tension that used to make my skin hum. Heavy footsteps on worn floorboards.

"Problem here?"

That voice. Deeper than I remembered, rougher around the

edges. Five years of mountain air and whatever demons he'd been carrying.

I turned around.

Beckett fucking Morrison stood in the doorway, filling it like he owned the space and everything in it. Broader through the shoulders, beard covering the jaw I used to trace with my finger-tips, eyes the same impossible blue that used to look at me like I was his whole world.

He saw me and went absolutely still.

My breath caught. For one traitorous second, I was twenty-six again, watching him work shirtless in the summer heat, thinking *mine, mine, mine* like a heartbeat. Then reality crashed back. Five years collapsed into five seconds—the white dress I never got to wear, the ring he'd mailed back in a box with no note, the phone calls that went straight to voicemail until I stopped making them.

"Hello, Beckett."

His name on my lips sounded like a warning. Maybe it was.

He flinched. Actually flinched, like I'd slapped him.

"Riley." He said it quiet, careful. Like my name might break if he handled it wrong.

"Seems we're partners." I kept my voice level, professional. The same tone I'd use to discuss weather patterns or equipment fail-ure. "I trust you can keep this professional."

Something flickered in his eyes. Pain, maybe. Or regret. I didn't care enough to figure out which.

"Of course."

"Good." I turned back to Nash. "When do we start?"

"Tomorrow. Dawn patrol." Nash looked between us like he was watching a bomb countdown. "You two can work out the details."

I nodded and headed for the door. Made it three steps before Beckett's voice stopped me.

"Riley, wait—I never stopped—"

He cut himself off so hard I heard his teeth click.

I didn't turn around. "Tomorrow, Morrison. Dawn patrol."

I walked out of that cabin and didn't look back. But I felt his eyes on me the whole way to my truck, heavy as a hand on my spine.

Five years I'd spent getting over him. Five years of building walls and moving on and convincing myself I was fine.

One look at him and every brick crumbled to dust.

BECKETT

I stood in that doorway and watched Riley Chen walk out of my life for the second time.

She looked the same. Different. Same storm-cloud eyes, same way of holding herself like she could take on the world and win. But there was something harder about her now, sharper edges where there used to be softness.

I'd done that to her. Put those edges there the day I chose cowardice over courage.

"Well," Sawyer said into the silence. "That was fucking awkward."

Nash shot him a look. "Back to work. All of you."

The crew scattered, but I caught the glances, the whispers. Everyone knew the story. Hard not to, in a place this small. Beckett Morrison left his fiancée at the altar. Disappeared for six months. Came back different.

Nobody knew why. I'd never told them about Jake, about the rookie who'd died because I'd made the wrong call. About how I'd spent our wedding morning staring at myself in the mirror, knowing I didn't deserve the happiness waiting for me at the end of that aisle.

Nash waited until we were alone. "You want to tell me what the hell that was?"

"Ancient history."

"Bullshit." He leaned against the table, arms crossed. "You two have a history that could level this mountain. You sure you can work together?"

I thought about the way she'd said my name. Like it tasted bitter. Like she hated having it in her mouth.

"She's the best surveyor in the region," I said. "I know that terrain better than anyone. It makes sense."

"That's not what I asked."

I looked out the window. Her truck was gone, but I could still feel the ghost of her presence in the room. Still hear the ice in her voice when she'd said my name.

"I can handle it."

Nash studied me for a long moment. "What about her?"

That was the question, wasn't it? Riley had always been strong, stronger than me in all the ways that mattered. But I'd broken something between us, something that might not be fixable.

"She'll be fine," I said. "She always is."

But even as I said it, I knew I was lying. Riley Chen might be a lot of things, but fine wasn't one of them. Not after what I'd done.

Not after I'd left her standing in a white dress, waiting for a man who'd already decided he didn't deserve her.

I grabbed my gear and headed for the door. Tomorrow I'd have to look her in the eye and pretend my chest wasn't caving in. Pretend I hadn't spent five years carving her name into trees and cabin walls like some lovesick teenager.

Pretend I didn't still love her enough to burn down the whole mountain if she asked me to.

The door swung shut behind me, and I walked into the cold

mountain air. Tomorrow, I'd face the woman I'd destroyed us both to protect.

Tomorrow, I'd find out if she hated me more than I hated myself.

2

FORCED PROXIMITY

RILEY

I spent the night in my truck.

Not because I couldn't afford the motel in town, but because I needed the distance. The isolation. The reminder that I could leave anytime I wanted.

Except I couldn't. The contract was ironclad—three months, minimum. And the money was too good to walk away from, even if it meant working alongside the man who'd turned my life into wreckage.

Dawn crept over the mountains like a bruise, purple and gold bleeding into gray. I climbed out of the truck, muscles protesting from sleeping on vinyl seats, and grabbed my gear. Coffee first. Then I'd face whatever fresh hell this partnership promised.

The main cabin was already buzzing. Nash looked up from his maps when I walked in, took one look at my rumpled clothes and truck-bed hair, and slid a mug across the table without a word.

"Sleep well?" Sawyer asked, grinning.

"Like a baby." I took a sip of coffee. It was strong enough to wake the dead. "Where's my partner?"

"Right here."

Beckett's voice came from behind me, low and rough. I didn't turn around, but I felt him fill the space at my back. The same way he used to stand when we cooked breakfast together, close enough that I could lean into him if I wanted.

I didn't want to. Much.

"You still know how to walk uphill?" he asked.

"I've been ready for twenty minutes." I drained my coffee and grabbed my pack. "Let's go."

The trail to Cascade Ridge was a bastard. Steep switchbacks through loose scree, drop-offs that would kill you if you missed a step, terrain that changed from stable to treacherous without warning. It was exactly the kind of survey work that required two people—one to map, one to watch for hazards.

It was also exactly the kind of work that meant spending the next three months alone with Beckett Morrison.

We hiked in silence for the first hour. He kept a respectful distance behind me, close enough to catch me if I fell but far enough that I couldn't smell his soap or hear the rhythm of his breathing. Professional. Careful.

I hated it.

"Stop being weird," I said without turning around.

"I'm not being weird."

"You're walking like I might explode if you get too close."

His laugh was bitter. "Might not be wrong about that."

I stopped so suddenly that he almost crashed into me. Turned to face him on the narrow trail, close enough that I had to tip my head back to meet his eyes.

"Let's get something straight," I said. "I don't explode. I don't break. I don't need you to handle me with kid gloves because you feel guilty about ancient history."

Something flickered in his expression. "Riley—"

"I'm here to do a job. You're here to keep me from falling off a cliff. That's it. We don't need to talk about anything else."

"And if I want to?"

The question hung between us like a blade. I stared up at him, at the face I used to trace in the dark, and felt something crack inside my chest.

"Then you should have thought of that five years ago."

I turned and started walking. This time, he didn't follow at a distance.

Thirty minutes later, I caught him watching me.

Not just glancing. Watching. The kind of look that used to make my skin burn when we were together. The kind of look that said he was remembering things he had no right to remember.

I stopped and turned around. "You looking for something?"

He didn't even have the grace to look embarrassed. "Maybe."

"Well, stop. It's creepy."

"Is it?" He stepped closer, close enough that I had to resist the urge to back up. "Or does it just remind you of things you'd rather forget?"

Heat flashed through me—anger, not arousal. Definitely not arousal.

"Data's clean," I said, shouldering my pack. "Let's move."

BECKETT

She was trying to kill me.

Had to be. Because there was no other explanation for the way she moved ahead of me on the trail, all confident grace and curves that her hiking gear couldn't hide. The same way she'd moved through our apartment, through my life, like she belonged there.

Like she'd always belonged there.

I watched her navigate a tricky section of loose rock, sure-footed and fearless, and felt the familiar ache in my chest. Five years of missing her, of waking up in empty beds and carving her name into wood like some kind of obsessed monk.

Five years of telling myself I'd done the right thing.

"GPS is acting up," she called back to me. "We need to get higher for a clear signal."

I moved up beside her, close enough to see the map spread across her palm. Close enough to catch the scent of her shampoo under the mountain air.

"There's an outcrop about half a mile up," I said, pointing to the ridge. "Clear sight lines in all directions."

She nodded and folded the map. Started up the steep section without waiting for me to lead.

That was Riley. Never waited for anyone to lead when she could do it herself.

The outcrop was a narrow shelf of granite jutting out from the mountainside. Stable, but not much room to maneuver. Riley pulled out her equipment, setting up the GPS unit and survey markers with the kind of efficiency that came from years of practice.

I watched her work and tried not to remember the way those same hands used to map my body in the dark.

"I need you to hold this steady," she said, not looking at me.

I moved to where she pointed, close enough that our shoulders brushed when she adjusted the equipment. She went rigid at the contact, then forced herself to relax.

Professional. Controlled.

"Riley."

"Don't."

"We have to talk about this eventually."

"No, we don't." She bent over the GPS unit, hair falling forward to hide her face. "We have to work together. That's all."

I reached out before I could stop myself, caught a strand of her hair between my fingers. She went absolutely still.

"I still dream about—"

The loose rock under her feet gave way.

She pitched forward, off-balance, toward the edge of the outcrop. I lunged, caught her around the waist, and hauled her back against my chest. We went down hard, her back pressed to my front, my arms locked around her like bands of steel.

For a heartbeat, we didn't move. Didn't breathe. Her body was soft and warm against mine, familiar in a way that made my chest seize. I could feel her pulse racing, could smell the scent of her skin.

Could remember exactly what it felt like to have her in my arms when it mattered.

Her hands clutched at my forearms, fingers digging in like anchors. She was shaking—from the fall, from the fear, from something else entirely.

"You still trust me to catch you. Say I'm wrong," I said against her ear.

She drew in a shuddering breath. Then another. Her grip on my arms loosened, but she didn't pull away. Not yet.

"I'm—" Her voice cracked. She cleared her throat, tried again. "I'm fucking fantastic."

The venom in her tone was pure overcompensation. We both knew it.

"Riley."

"Let go of me."

But she still wasn't pulling away. Still wasn't moving. For one perfect, terrible moment, she let herself lean into me. Let herself remember what it felt like to be held by someone who'd once loved her more than breathing.

Then reality hit.

She twisted out of my arms, scrambled to her feet, put three feet of distance between us in the span of a breath. Her face was flushed, her breathing too fast.

"I'm fine." She wouldn't look at me. "I'm fine."

But she wasn't fine. Her hands were trembling as she checked her equipment, her movements sharp and jerky. I'd felt the way she'd melted against me for that split second, the way her body had remembered mine.

I stood up slowly, brushed dirt and granite dust off my shirt. She was still pointedly not looking at me, all sharp angles and barely controlled fury.

Without thinking, I reached out and brushed a smudge of dirt off her shoulder.

She froze like I'd electrocuted her.

The touch was nothing—barely contact, over in a second. But her eyes snapped to mine, wide and dark and full of something that looked dangerously close to want.

"Don't," she whispered.

I used to know every way she liked to be touched. Now I couldn't even brush her shoulder without making her flinch.

"Sorry." I pulled my hand back. "You had—"

"I know what I had." Her voice was rough. Raw. "Just don't."

She turned away, started packing up her gear with movements that were too controlled, too careful. Like she was afraid she might break something if she wasn't careful.

Like she was afraid she might break.

"Data's clean," she said without looking at me. "Let's move."

As we hiked back down the mountain, I couldn't stop thinking about the way she'd felt in my arms. The way she'd let herself lean into me, just for a second. The way her pulse had jumped when I'd touched her shoulder.

She still fit like she was made for me. And maybe I hadn't ruined it completely.

Not yet.

3

FIRELINE

RILEY

Three days of this bullshit, and I was ready to push him off a cliff myself.

Not the accidental kind. The deliberate, satisfying kind where I got to watch him fall.

Beckett had spent seventy-two hours being the perfect professional. Polite. Careful. Treating me like I was made of glass and might shatter if he breathed too hard in my direction.

It was driving me insane.

"The elevation readings don't match the topographic," I said, squinting at my tablet. We were on a narrow ledge halfway up Devil's Backbone, the kind of place that required absolute focus. "We need to re-survey this entire section."

"That'll add two days to the timeline."

"Then we add two days." I didn't look at him. Couldn't. Three days of watching him move through the mountains like he owned them, of catching glimpses of the man I used to know buried under all that careful politeness, and I was hanging on by a thread. "Unless you have somewhere more important to be."

"No." His voice was flat. "Nowhere more important."

The way he said it made something twist in my chest. Like he was talking about more than just work schedules.

"Good," I said. "Then we do it right."

I started setting up the equipment for another reading, movements sharp with frustration. The GPS unit slipped out of my hands. I caught it before it could fall, but barely.

"Careful," Beckett said.

"I'm always careful."

"Are you?"

Something in his tone made me look up. He was watching me with an expression I couldn't read, intense and focused in a way that made my skin feel too tight.

"What's that supposed to mean?"

"Nothing." He looked away. "Forget it."

"No, say what you mean." I stood up, tablet clutched in my hands like a weapon. "You think I'm not being careful? You think I can't handle my job?"

"That's not what I said."

"Then what are you saying?"

He was quiet for so long, I thought he wouldn't answer. When he finally spoke, his voice was rough.

"I'm saying you're acting like you have something to prove."

Heat flashed through me, sharp and bright. "Maybe I do."

"To who?"

"To you." The words came out before I could stop them, raw and honest and too revealing. "To everyone who thinks I'm the pathetic girl who got left at the altar. To myself."

His face went carefully blank. "Riley—"

"Don't." I turned away, started shoving equipment back into my pack. "Just don't."

"You want to know what I think?"

I stopped moving. "No."

"I think you're scared."

The words hit me like a slap. I turned around slowly, fury building in my chest like a storm.

"Excuse me?"

"You heard me." He stepped closer, close enough that I could see the flecks of gold in his blue eyes. "You're scared that being up here with me means something. That working together, being this close, might crack that wall you've built around yourself."

"You don't know anything about my walls."

"I know I helped build them."

The quiet admission hung between us like a blade. I stared at him, at the face I used to love more than breathing, and felt five years of carefully controlled rage finally break free.

"You're right," I said. "You did help build them. "You built them when you made me stand in front of three hundred people and explain why my fiancé had vanished. When you made me return wedding gifts and cancel a honeymoon and pretend like my heart wasn't completely fucking shattered."

"Riley—"

"I'm not finished." I stepped closer, close enough to see the guilt written across his features.

"When you stopped answering my calls. When you mailed my ring back like I was some stranger you'd met at a bar."

His jaw clenched. "You think I don't know that? You think I don't live with that every goddamn day?"

"I think you're a coward."

The words came out quiet, deadly. He flinched like I'd hit him.

"I think you ran when things got hard instead of fighting for us," I continued. "I think you took the easy way out and left me to clean up the mess."

"Easy?" His voice cracked on the word. "You think leaving you was easy?"

"Wasn't it?"

Something dangerous flickered in his eyes. "You want to know what was easy? Staying away. Not calling. Not showing up at your apartment drunk at three in the morning because I missed you so much I couldn't breathe."

My heart stuttered. "Beckett—"

"You want to know what was hard?" He stepped closer, crowding me against the rock wall. "Watching you walk into that cabin and realizing you were still the most beautiful thing I'd ever seen. Realizing I was still so fucking gone for you that it hurt to look at you."

The air between us crackled with tension, with five years of unspoken words and buried feelings. I could feel his heat, could smell the familiar scent of his skin under the mountain air.

Could remember exactly what it felt like when he used to look at me like that.

"You don't get to say things like that," I said. My voice came out breathless. "Not anymore."

"Why not?"

"Because you lost the right when you left me."

"Maybe." His hand came up to cup my face, thumb brushing across my cheekbone. "But I never stopped loving you."

The words broke something open inside me. Something I'd kept locked away for five years.

I kissed him.

Hard. Desperate. Like I was trying to hurt him as much as he'd hurt me. His lips were warm and familiar and wrong, so wrong, but I couldn't stop. Couldn't think past the need to feel something other than this endless, aching emptiness.

He kissed me back with the hunger of a starving man. His hands tangled in my hair, tilted my head back so he could take my mouth deeper, harder. I bit his lower lip, and he groaned, pressing me back against the rock wall.

"Riley." My name came out like a prayer, like a curse. "God, I've missed—"

"Shut up." I grabbed his shirt, pulled him closer. "Just shut up."

We tore at each other like we were drowning. His hands were everywhere—in my hair, on my face, sliding under my jacket to find skin. I worked at his shirt, desperate to feel the body I'd once known by heart.

When my fingers found the warm skin of his chest, he made a sound low in his throat that sent heat straight through me.

"Here?" he asked against my mouth.

"Here."

It was insane. We were on a narrow ledge halfway up a mountain, visible to anyone with binoculars and a clear sight line. But I didn't care. Five years of anger and want and grief had finally found an outlet, and I wasn't stopping.

Not when his hands found the hem of my shirt and pulled it over my head in one smooth motion. Not when he pressed his mouth to my throat and made me gasp. Not when he whispered my name like it was the only word he remembered.

"I hate you," I said as he worked at my belt.

"I know." His teeth found my earlobe, bit down gently. "I hate me too."

My hiking pants hit the ground. His followed. Cool mountain air hit my skin, but his hands were warm, reverent, mapping the body he'd once known better than his own.

"You're so fucking beautiful," he said against my collarbone. "Still so beautiful."

I wanted to tell him to shut up again. Wanted to tell him I didn't want his words, his praise, his wonder. But when he dropped to his knees and pressed his mouth to my hip, when he looked up at me with eyes gone dark with want, the words died in my throat.

"Riley." He said my name like a question.

I answered by threading my fingers through his hair and pulling him closer.

BECKETT

She tasted like sunlight and fury. Like five years of longing made real.

I'd dreamed about this moment so many times, I'd lost count. Dreamed about having her in my arms again, about the way she'd feel against me, about the sounds she'd make when I touched her in all the places that used to drive her wild.

The reality was better and worse than anything I'd imagined.

Better because she was here, real, solid, warm, and alive under my hands. Because she wanted this as much as I did, even if she hated herself for it.

Worse because I could feel her anger in every kiss, every touch. She wasn't making love to me. She was trying to exorcise something, to burn it out of her system so she could go back to hating me in peace.

I didn't care.

If this was all I got—angry sex on a mountain ledge with the woman I'd never stopped loving—then I'd take it. I'd take whatever she was willing to give me and be grateful for it.

She came apart in my arms like she was made for it. Head

thrown back, fingers digging into my shoulders, my name on her lips like a curse and a benediction. When she shattered, she took me with her, pulled me up and into her arms, and whispered "now" against my ear like it was an order.

I'd have followed that order straight to hell.

After, we stayed pressed together against the rock wall, breathing hard, not looking at each other. Her head was tucked against my shoulder, hair damp with sweat despite the cool air.

I wanted to stay like that forever. Wanted to hold her until the sun went down and the stars came out and she remembered what it felt like to be loved by someone who'd burn down the world for her.

Instead, she pulled away.

"Fuck." The word came out quiet, devastated. She reached for her clothes, started dressing with sharp, angry movements. "Fuck, fuck, fuck."

"Riley—"

"Don't." She pulled on her shirt, wouldn't meet my eyes. "Just don't."

I started getting dressed, watched her pace the narrow ledge like a caged animal. "We should talk about this."

"No, we shouldn't." She was stuffing equipment into her pack with barely controlled violence. "This was a mistake. A stupid, pointless mistake."

The words hit me like a physical blow. "Was it?"

"Yes." She swallowed. Looked away. "Because nothing's changed, Beckett." The pause said otherwise. Her voice didn't. "You're still the man who left me. I'm still the woman who wasn't enough to make you stay."

"That's not—"

"It is." She shouldered her pack, started toward the trail. "And fucking you against a rock wall doesn't change that."

I watched her walk away from me for the third time in a week. This time, I didn't let her go alone.

I caught up to her on the switchback, fell into step beside her. She kept her eyes fixed on the trail ahead, jaw set in a line I recognized.

"You're wrong," I said.

"About what?"

"About not being enough." I stopped walking, waited until she had to turn around to face me. "You were everything, Riley. You were more than I deserved, and I knew it."

Something cracked in her expression. "Then why—"

"Because I was fucked up and scared and convinced that loving you was the most selfish thing I could do." The words came out raw, honest. "Because I thought you deserved better than a man who couldn't save the people he was supposed to protect."

She stared at me for a long moment. When she spoke, her voice was quiet, deadly.

"You don't get to decide what I deserve. You don't get to protect me from yourself by destroying us both." Her voice cracked. "I was ready to marry you. *But you made me choose centerpieces alone.*"

The words hit me like a punch to the gut. I remembered that day—remembered her calling me, excited about some detail she wanted to share, and me letting it go to voicemail because I'd been too deep in my own guilt to answer.

I'd made her plan our wedding alone while I'd been planning my escape.

"You don't get to decide what I deserve. You don't get to protect me from yourself by destroying us both."

"I know."

"Do you?" She stepped closer, and I could see the fury and hurt and love warring in her eyes. "Because you did it anyway. You made the choice for both of us, and you broke something that can't be fixed."

The words hung between us like a sentence. Final. Absolute.

I wanted to argue. Wanted to tell her that some things could be fixed, that some wounds could heal if you were willing to do the work. But the look in her eyes told me she was done listening.

Done hoping.

Done with me.

"The data's clean," she said, turning away. "We can head back."

I followed her down the mountain in silence, watching the way she held herself apart, untouchable. Like the last hour had never happened. Like she hadn't fallen apart in my arms and whispered my name like a prayer.

Like she hadn't kissed me back with five years of accumulated longing.

But I'd felt it. The way she'd trembled when I touched her. The way she'd looked at me in that moment before everything went sideways.

She could pretend this didn't change anything.

I knew better.

4

WHAT BROKE

RILEY

I didn't sleep.

Couldn't. Every time I closed my eyes, I felt his hands on my skin, heard the way he'd said my name like it was something sacred. Tasted him on my lips like a ghost I couldn't exorcise.

By dawn, I was furious all over again.

Not at him this time. At myself. For being weak. For letting five minutes of good sex make me forget five years of hell. For the way my body had betrayed me, coming apart under his touch like no time had passed at all.

Like I hadn't spent months learning to sleep alone again. Learning to cook for one. Learning to stop reaching for someone who wasn't there.

I found him by the equipment shed at first light, checking gear with the kind of focused intensity that meant he hadn't slept either. Good. I wanted him as wrecked as I felt.

"We need to talk," I said.

He looked up, and I saw my own sleepless night reflected in his eyes. "Do we?"

"Yes." I crossed my arms, kept my distance. Close enough to talk, far enough that I couldn't smell his soap. "About yesterday."

"What about it?"

"It can't happen again."

Something flickered in his expression. "Can't? Or won't?"

"Both." I kept my voice steady, professional. "We have a job to do. I won't let personal history compromise that."

"Is that what you're calling it? Personal history?"

Heat flashed through me. "What would you call it?"

"Unfinished business."

The words hung between us, loaded with implication. I wanted to argue, to tell him we were as finished as two people could be. But my body was still humming from his touch, still craving things I had no right to want.

"There's nothing unfinished about us," I said. "You made sure of that five years ago."

"Did I?" He set down the rope he'd been coiling, took a step closer. "Because it doesn't feel finished. Not when you kiss me like that. Not when you say my name like—"

"Stop."

"Like you're dying for me to touch you again."

My pulse jumped. "You're delusional."

"Am I?" Another step. "Then why are your hands shaking?"

I looked down. Fuck. He was right. I shoved my hands into my pockets, lifted my chin. "I'm angry."

"You're scared."

"I'm not—"

"You're scared because yesterday meant something, and you don't want it to." His voice was quiet, certain. "You're scared because you felt it too. That spark. That connection. Everything we used to have."

"What we used to have is dead." The words came out harsher than I intended. "You killed it."

He flinched like I'd slapped him. Good. I wanted him to hurt.

"I know," he said quietly.

"Do you know what it was like to see you at Nash's birthday party two years later, laughing with the crew like nothing had happened? Like you hadn't destroyed everything good between us?"

His face went pale. "You were there?"

"I left before you saw me." I wrapped my arms around myself, suddenly cold despite the morning sun. "I couldn't... I wasn't ready to face you."

"Why didn't you—"

"What? Say hello? Ask how you'd been? Pretend we were old friends who'd just drifted apart?" I laughed, but there was no humor in it. "I wasn't that strong."

He was quiet for a long moment. When he spoke, his voice was rough with something that might have been regret.

"I looked for you."

"What?"

"At Nash's party. I heard you were coming, and I..." He ran a hand through his hair. "I spent the whole night looking for you. Hoping I'd get a chance to explain."

My chest tightened. "Explain what?"

"Why I left. Why I couldn't..." He trailed off, looked away. "Why I couldn't be the man you deserved."

"I didn't want someone perfect and unrealistic," I said quietly. "I wanted you."

The admission hung between us, raw and honest. He looked at me like I'd gutted him.

"Riley."

"But you didn't want me." I forced the words out, made myself say them. "Not enough to stay. Not enough to fight for us. Not enough to trust me with whatever was eating you alive."

"That's not true."

"Isn't it?" I stepped back, put distance between us before I did something stupid like reach for him. "Then tell me. Tell me why you left. What was so terrible that you'd rather break both our hearts than let me help you carry it?"

He went very still. I could see the war playing out across his face—the need to confess battling against years of self-imposed silence.

"Riley—"

"Tell me." My voice cracked on the words. "Please. I need to understand."

BECKETT

She deserved the truth.

Had always deserved it. But I'd been too much of a coward to give it to her, too convinced that my guilt was mine alone to carry.

Looking at her now—seeing the pain I'd put in her eyes, the way she held herself like she was bracing for another blow—I realized my silence had been just another kind of cruelty.

"There was a fire," I said quietly. "Three weeks before our wedding. Bad one, up on Salmon Creek Ridge."

Her expression shifted, some of the anger fading into concern. "I remember. You were gone for four days."

"I was the crew boss. Had a rookie with me—Jake Morrison. Kid was twenty-two, eager, wanted to prove himself." I swallowed hard, forced myself to continue. "I sent him in to clear a firebreak on the north flank. Told him it was safe, that the wind wouldn't shift."

Riley went very still. "Beckett."

"It shifted." The words came out flat, matter-of-fact. Like I was giving a report instead of confessing the thing that had eaten me alive for five years. "Caught him in a chimney. By the time we got to him..."

I couldn't finish. Couldn't say the words that had played in my head every night since. Riley's hand came up to cover her mouth.

"Oh God."

"He had a girlfriend. Sarah. They were talking about getting married after fire season." I looked at my hands, still saw soot under my nails sometimes. "I had to call her. Had to tell her that the man she loved was dead because I made the wrong call."

"Beckett, that's not—"

"It is." The words came out harsher than I intended. "I was the crew boss. My call, my responsibility. That kid died because I fucked up."

"Accidents happen—"

"This wasn't an accident." I met her eyes, let her see the truth I'd been carrying. "I knew the wind was unpredictable. I sent him anyway because I was thinking about our wedding, about the honeymoon, about how I couldn't wait to get off that mountain and marry you."

Understanding dawned in her expression. "So you think it's your fault."

"I know it is."

"And you think that means you don't deserve to be happy."

I didn't answer. Didn't need to. She could see it written across my face.

"So you left me," she said quietly. "You decided that marrying me would be... what? Disrespectful to his memory?"

"I decided that I didn't deserve you." The admission came out rough, honest. "That a man who'd gotten someone killed because he was too distracted by his own happiness didn't get to have a happily ever after."

She stared at me for a long moment. When she spoke, her voice was deadly quiet.

"You fucking idiot."

I blinked. "What?"

"You absolute, fucking idiot." She stepped closer, eyes blazing. "You think Jake would have wanted this? You think he would have wanted you to destroy your life because of something that wasn't even your fault?"

"It was my fault—"

"Bullshit." She was in my face now, furious and magnificent. "You think you're the first crew boss to lose someone? You think Nash has never made a call that went sideways? That Sawyer hasn't sent someone into danger?"

"That's different—"

"How? How is it different?"

"Because they don't have blood on their hands."

"And neither do you." Her voice cracked. "God, Beckett, don't you see? You're not responsible for every bad thing that happens on your watch. You're not God. You can't control the wind or the fire or the thousand things that can go wrong on any given day."

I wanted to believe her. Wanted to let her words wash away five years of guilt and self-recrimination. But it wasn't that simple.

"I should have known—"

She looked away, blinked hard. "You should have trusted me." Her voice cracked on the words, then came back stronger, deadlier. "You should have come home and told me what happened and let me help you carry it. That's what partners do. That's what marriage is."

She was right. I knew she was right. But knowing it and feeling it were two different things.

"I couldn't," I said. "I couldn't look at you in your wedding dress and know that I'd killed someone. I couldn't stand at that altar and promise to love and protect you when I'd failed to protect him."

"So you protected me by abandoning me." There was no anger in her voice now, just a tired kind of sadness. "You decided what I could and couldn't handle without giving me a choice."

"I thought—"

"You thought wrong." She stepped back, wrapped her arms around herself. "You took away my right to make my own decisions about my own life. You decided that your guilt was more important than our love."

The words hit me like a physical blow. Because she was right. I had decided for both of us. Had played God with our relationship just like I thought I'd played God with Jake's life.

"I was trying to protect you," I said weakly.

"From what? From loving someone who'd been through trauma? From being married to someone who made a mistake?" She laughed, but there was no humor in it. "Newsflash, Beckett—life is messy. People get hurt. Bad things happen to good people every single day. That doesn't mean you stop living."

I stared at her, at this woman who'd always been stronger than me, braver than me, better than me in every way that mattered.

"I'm sorry," I said. The words felt inadequate, but they were all I had. "Riley, I'm so fucking sorry."

"I know you are." Her voice was soft, broken. "But sorry doesn't fix this. Sorry doesn't give us back five years. Sorry doesn't make me trust you not to run again the next time something hard happens."

She was right. About all of it. I'd destroyed something

precious, something irreplaceable, because I'd been too cowardly to face my own demons.

"What can I do?" The question came out desperate. "Tell me what I can do to fix this."

She looked at me for a long moment, and I saw my answer in her eyes before she spoke.

"Nothing," she said quietly. "There's nothing you can do. Some things can't be fixed, Beckett. Some things, once broken, stay broken."

She turned and walked away, leaving me standing by the equipment shed with the taste of my own failures in my mouth.

She didn't cry. Didn't pause. Just walked away like five years and one confession hadn't changed a damn thing.

This time, I didn't follow.

Because maybe she was right. Maybe some things couldn't be fixed.

Maybe I'd broken us beyond repair, and the kindest thing I could do was let her go. Again.

5

GHOSTS AND GRAVES

RILEY

Iran.

Not literally—I had more pride than that. But I grabbed my gear, told Nash I needed to check the southern boundary markers alone, and got the hell away from base camp before I did something stupid.

Like cry. Or scream. Or march back to that equipment shed and tell Beckett Morrison exactly what I thought about his martyr complex.

The trail to Widow's Peak was brutal—steep switchbacks through dense forest, the kind of hike that demanded every ounce of focus just to stay upright. Perfect for drowning out the sound of my own thoughts.

Except it wasn't working.

You should have trusted me.

The words echoed in my head with every step. Five years too late, but still true. Still devastating. He should have trusted me.

Should have come home covered in soot and grief and let me hold him while he fell apart.

Instead, he'd decided I was too fragile to handle his trauma. Too weak to love him through the hard parts.

The trail leveled out at a small clearing, and I stopped to catch my breath. Check my GPS. Try to pretend my chest wasn't tight with something that felt dangerously close to hope.

Because part of me—the stupid, naive part that still remembered what it felt like to love him—wanted to believe his story changed something. Wanted to think that finally knowing the truth could somehow bridge the canyon he'd carved between us.

But the truth didn't erase abandonment. Understanding didn't fix betrayal.

And knowing why he'd left me didn't make me trust him not to do it again.

I pulled out my phone, checked for signal. One bar. Enough to send Nash a quick text that I'd be back late. Enough to keep hiking and pretend I wasn't running from a conversation that had stripped me raw.

The weather was turning. Dark clouds were building over the peaks, the kind of mountain storm that could trap you if you weren't careful. I should have turned back. Should have played it safe.

Instead, I kept climbing. Because I needed to hurt as much on the outside as I did inside, and the only way through hell was to run straight at it.

The storm hit an hour later.

Wind first, howling through the pines like something alive and angry. Then rain, heavy drops that turned to sleet as the temperature plummeted. I was still two miles from the cabin when the visibility dropped to nothing.

I found the emergency cache by pure luck—a weathered

supply box tucked under an overhang, the kind the Forest Service maintained for situations exactly like this. Basic shelter, emergency food, radio equipment.

I fumbled with the lock, fingers numb with cold, and got the metal box open just as the sleet turned to snow.

Inside: space blankets, protein bars, a radio that might work if I could get it high enough for signal. And at the bottom, wrapped in oilcloth like something precious—

A small wooden box.

My hands shook as I lifted it out. Unmarked, smooth from years of handling. It looked like something someone had carved by hand, ding hours to make it perfect.

I knew I shouldn't open it. Knew it belonged to someone else, some ranger or trail worker who'd left personal items in the cache for safekeeping.

I opened it anyway.

The ring sat nestled in faded velvet, exactly as I remembered it. White gold band, three small diamonds, simple and perfect and mine. The ring Beckett had slipped onto my finger on a snowy night three months after we'd met, his hands shaking as he'd asked me to marry him.

The ring he'd mailed back in a box with no note, no explanation, nothing but the return address and the weight of everything we'd lost.

My fingers were trembling as I lifted it out. There was an inscription inside the band—our initials and a date. The night he'd proposed. The night I'd thought my life was finally beginning.

But that wasn't what broke me.

What broke me was the piece of paper tucked beneath the ring. Folded small, worn soft from handling. My handwriting, faded but still legible:

Things to remember when you're being stubborn: 1) I love you exactly as you are. 2) Your guilt doesn't define you. 3) I'd rather weather every storm with you than dance in someone else's sunshine. 4) Come home to me. Always come home to me.

A list I'd written after our first real fight, when he'd tried to pull away because he thought I deserved better. A list I'd tucked into his gear bag as a reminder.

A list he'd kept for five years.

The sob came out of nowhere, raw and broken. I pressed my hand to my mouth, tried to hold it back, but five years of buried grief finally found its escape route.

He'd kept it. Through everything—the guilt, the self-recrimination, the decision to leave—he'd kept my words. Had carried them with him like a talisman.

Had carved this box to hold them safe.

The storm raged outside the shelter, but I barely heard it over the sound of my own heart breaking. Not for what we'd lost, but for what we'd never really had.

For the love that had been strong enough to survive his leaving, but not strong enough to make him stay.

I sat in that tiny shelter with his ring in my palm and my words in my lap, and finally let myself grieve. Not just for the wedding that never happened or the life we'd never lived.

For the man who'd loved me enough to keep my words, but hadn't loved himself enough to believe them.

BECKETT

I found Nash in the main cabin, bent over supply manifests like they held the secrets of the universe.

"She's not back yet," he said without looking up.

I checked my watch. Nearly sunset, and the storm was getting worse. "How long has she been gone?"

"Six hours." Nash finally looked up, and I saw my own worry reflected in his expression. "Got a text around noon saying she'd be late. Nothing since."

My chest tightened. Riley was experienced, capable. But mountain weather could turn lethal fast, especially for someone hiking alone.

Especially for someone running from a conversation that had left her raw.

"I'm going after her," I said.

"In this weather? You'll be lucky to find your own ass, let alone—"

"I know where she went." I was already moving toward the gear room, grabbing my pack, emergency equipment. "Widow's Peak. Southern boundary markers."

"Beckett." Nash's voice stopped me at the door. "What the hell happened between you two?" I thought about lying. About keeping my demons buried the way I had for five years. But I was tired of carrying this alone.

"I told her about Jake."

Understanding dawned in his eyes. Nash had been there that day, had helped carry what was left of the kid down the mountain. Had never asked why I'd disappeared afterward, but he'd known.

"And?"

"And she's right. I should have trusted her." I shouldered my pack, checked my radio. "I should have come home instead of running."

"So why didn't you?"

The question I'd been asking myself for five years. The answer I'd never been brave enough to speak out loud.

"Because loving her was the best thing I'd ever done," I said quietly. "And I didn't think I deserved to keep doing it."

Nash nodded slowly. "You think she's in trouble?"

"I think she's hurt and angry and stuck in a storm because I'm a fucking coward." I headed for the door. "And I think if something happens to her, I'll never forgive myself."

The trail to Widow's Peak was barely visible in the driving snow. I followed it by memory and instinct, headlamp cutting through the white-out in narrow circles. The wind howled through the trees, covering any sound that might lead me to her.

I'd hiked this trail a hundred times. Could walk it blindfolded in good weather. But the storm had transformed the landscape into something alien and treacherous.

I found her tracks at the three-mile marker, already half-filled with snow but still visible. Relief flooded through me—she'd made it this far. But the tracks continued up the mountain, toward terrain that would be deadly in this weather.

Unless she'd found shelter.

The emergency cache was tucked under a granite overhang, invisible unless you knew where to look. I saw the light first—the faint glow of a headlamp through the storm. Then I heard it.

Crying.

Not just tears. The kind of broken sobbing that came from somewhere deep and wounded. The kind of crying that said someone had finally reached their breaking point.

I found her huddled in the small shelter, knees drawn up to her chest, something clutched in her hands. She looked up when my light hit her. "You kept it," she said. Her voice was rough from crying.

"You shouldn't be out in this—" But then he saw the ring. And whatever he was going to say died in his throat.

I dropped my pack, knelt beside her in the cramped space. "I kept everything."

She held up a piece of paper—my list, the one she'd written

after our first fight. The one I'd read so many times that the words were burned into my memory.

"Even this."

"Especially this." I reached out slowly, like she might bolt if I moved too fast. "Riley—"

"You loved me." It wasn't a question.

"I never stopped."

She stared at me for a long moment. Then she took off the ring.

For a heartbeat, I thought she was giving it back. Thought this was her way of saying we were finally, truly finished.

Instead, she held it out to me.

"Put it on," she said quietly.

"Riley—"

"Put it on my finger, Beckett. The way you should have five years ago."

My hands were shaking as I took the ring. As I reached for her left hand and found the place it had always belonged.

"I can't promise I won't break again," I said as I slid it home. "I can't promise I won't fuck this up."

"I'm not asking for promises." Her fingers curled around mine. "I'm asking for honesty. For partnership. For the chance to carry your demons with you instead of watching you carry them alone."

The ring caught the light from her headlamp, sending small sparkles dancing across the shelter walls. Like stars. Like hope.

"What does this mean?" I asked.

She leaned forward, pressed her forehead against mine. "It means we try again. It means we build something new from the wreckage of what we had."

"And if I run again?"

"Then I'll come after you." Her voice was steady, certain. "And

I'll keep coming after you until you believe you're worth fighting for."

Outside, the storm raged on. But inside our tiny shelter, something fragile and precious was being born from the ashes of everything we'd lost.

Something that might, with time and work and forgiveness, become stronger than what we'd had before.

Something that might last.

6

THROUGH THE FIRE

RILEY

We made it back to base camp before dawn, moving through the dying storm in careful silence. The ring sat heavy on my finger—familiar weight in an unfamiliar place. Five years of scar tissue around a wound that had never properly healed.

I didn't know what putting it back on meant. Didn't know if we were engaged again or just carrying ghosts or something else entirely. But when Beckett's hand had shaken as he'd slipped it onto my finger, when his voice had cracked on my name, something in my chest had finally stopped bleeding.

That didn't mean I trusted him. Didn't mean I'd forgotten five years of hell.

It just meant I was willing to see what we could build from the wreckage.

Nash was waiting in the main cabin, coffee already brewed,

relief written across his weathered face. "Glad you made it back. Storm's supposed to clear by noon."

"Good." I shrugged out of my wet jacket, tried to ignore the way Beckett's eyes tracked my movements. "We can finish the boundary survey in the area this afternoon than continue on."

"Actually," Nash said carefully, "I was thinking you two could use a day off. After yesterday's weather."

I shot him a look. Nash Morrison didn't believe in days off. Not during survey season.

"We're fine," I said.

"Are you?"

The question hung in the air, loaded with implication. Nash's eyes flicked to my left hand, where the ring caught the cabin's overhead light.

I'd forgotten he'd know it. Forgotten that Nash had been there the night Beckett proposed, had helped him pick it out, had been planning to stand as best man at a wedding that never happened.

"We're fine," I repeated, but my voice had lost some of its edge.

Nash nodded slowly. "Crew's having a bonfire tonight. You should come."

It wasn't really a suggestion. In Nash Morrison's world, crew meant family, and family showed up for each other. Even when things were complicated.

Especially when things were complicated.

"I'll think about it," I said.

But I was already thinking about something else. About the way Beckett had looked at me in the storm shelter. About the careful distance he'd maintained on the hike back, like he was afraid to push too hard too fast.

About the fact that I was wearing his ring and had no idea what that made us.

I spent the day avoiding him.

Not obviously. Just strategically. Found reasons to be wherever he wasn't. Helped Nash with inventory while Beckett worked on equipment maintenance. Went for a solo run when he was in the main cabin. Took a shower when he was setting up for the bonfire.

Professional avoidance disguised as productivity.

By evening, the storm had cleared completely, leaving the mountain air crisp and clean. The crew had built a massive fire in the clearing behind the main cabin, logs arranged in a wide circle, beer coolers strategically placed for easy access.

I watched from my cabin window as they gathered. Sawyer telling some story that had everyone laughing. Frankie quietly tuning a guitar. Nash moving between groups with the easy authority of a man who'd been managing mountain men for decades.

And Beckett, sitting slightly apart from the others, staring into the fire like it held answers to questions he hadn't learned how to ask.

I could stay inside. Could claim exhaustion or a headache, or simple antisocial tendencies. Could avoid the inevitable conversations, the questions, the weight of everyone's eyes on the ring I was still wearing.

Instead, I grabbed a jacket and walked outside.

The crew looked up as I approached the fire circle. Conversations paused, resumed at lower volumes. They knew something had shifted between Beckett and me—could probably smell the emotional upheaval from fifty yards away.

Mountain men weren't exactly subtle.

"Riley!" Sawyer waved me over to an empty log beside him. "Just in time. Frankie was about to play something that isn't completely terrible."

I settled beside him, accepted the beer he pressed into my hands. The fire was warm against my face, the familiar crackle of burning wood a soundtrack to countless nights just like this one.

Except nothing about this night was familiar.

Beckett was directly across the fire from me, close enough that I could see the reflection of flames in his eyes. Close enough to feel the weight of his attention every time I moved.

Close enough that when he finally stood up and started walking around the fire toward me, I felt my pulse jump like a startled animal.

"Riley," he said when he reached me. His voice was quiet, careful. "Can we talk?"

Every conversation in the circle stopped. Fourteen pairs of eyes locked onto us like we were the evening's entertainment.

"Here?" I asked.

"Privately."

I could feel the crew's collective held breath. Could practically hear them taking mental notes for later gossip sessions. But Beckett was looking at me like my answer mattered more than their curiosity.

Like maybe I mattered more than their curiosity.

"Okay," I said.

We walked to the edge of the clearing, far enough from the fire that the conversations resumed behind us. Close enough that the light still reached us, painting everything in warm gold.

"I've been thinking," he said.

"Dangerous habit."

His mouth quirked up at one corner. "About what happens next."

"And?"

"And I don't want to assume anything." He ran a hand through his hair, a gesture so familiar it made my chest ache. "About the ring. About us. About what putting it back on means."

I looked down at my left hand. The diamond caught the firelight, throwing tiny rainbows across my skin.

"I don't know what it means," I said honestly.

"Then let me tell you what I want it to mean."

Something in his tone made me look up. Made me really look at him for the first time since we'd left the shelter.

He looked different. Lighter, somehow. Like confessing his demons had lifted a weight he'd been carrying for so long he'd forgotten what it felt like to stand straight.

"I want it to mean we try again," he said. "Not where we left off —we can't go back. But something new. Something built on honesty instead of assumption."

"Beckett—"

"I want it to mean I get to love you without apology. That I get to build you things instead of tear them down. That when something scares me, I come to you instead of running away."

My throat was tight. "And if you can't? If old habits are stronger than good intentions?"

"Then you call me on my bullshit. You hold me accountable. You make me do the work." He stepped closer, close enough that I could smell his soap, see the flecks of gold in his blue eyes. "You don't let me hide from you again."

"That's a lot to ask."

"It is." He reached up, cupped my face in his palm. "But I'm not asking for easy. I'm asking for real."

I leaned into his touch before I could stop myself. "What if real isn't enough?"

"Then we'll find out together." His thumb brushed across my cheekbone. "But Riley—what we had before wasn't real. Not completely. It was me hiding from you and you loving a version of me that didn't exist."

He was right. I'd loved the man I thought he was—confident, unshakeable, whole. I'd never seen his cracks, never been allowed close enough to his darkness to understand what lived there.

Maybe that wasn't love. Maybe it was just projection.

"So what are you asking me?" I said.

"To let me love you properly this time. All of you—the parts that are easy and the parts that scare me. The way you should have been loved from the beginning."

"And in return?"

"You get the real me. Broken parts, sharp edges, survivor's guilt, and all." His voice was rough with something that might have been hope. "You get a man who's learning to believe he's worth fighting for."

Behind us, Frankie had started playing something soft and instrumental. The crew's voices had settled into comfortable murmur, the kind of easy camaraderie that came from shared work and mutual respect.

This was what Beckett was offering me. Not just himself, but this life. This place. This family of mountain men who built things that lasted.

"I'm scared," I said.

"Good." He smiled, and for the first time in five years, it reached his eyes. "Scared means it matters."

"I'm scared you'll run again."

"I'm scared I'll disappoint you. That I'll fuck this up so badly you'll wish you'd never given me a second chance."

"And we're doing this anyway?"

"We're doing this anyway."

I looked at him—really looked. At the man I'd loved and lost and found again. At the scars he was finally letting me see. At the hope in his eyes that matched the hope building in my chest.

"Okay," I said.

"Okay?"

"Okay, we try again. We build something new." I reached up, covered his hand with mine. "Beckett—if you run, I'll come after you." My voice was steady, certain. "And I'll keep coming after you until you believe you're worth fighting for."

"Understood."

"And I want a ring."

He blinked. "You have a ring."

"I want a new ring. This one—" I held up my left hand "—belongs to who we were. I want one that belongs to who we're becoming."

His smile was soft, wondering. "You want me to propose again."

"I want you to propose for the first time. To me. The real me. Not the version of me you thought you had to protect."

"And when I do?"

"Then we'll see if the real us is strong enough to last."

Around us, the fire crackled and the mountains rose like silent sentinels and the crew continued their easy conversation. But in our small circle of firelight, something precious was taking shape.

Something that felt like possibility.

Something that felt like home.

BECKETT

She said yes before I even asked.

Not to marriage—not yet. But to trying again. To building something real from the foundation of everything we'd lost.

It was more than I'd dared to hope for. More than I deserved.

But as I looked at her in the firelight, at this woman who'd always been braver than me, I made myself a promise. I would do the work. I would face my demons instead of running from them. I would love her the way she deserved to be loved—openly, honestly, without reservation.

I would be worthy of the chance she was giving me.

"There's something else," I said.

"What?"

I reached into my pocket, pulled out the small piece of wood I'd been carrying. A simple carved heart, no bigger than my thumb. Rough around the edges but smooth where it mattered.

"I made this for you," I said, pressing it into her palm. "Five years ago. The night before I left."

She stared down at it, traced the grain with her fingertip. "You kept it."

"I kept everything that mattered. Everything that was ours." I closed her fingers around the carving. "I know it's not much. But it's honest. It's what I had to give when I didn't think I had anything left."

She was quiet for so long, I started to worry I'd pushed too hard, too fast. Then she looked up at me, and her eyes were bright with unshed tears.

"It's perfect," she said. "It's exactly right."

"Riley—"

She kissed me. Soft, tentative, like she was testing whether this new thing between us could hold the weight of physical affection. When I kissed her back—gentle, careful, grateful—she made a small sound in the back of her throat.

"Not here," she whispered against my mouth.

"Where?"

"Your cabin. After the crew goes to sleep. After we figure out how to do this without an audience."

I smiled against her lips. "Think you can wait that long?"

"I've waited five years. I can wait a few more hours."

But the way she was looking at me—hungry, hopeful, alive—said the waiting might kill us both.

Behind us, someone started whooping. We broke apart to find the entire crew watching us with varying degrees of amusement and satisfaction.

"About fucking time!" Sawyer called out.

"Took you long enough," Nash added, but he was smiling.

Riley laughed, the sound bright and uninhibited. "Subtle as a brick, all of you."

"Subtlety's overrated," Frankie said, not looking up from his guitar. "Besides, some of us had money on when you'd figure your shit out."

"You bet on us?" I asked.

"Twenty bucks says you're engaged again by Christmas," Sawyer said cheerfully.

Riley shot me a look. "No pressure."

"None at all," I agreed. But I was already thinking about rings. About proposals that honored who we'd become instead of who we'd been. About the kind of wedding that would be ours—small, honest, real.

About the life we could build if we were brave enough to try.

The fire burned lower, conversations shifted to quieter topics, and gradually the crew began drifting back to their cabins. Until it was just Riley and me and the dying embers and the weight of everything we'd finally said out loud.

"Your cabin," she said. It wasn't a question.

"If you're sure."

"I'm sure." She stood, brushing ash from her jeans. "But Beckett—when we get there, when we're alone—I need you to know this isn't just about sex."

"I know."

"I need to know you see me. All of me. Not the woman you left, not the woman you remember, but the woman I am now."

I stood too, caught her hand in mine. "That's all I want to see."

"Good." She smiled, and it was like sunrise after the longest night. "Because she's pretty fucking amazing."

She was right. She was amazing. And if I spent the rest of my life proving I was worthy of her amazingness, it still wouldn't be enough.

But it would be a hell of a good start.

RELENTLESS

RILEY

Three weeks later, I woke up in Beckett's cabin to the sound of hammering.

Not unusual. The man built things when he was thinking, carved wood when he was working through problems, fixed what was broken because that's what mountain men did.

What was unusual was the hour. Five in the morning, barely light outside, and he was already up and working on something that required serious construction.

I pulled on his flannel shirt and padded barefoot to the kitchen window. Found him in the small clearing behind the cabin, bent over a workbench he'd dragged outside, tools scattered around him like he'd been at this for hours.

Coffee first. Then investigation.

By the time I made it outside with two steaming mugs, he'd stopped hammering and was examining something small in his palm. His hair was messed up, stubble dark on his jaw, flannel sleeves rolled up to reveal forearms that still made my pulse skip.

"Morning," I said, offering him coffee.

He looked up, startled. Like he'd been so absorbed in his work that he'd lost track of time completely.

"You're up early," he said, accepting the mug.

"So are you. What are you building?"

"Something for you." He set down his coffee, held out his hand. "Close your eyes."

"Beckett—"

"Trust me."

I closed my eyes, held out my palm. Felt him place something small and warm in it. Wood, smooth and perfectly fitted.

"Open."

The ring was unlike anything I'd ever seen. Not carved from a single piece, but built—layers of different woods fitted together in a pattern that reminded me of topographical lines. Mountain ash and cedar, and something darker I couldn't identify, all flowing together like the contours of the land we'd mapped together.

"You made this," I breathed.

"I built it." He took it from my palm, held it up to catch the early light. "Each piece represents something. The ash is for resilience—how you bend without breaking. The cedar is for endurance—how you weather every storm. The walnut is for strength—how you hold everyone else together."

My throat was tight. "Beckett."

"It's not perfect. The joins aren't quite seamless, and the finish could be smoother." He met my eyes. "But it's honest. It's made from pieces that shouldn't fit together but do. Like us."

I stared at the ring, at this thing he'd built with his hands for me. Not bought, not inherited, not chosen from a case in some jewelry store. Made. Crafted. Born from his understanding of who I actually was.

"Riley Chen," he said, and his voice was steady, sure. "You're the strongest person I know. You're brilliant and stubborn and brave enough to love a broken man back to wholeness. You see through my bullshit, call me on my cowardice, and make me want to be worthy of the way you look at me."

He dropped to one knee in the dirt behind his cabin, ring held between us like an offering.

"I'm not asking you to save me. I'm asking you to build a life with me. To map new territory together. To let me love you the way you deserve—completely, honestly, without reservation."

My heart was hammering so hard I was sure he could hear it.

"I'm asking you to marry me. Not the man you thought I was, but the man I'm becoming. Will you?"

I looked down at him—at this man who'd learned to face his demons instead of running from them, who'd built something beautiful from broken pieces, who was offering me not perfection but truth.

"Yes," I said. "God, yes."

He slipped the ring onto my finger, and it fit perfectly. Like it had been made for me. Like everything we'd been through had led to this moment.

"It's beautiful," I said, admiring the way the different woods caught the light.

"It's yours." He stood, pulled me into his arms. "You're mine. If you'll have me."

"I'll have you." I went up on my toes, kissed him soft and deep. "Broken pieces and all."

BECKETT

Six months later, I married Riley Chen on the ridge where we'd first kissed.

No church, no three hundred guests, no white dress that cost more than my truck. Just us and Nash as officiant and a handful of crew members as witnesses. Riley wore jeans and boots and a soft blue sweater that brought out her eyes. I wore my cleanest flannel and the smile that hadn't left my face since she'd said yes.

The vows we wrote ourselves were simple, honest. Promises to choose each other daily, to weather whatever storms came, to build something lasting from the foundation of everything we'd learned.

When Nash pronounced us married, Sawyer whooped loud enough to echo off the peaks. Frankie played something soft on his guitar while we kissed. And somewhere in the distance, I heard the sound of hammering—probably Walker Boone working on another project, building something beautiful for someone he cared about.

Mountain men built things that lasted. I'd finally learned to build something worth keeping.

"What now?" Riley asked as we walked back down the trail, her hand warm in mine.

"Now we go home," I said. "And I spend the rest of my life proving I'm worthy of you."

"You already are." She squeezed my fingers. "But I'll let you keep trying anyway."

I laughed, pulled her close, breathed in the scent of her hair and mountain air and possibility.

We had work to do. Trails to map, mountains to climb, a life to build together. But for the first time in five years, I wasn't running from my future.

I was running toward it.

With the woman who'd taught me that some things, once broken, could be made stronger in the healing.

Some things were worth fighting for.

Some things were relentless.

THE END

Did you enjoy *Mountain Men Trail Builders*?

Please consider reviewing it on Goodreads, Bookbub or your favorite retailer. Reviews help me reach new readers.

Read *all the stories* in the **Bitterroot Ridge Trail Crew** series!

Have you read the FREE prequel?

Click below, or find the link on my website at www. peytonlawsonromance.com

Rugged Mountain Man

ALSO BY PEYTON LAWSON

Bitterroot Ridge Trail Crew

Rugged Mountain Man (FREE Reader Magnet)

Forbidden Mountain Man

Devoted Mountain Man

Untamed Mountain Man

Irresistible Mountain Man

Relentless Mountain Man

Carved by the Mountain Man

Branded Mountain Man

The Virgin Mountain Man who Falls First

Christmas with the Trail-Building Mountain Man

Christmas Vows for the Mountain Man

Burn Ridge

Bitter

Hot Vikings

A Viking's Honour (FREE Reader Magnet)

The Jürgensen Vikings

Sören: Healed by a Highland Witch

Abjörn: Lured by an English Rose

Erik: Humbled by the Runemaster

Ryker: Bested by the Valkyrie

ABOUT PEYTON LAWSON

Peyton Lawson writes steamy romance that burns hard and loves harder—Viking warriors, grumpy mountain men, and the curvy heroines who bring them to their knees. Her stories deliver action, emotion, and no-fade heat with guaranteed HEAs. When she's not writing, she's reading, hiking, or chasing her next wild escape.

www.peytonlawsonromance.com

www.ingramcontent.com/pod-product-compliance
Lightning Source LLC
Chambersburg PA
CBHW020644030726
47498CB00002B/362